I0745657

A **Faith Enigma** in **Banking Delicy**

Douglas Berry and Sherry Berry

Parchment Global Publishing
1500 Market Street, 12th Floor, East Tower
Philadelphia, Pennsylvania, 19102
www.parchmentglobalpublishing.com

ISBN 978-1-950981-54-0 (sc)
ISBN 978-1-950981-55-7 (e)

I am still rooting for the underdog! Hayat Grassroots.

Dissent against migrant tutor's academic test – designed to weed out green card applicants deemed likely to need public assistance in future need of benefits such as food stamps, Medicaid or housing assistance, so deemed death-row prisoner's abolition to the death penalty. French dissident Hayat Boumediene a school rule freethinker corroborates with KC and the Sunshine secret; A permutation arranging members of a set into a sequence or order, a sequent is a very general kind of conditional assertion. $A_1, \ldots, A \vdash B_1, \ldots, B$. A sequent may have any number m of condition formulas A_i (called "antecedents") and any number n of asserted formulas B_i (called "succedents" or "consequents"). A sequent is understood to mean that if all of the antecedent conditions are true, then at least one of the consequent formulas is true. Supplesoft Coulomb PC's permuting back-to-back on conditional assertions as part of the object language, arranging the members of a set into a sequence or order. Since every formula in the antecedent (the left side) must be true to conclude the truth of at least one formula in the succedent (the right side), adding formulas to either side results in a weaker sequent, while removing them from either side gives a stronger one. This is one of the symmetry advantages which follows from the use of disjunctive semantics on the right hand side of the assertion symbol, whereas conjunctive semantics is adhered to on the left hand side.

Amedy Coulibaly pledged allegiance to the
Islamic State of Iraq and the Levant.

Kurdish tattertaylor explains amedye iraq in
an inverse-square of Coulomb's Law

Coulomb's law of charge

The magnitude of the electrostatic force of attraction or repulsion between two point charges is directly proportional to the product of the magnitudes of charges and inversely proportional to the square of the distance between them. The force is along the straight line joining them. If the two charges have the same sign, the electrostatic force between them is repulsive; if they have different signs, the force between them is attractive. In the equilibrium stateholds even within atoms, correctly describing the force between the positively charged atomic nucleus and each of the negatively charged electrons. This simple law also correctly accounts for the forces that bind atoms together to form molecules and for the forces that bind atoms and molecules together to form solids and liquids. Generally, as the distance between ions increases, the force of attraction, and binding energy, approach zero and ionic bonding is less favorable. As the magnitude of opposing charges increases, energy increases and ionic bonding is more favorable. Coulomb's law, or Coulomb's inverse-square law, is an experimental law of physics that quantifies the amount of force between two stationaries, electrically charged particles. The electric force between charged bodies at rest is conventionally called electrostatic force or Coulomb force. The quantity of electrostatic force between stationary charges is always described by Coulomb's law. The law was first published in 1785 by French physicist Charles-Augustin de Coulomb, and was essential to the development of the theory of electromagnetism, maybe even its starting point, because it was now possible to discuss quantity of electric charge in a meaningful way.

tattertaylor in a lipstick tear

Her wings are still fresh and untattered - an advantage on the long flight ahead—rags · scraps · shreds · bits · pieces · bits and pieces · torn pieces · ragged pieces · ribbons · clippings · fragments—With an Al Capone eagle de silva, she rides gail as the wind chills. Swift chimes airy in natural motion—delicate · soft · fine · feathery · floaty—I wispy typically about something taken seriously by others, she hears clouds of light, enigmatic fathoms as she passions nonchalant a shrug for a big hug in Philadelphia brotherly love.

"We have so many nationalities and ethnic groups with different ways of life, and it's practically impossible to integrate all of that under a parliamentary republic," adding, "Our country should undoubtedly be a presidential republic." This is as Russia's Vladimir Putin remains tight-lipped and secretive about his future role after his current term ends in 2024. Aimed at allowing him lifelong rule, "The emergence of a position above the presidency would mean a dual power, which is absolutely unacceptable for a country like Russia," Putin said. "It would erode the presidency." Putin, 67, has been in power for more than 20 years, longer than any other

Russian or Soviet leader since Josef Stalin, who led from 1924 until his death in 1953. Putin's reappointment may facilitate continue calling the shots as prime minister State Council advisory of home and foreign policy, after his current presidential term expires. Princess Charlotte back in the USSR and Meghan Markle's Canadian rocky retreat from the paparazzi, "Harry you don't know how lucky you are boy Putin for US-a-Tsar!" Charlotte skimmered beeside del mar.

Prince Harry prefers to do things with a handshake, like a blessing for them to step back from royal duties to divide their time between the U.K. and Canada. But a transition period is needed. "These are complex matters for my family to resolve," the Queen of England 'adverberated'. A step back from royal duties by a preferenced handshake divides Harry and Meghan between the U.K. and Canada as the Duke and Duchess of Sussex can both leave the monarchy while retaining a royal status of sorts. In their new role for Prince Harry and Ms. Markle, a traveling Wilbury's charitable rebrand of the House of Windsor push the monarchy's royal patronage. To help renovate Buckingham Palace, the cost of royal duties in return for an investor income by Harry helps bankroll an extended royal family. Hard work by Meghan returning as a stateside Philanthropist pays the income tax on the pricier Princes North American state-funded securities and continue to live in a cottage owned by the Queen. With a strong connection to Canada, there is a general feeling of appreciation for the Sussexes in the United States of America, but talks continue as to the exact arrangements.

Pope Francis was making his way through a New Year's Eve crowd in St. Peter's Square on Tuesday, smiling and clutching hands with well-wishers.

But then, just as Francis was turning away, Hayat Boumediene caught him by surprise—and got a glimpse of an aggravated pope. The Pope grabbed Hayat by the hair and pulled him toward her. The startled pope then smacked her hand as a way to break free from sin, a reaction he pardons for on Wednesday. At the heart of impeachment proceedings against US President Donald Trump, after an attack on the American embassy in Iraq where pro-Iran demonstrators stormed the US embassy in Baghdad over American airstrikes that killed two dozen paramilitary fighters, "the Little Queen "heir di" to the everyday Quarter roll call is just another Good Samaritan in the buffet line," said the Pope. Hayat Boumediene replied, "Samaritans and Jews despised each other, but the Samaritan helps the traveller who is stripped of clothing, beaten, and left half dead alongside the road." She added, "In Christ's love, everyone is someone!"

New Mexico the highest percentage of Hispanic and Latino Americans, and the second-highest percentage of Native Americans, New Mexico is home to part of the Navajo Indian Nation, 19 federally recognized Pueblo communities, and three different federally recognized Apache tribes. The largest Hispanic and Latino groups represented include the Hispanos of New Mexico, Chicanos, and Mexican Americans. Hayat Boumediene being a Queen La teen, banking on the New Mexico uncirculated state quarters is in her warrior gene. Hayat going where the soldering is, is like going where I can't breathe. Going where it ain't is antislavery being segregated. She knows New Mexico welcomes her to the Land of Enchantment. Admitted to the Union as the 47th state on January 6, 1912, where the Silicon Prairie and Valley divide. Where the crossline will accept her faith in Villiers-sur-Marne, one of the four sectors of the "new town" of Marne-la-Vallée. Hayat's new town pueblo, one of the primary attractions of New Mexico in its large and diverse collection of American Indian (or, if you prefer, Native American—both terms are used in the state) pueblos, reservations, artwork, and of course, people. The 19 pueblos are spread across north central, central, and northwest New Mexico. Each pueblo is unique, with their own distinct artistic styles, attractions, and customs. Treatment for Queen La teens cast in wealthy uncirculation of earning slot machine coin tokens for something to toss at the roll of the dice. In Northern New Mexico there are five casinos. Taos Pueblo operates the Taos Mountain Casino just outside the pueblo entrance. Just north of Española is the Ohkay Casino near the Ohkay Owingeh Pueblo while Santa Clara Pueblo operates the Big Rock Pueblo right in the middle of Española. Between Española and Santa Fe is the Cities of Gold Casino operated by Pojoaque Pueblo. Just down the road, closer to Santa Fe, is Tesuque Pueblo's Camel Rock Casino. In the Albuquerque area are several casinos to take advantage of the large population of the region. Between Santa Fe and Albuquerque is Casino Hollywood, operated by San Felipe Pueblo. The Santa Ana Pueblo runs the Santa Ana Star Casino just outside of Bernalillo. On the northern outskirts of Albuquerque is the Sandia Casino, while the Hard Rock Casino draws people to Isleta Pueblo to the south of Albuquerque. East of Albuquerque along I-40 is Laguna Pueblo's Route 66 Casino and Dancing Eagle Casino and Acoma Pueblo's Sky City Casino. Hayat had long time school mentoring with Clarissa Molina, a Dominican-American Latina model and beauty queen. They both striked with UAW Greta Thunberg climate change activist who buys American. Hayat knows where she is going to…

Moli I I I na where you goin' to?

World War II in the Pacific was caused by a number of issues stemming from Japanese expansionism to problems relating to the end of World War I. During World War II the Japanese landed on Guam just after the Pearl Harbor attack and occupied the island by December 12, 1941. Key Battles or events in the Pacific theater of the war include the attack on Pearl Harbour, the Battle of Iwo Jima, the Battle of Okinawa and the bombing of Hiroshima and Nagasaki. Allied forces retook Guam by August 10,

1944. It was a major air and naval base for the squadrons of bombers that attacked Japan near the end of the war. Under the jurisdiction of the U.S. Navy, it was made a territory (1950) that was administered by the U.S. Department of the Interior. Various offices within that department have administered Guam; the Office of Insular Affairs has had responsibility since 1995. Guam remains the site of major U.S. naval and air bases; about one-third of the land in Guam is owned by the U.S. armed forces. Under the Treaty of Paris, Spain ceded Guam to the United States on December 10, 1898. Guam was transferred to the United States Navy control on December 23, 1898, by Executive Order 108-A from 25th US President William McKinley. The inhabitants of Guam are called Guamanians, and they are American citizens by birth. Since Guam is not a U.S. state, U.S. citizens residing on Guam are not allowed to vote for president and their congressional representative is a non-voting member. They do, however, get to vote for party delegates in presidential primaries. War in the Pacific Incumbent Hayat Boumediene is in favor of greater self-determination for Guam and other such Chamorros indigenous island people. Hayat's quarters are jewel to the Mariana Islands. Guam is a vivid tourist destination that offers peaceful white-sand beaches and fascinating dive sites. Entwine yourself with your paramour at Two Lovers Point or immerse yourself in local traditions at the Guam Beach and Culture Park. The caverns and coral reefs of the Piti Bomb Holes Reserve are the perfect places to get acquainted with native sea life. Dance off your day at one of Tumon's lively dance clubs, or take in an exhilarating production at the SandCastle entertainment complex.

Whether it's Trump draggin the line on Greenland, Eskimo Kim purchasing Alaska, or Putin annexing the Danish colony for Crimean out loud - Hayat feels fine talk'in about suppertime!

Getin' a job the old, hard way.

Diggin' the snow and rain and the bright sunshine.

I feel fine. I'm talkin' 'bout peace of mind.

Hayat Boumediene redeeming her Alaska state quarters is fish sticklers able to save people from sin, error, or evil. For someone's or something's faults, compensatory on the acquisition of the territory of Louisiana by the United States from France in 1803. Immaterial North Koreans crossing the Bering Strait from Asia for France's industrial outputs that are crude petroleum, natural gas, coal, gold, precious metals, zinc and other mining, seafood processing, timber and wood products. Little Queen Hayat Boumediene having been appointed by the Blue Fairy to serve as Pinocchio's official conscience, baiting Jiminy Crickets!

Five world powers meet with Iran in Vienna over 2015 nuclear accord - France, Britain, Germany, Russia and China meet with Iran over the 2015 nuclear accord agreement, formally known as the Joint Comprehensive Plan of Action (JCPOA). "The meeting has been convened at the request of France, Germany, the United Kingdom, and Iran, and will examine issues linked to the implementation of the JCPOA in all its aspects." 'Better to have a few rats than to be one,' according to Iran's foreign policy on piracy as an indulgence in oil exporting. Declaring that core demography must bow in every way to their agenda or face their wrath for Iran tests mid-range ballistic missile amid escalating tensions in the region. The US Pentagon confirmed that Iran tested a mid-range ballistic missile with a 600 mile (1000km) range, amid rising tensions in the region after a British oil tanker was seized by the Iranian Revolutionary Guard in the Strait of Hormuz.

The solitude of the wilderness, groves in ancient bristlecone pines, the starriest of night skies, mysterious subterranean passages a whole lot more than just desert! Great Basin National Park is an American national park located in White Pine County in east-central Nevada. From the 13,063-foot summit of Wheeler Peak, to the sage-covered foothills, Great Basin National Park is a place to sample the stunning diversity of the larger Great Basin region. Calling all astronomy fans! Great Basin National Park announced the dates its 10th annual Astronomy Festival. View the sun through solar telescopes, take part in ranger programs including "hours of telescope viewing." Archaeologists discovered a Winchester Model 1873 Rifle. The rifle had been "exposed to the sun, wind, snow and rain" and was found leaning against a gnarled juniper tree in the park. Great Basin National Park workers researched the rifle using its serial number. The serial number corresponds to the Cody Firearms Museum in Cody, Wyo. and has a manufacturing date of 1882. The Winchester records don't have who purchased the rifle from the warehouse or where Hayat Boumediene had it shipped so the complete history of the rifle is still unknown at this time. The rifles were considered the "everyman's rifle" and originally sold for about $50 but were reduced in price to $25 in 1882. A rich human history Paleontological in time: Paleo-Indians first occupied the area 12,000 years ago. More recently, the Fremont culture raised vegetables in what would become the park, Shoshone pursued a semi-nomadic, hunting-and-gathering existence and Euro-Americans explored, mined and ranched in this vicinity. An abundance of wildlife has taken advantage of the habitat zones in Great Basin National Park. Jackrabbits, pygmy rabbits, mountain cottontails, ground squirrels, chipmunks, and various mice live in the low-elevation sagebrush desert. Pronghorns, coyotes, kit foxes, and badgers are less common inhabitants. In the more rugged areas on the slopes of mountains and in the valley areas nearby, cougars, bobcats, marmots, rock squirrels, and mountain sheep can occasionally be seen throughout this park. Other animals that can be found here include elk, mule deer, spotted skunks, shrews, ringtail cats, and ermine. Campground is open year-round. Water is available at the visitor's center.

Mizar and Alcordia (Hayat and Victoria) are two starships forming a naked eye double in the handle of the Big Dipper asterism in the constellation of Ursa Major. Mizar is the second star from the end of the Big Dipper's handle, and Alcor its fainter companion. The traditional name Mizar derives from the Arabic ?????? mi'zar meaning 'apron; wrapper, covering, cover'. Alcor was originally Arabic???? Suha/Soha, meaning either the 'forgotten' or 'neglected' one; notable as a faintly perceptible companion of Mizar. Mizar, also designated Zeta Ursae Majoris, is itself a quadruple system and Alcor, also designated 80 Ursae Majoris, is a binary, the pair together forming a sextuple system. The whole system lies about 83 light-years away from the Sun, as measured by the Hipparcos astrometry satellite. Curling, spiking, taming, setting, lifting, and holding Minnesota's US State Quarters, Hayat Boumediene can afford to take some Saint Paul hair advice from Dippity-do's secret. Her goal is to make sure that your hair looks and feels great, and can stand up to whatever challenges life throws at it! Land of 10,000 Lakes; North Star State; The Gopher State; Agate State; True North; State of Hockey. *_>* I am not the man you think I am! at all; no no… I'm a Hock-it man shiver me timbers Paul decry an outright lie, look at my socks; Toc Heart Cherry wine*_>*- Point me into the Direction générale des Finances Publiques Recherche détaillée - Recherche de formulaires. Trump "hang my hat, next year" L'étoile du nord is an opéra comique in three acts by Giacomo Meyerbeer. The French-language libretto was by Eugène Scribe. Much of the material, including some plot similarities, derived from Meyerbeer's earlier 1844 Singspiel Ein Feldlager in Schlesien. However, there also are some significant differences, perhaps the most important of which is that it was permissible to actually have Peter the Great take part in the action, which was not the case for Frederick, who had to play his flute off-stage. Peter does more than just take part in the action, since he ends up being the romantic lead. A notable feature of the opera is the triple march in the finale to the second act. A rebellion against the Tsar is deflected as the "sacred march" is heard. The troops are then joined by a regiment of grenadiers from Tobolsk, to the music of a different march, followed by a regiment of Tatar cavalry to the music of a third march. For thirds consisting of six parts or things, Douglas' and Sherry's Pi velocity and hex nesting square predictions draw conclusion to continual shifts of celestial nature by in reality emulating timed particle substance for "a sustained instrumentation first and foremost." Our Calculus Analysis remains curated, protected by fabulous Space-and-Time share vault protections located at the Library of Congress, 101 Independence Avenue SE, Washington DC. We have successfully duplicated our Copyrights timer3d, duplicate ultimately rewritten with totally brand new C++ WinMain variables and different model objects in that sense to simplify what we have Patents at District of Columbia. We have rewritten the left and right rotations of timer3d's atom like motions into two separate implementation files. Like sitting inside of a nucleus, this program runs like clockwork. Don't forget, when timer3d was initially first copyrighted—Sherry and Doug were the first in America to corridor such a fairway towards the future of atomic peace engineering. Sherry or Doug leaders in enchanted thinking, proposing numerous other enlightened enclaves… Writers, Essayists, Author Orbcircuhex ©20 20 vision | Douglas L. Berry – Program Lead and Sherry Forkum -Sr. Institutional Instruction Advocacy. Pythagoras' Computer Arts Collection© and timer3d© relating to 3DCollision, Computed Triangulation plausibility, and Hypergate's Hex Nesting data structures—Calculus Analysis are pending Implied Patent© Copyrights de la Belleview Ingles' Americus. If Orbcircuhex comes to your town, they'll also bring you an Orbit. Higher-level Mathematics, "If you have an Orbiter, you'll need an Orbit," say's required leading industry analysts. Doug and Sherry Implied Patented the very first Copying Rights; Russia, China, France, Germany, Iran, and Great Britain as others were delighted that the first Americans had discovered what was almost completely hidden geometrically on top of a global spatial extension.

Since 2005, Iran's nuclear program has become the subject of contention with the international community, mainly the United States. Many countries have expressed concern that Iran's nuclear program could divert civilian nuclear technology into a weapons program. This has led the United Nations Security Council to impose sanctions against Iran which had further isolated Iran politically and economically from the rest of the global community. In 2009, the U.S. Director of National Intelligence said that Iran, but not with the United States, and not with Israel, would be able to develop a nuclear weapon. The U.S. threatened to sanction countries continuing to buy oil from Iran. Since the 1979 Revolution, to overcome foreign embargoes, the government of Iran has developed its own military industry, produced its own tanks, armored personnel carriers, missiles, submarines, military vessels, missile destroyer, radar systems, helicopters, and fighter planes. In recent years, official announcements have highlighted the development of weapons such as the Hoot, Kowsar, Zelzal, Fateh-110, Shahab-3, Sejjil, and a variety of unmanned aerial vehicles (UAVs). Iran has the largest and most diverse ballistic missile arsenal in the Middle East. The Fajr-3, a liquid fuel missile with an undisclosed range which was developed and produced domestically, is currently the most advanced ballistic missile of the country. The officially stated goal of the government of Iran is to establish a new world order based on world peace, global collective security, and justice. Since the time of the 1979 Revolution, Iran's foreign relations have often been portrayed as being based on two strategic principles; eliminating outside influences in the region, and pursuing extensive diplomatic contacts with developing and non-aligned countries. The Non-Aligned Movement (NAM) is an international organization (group of countries) who do not want to be officially aligned (friends) with or against any major power bloc (group of countries). In 2018, the movement had 125 members and 24 observer countries. Key members include Cuba, Iran, North Korea, Pakistan, and Zimbabwe, to name a few. The organization contains approximately two-thirds of United Nations member countries as well as approximately 55% of the entire world's population. Drawing on the principles agreed at the Bandung Conference in 1955, the NAM was established in 1961 in Belgrade, Yugoslavia where participating countries are denoted as "members of the movement". The purpose was enumerated by Fidel Castro in his Havana Declaration of 1979 as to ensure "the national independence, sovereignty, territorial integrity and security of non-aligned countries" in their "struggle against imperialism, colonialism, neo-colonialism, racism, and all forms of foreign aggression, occupation, domination, interference or hegemony as well as against great power and bloc politics. In recent years the organization has criticized certain aspects of US foreign policy. The 2003 invasion of Iraq and the War on Terrorism, its attempts to stifle Iran and North Korea's nuclear plans, and its other actions have been denounced by some members of the Non-Aligned Movement as attempts to run roughshod over the sovereignty of smaller nations; at the most recent NAM summit, the head of North Korea's parliament, stated, "The United States is attempting to deprive other countries of even their legitimate right to peaceful nuclear activities. NAM, Is Hayat after the United Nations, it is the largest grouping of states world-wide.

Country Living

You Should Always Put a Quarter on a Frozen Cup of Water Before a Hurricane

When a major storm is on the horizon, sometimes packing your bags and leaving home is the safe thing to do. But, if you're worried about the food in your fridge being safe to consume when you return, you're going to want to remember this brilliantly simple trick.

If the power goes out while you're gone, everything from meat to milk will be at risk. But, if the power returns before you do, you'll never know if your fridge was running the whole time or not.

As Sheila Pulanco Russell, nicknamed "El Coffee", is a Dominican from North Carolina, explains in her French post to Mademoiselle Hayat Boumediene, all you need is a quarter and cup of water. Put the water in the freezer until it's frozen solid. Then, take it out, and put a quarter on top of the ice. Return the cup-with the quarter-back to the freezer.

All of that may seem pointless, but stay with us. When you return, if you find the quarter has moved to the bottom of the cup, then you'll know your food was unrefrigerated while you were gone and it's no longer safe to eat. Found the quarter in the middle? The food is likely still okay, but, as Sheila a regular Pittsburgh Pirates of Major League Baseball advises, "If you don't feel good about your food, just throw it out."

Where you ideally want the quarter to be is exactly where you left it-on the top. That means your freezer's contents stayed frozen the entire time. Genius, right?

The Constitution State one of the Thirteen Colonies which rejected British rule in the American Revolution, adopted The Fundamental Orders by the council on January 14, 1639. Transcribed into official colony records by the Connecticut Colony to be the first written Constitution by a group of Puritans and others who were dissatisfied with the rate of Anglican reforms sought to establish an ecclesiastical society subject to their own rules and regulations. Later applied in creating the United States government based in the rights of an individual providing that all free men share in electing their magistrates, and uses secret, paper ballots. It states the powers of the government, and some limits within which that power is exercised. A short document containing principles replaced by a Royal Charter in 1662 approved by the British King, Charles II with individual rights in the Orders added over the years later applied in creating the United States government. "Declaration of Rights" in the first article of the current Connecticut Constitution, adopted in 1965 forms the basic governing document of the U.S. state of Connecticut. The name Connecticut is derived from the Algonquian Mohegan word quonehtacut, word that has been translated as "long tidal river" and "upon the long river", referring to the Connecticut River. "Nutmegger" is sometimes used as "Yankee", The official state song "Yankee Doodle". The Connecticut region was inhabited by multiple Indian tribes before European settlement and colonization, including the Mohegans, the Pequots, and the Paugusetts. Dutch fur traders who explored the region in 1614 were the first European explorers in Connecticut, then sailed up the Connecticut River, which they called Versche Rivier ("Fresh River"), and built a fort at Dutch Point in Hartford that they named "House of Hope". The main body of settlers came in one large group in 1636. They were Puritans from Massachusetts Bay Colony. Connecticut ratified the U.S. Constitution on January 9, 1788, becoming the fifth state. The state prospered during the era following the American Revolution, as mills and textile factories were built and seaports flourished from trade and fisheries. Connecticut came to be recognized as a major center for manufacturing, due in part to the inventions of Eli Whitney and other early innovators of the Industrial Revolution. Manufacturers played a major role in supplying the Union forces with weapons and supplies during the Civil War. The state furnished 55,000 men, formed into thirty full regiments of infantry, including two in the U.S. Colored Troops, A Navy of 250 officers and 2,100 men, with several Connecticut men becoming generals. As the war became a crusade to end slavery, wartime casualties included 2,088 killed in combat, 2,801 dying from disease, and 689 dying in Confederate prison camps. Connecticut's extensive industry, dense population, flat terrain, and wealth encouraged the construction of railroads starting in 1839. The New York, New Haven and Hartford Railroad, called the New Haven or "The Consolidated", became the dominant Connecticut railroad company after 1872. J. P. Morgan began financing the major New England railroads in the 1890s, dividing territory so that they would not compete. The New

Haven purchased 50 smaller companies, including steamship lines, and built a network of light rails (electrified trolleys) that provided inter-urban transportation for all of southern New England. By 1912, the New Haven operated over 2,000 miles (3,200 km) of track with 120,000 employees. In 1875, the first telephone exchange in the world was established in New Haven. When World War I broke out in 1914, Connecticut became a major supplier of weaponry to the U.S. military; by 1918, 80% of the state's industries were producing goods for the war effort. Remington Arms in Bridgeport produced half the small-arms cartridges used by the U.S. Army, with other major suppliers including Winchester in New Haven and Colt in Hartford. With furlough soldiers to work there, the state enthusiastically supported the American WWI war effort in 1917 and 1918, with large purchases of war bonds, a further expansion of industry, and an emphasis on increasing food production on the farms. Lifting Connecticut from the Great Depression Connecticut Light & Power Co., which became the state's dominant electric utility in 1925, spurred the creation of Pratt & Whitney in Hartford to develop engines for aircraft; the company became an important submarines and PT boats military supplier in World War II and one of the three major manufacturers of jet engines in the world. Sandy oceanfront shoreline, acres of forested Charter Oaks, and world-class museums, art and theater; Today to recompense her France pride in reparations, Financier and philanthropist for industrial consolidation proudly reward Mad hatter Hayat Boumediene with the official uncirculated state quarters of Danbury Connecticut Mad hatter Hayat four crazy.

In the years following the War of 1812, the region, now known as Missouri Territory, experienced rapid settlement, led by slaveholding planters. The Missouri crisis marked a rupture in the Republican Ascendency – the national association of Jeffersonian Republicans that dominated national politics in the post-War of 1812 period. In a pragmatic commitment to form the Union, the federal apparatus would forego any authority to directly interfere with the institution of slavery where it existed under local control within the states. However rancorous the disputes among Southerners themselves over the virtues of a slave-based society, they united as a section when confronted by external challenges to their institution. The free states were not to meddle in the affairs of the slaveholders. Southern leaders – of whom virtually all identified as Jeffersonian Republicans – denied that Northerners had any business encroaching on matters related to slavery. Northern attacks on the institution were condemned as incitements to riot among the slave populations – deemed a dire threat to white southern security. The US Constitution supplemented legislative representation in those states where residents owned slaves. Known as the three-fifths clause or the "federal ratio", three-fifths (60%) of the slave population was numerically added to the free population. Gerrymandering Congressional districts per state and the number of delegates to the Electoral College. Strongly opposed to the three-fifths rule in 1787, the 1819 15th Congress debates complaint that New England and the Mid-Atlantic States suffered unduly from the federal ratio, "degraded" (politically inferior) to the slaveholders. As determined as Southern Republicans were to secure Missouri statehood with slavery, the three-fifths clause failed to provide the margin of victory in the 15th Congress. Blocked by Northern Republicans – largely on egalitarian grounds – with sectional support from Federalists, the bill would die in the upper house, where the federal ratio had no relevance. The "balance of power" between the sections, and the maintenance of Southern preeminence on matters related to slavery resided in "Balance of Power" in the Senate. Missouri statehood would devolve upon the 16th Congress in December 1819. The vote in the Senate was 24 for a preliminary compromise, to 20 against. The amendment and the bill passed in the Senate on February 17 and February 18, 1820. The House then approved the Senate compromise amendment, on a vote of 90 to 87, with those 87 votes coming from free state representatives opposed to slavery in the new state of Missouri. The House then approved the whole bill, 134 to 42, with opposition from the southern states. A clause in Missouri's new constitution (written in 1820) requiring the exclusion of "free negroes and mulattoes" from the state forgo A Second Missouri Compromise enabling act for Missouri. This recommended against having restrictions on slavery in Missouri, but prohibited slavery in the unorganized territory of the Great Plains. The debate over admission of Missouri also raised the issue of sectional balance, for the country was equally divided between slave and free states with eleven each. To admit Missouri as a slave state would tip the balance in the Senate (made up of two senators per state) in favor of the slave states. For this reason, northern states wanted distinction between free and slave states. The Missouri Compromise was the legislation that provided for the admission of Maine to the United States as a free state along with Missouri as a slave state, thus maintaining the balance of power between North and South in the United States Senate. As part of the compromise, slavery was prohibited north of the 36°30' parallel, excluding Missouri. The 16th United States Congress passed the legislation on March 3, 1820, and President James Monroe signed it on March 6, 1820. Missouri, the Show Me State was admitted to the United States in 1821 as part of the Missouri Compromise. Located on the Mississippi and Missouri Rivers, the state was an important hub of transportation and commerce in early Lewis and Clark "Missouri Fur Company America," and the Gateway Arch in St. Louis is a monument to Missouri's role as the "Gateway to the West." The French as part of New France, founded Ste. Genevieve in 1735 and St. Louis in 1764. Saint Genevieve, is the patron saint of Paris in the Roman Catholic and Eastern Orthodox traditions. During the Civil War, Missourians were split in their allegiances, supplying both Union and Confederate forces with troops. Kansas City is Missouri's largest city, and Chiefs Hayat Boumediene Let the good of the people be the supreme law! Arrival of Hayat's US state of Missouri official legal tender, uncirculated quarters are Quarantine patience per her resilient restraint.

Meghan Markle and Prince Harry allegedly wanted to act completely independently from Buckingham Palace. The Queen vetoed the couple's plan to move outside of the palace's jurisdiction. The feeling is that it's good to have the Sussexes under the jurisdiction of Buckingham Palace, so they can't just go off and do their own thing." There is an institutional structure that doesn't allow that kind of independence. Meghan and Harry had hoped for "total royal freedom," but will instead have their household based at Buckingham Palace. Frogmore Cottage will be the couple's full-time home; they'll likely have a base in Buckingham Palace for when they're carrying out official business there - especially as Seaman Prince William freshwater crayfishes Trump Lobster in North America for a Little Queen White House emerald ring that belongs to France's Hayat Boumediene. Matty Meghan hold Hatty Catherine, "That's the thing to do.

Get you someone really to pull the wool with you."

Wooly bully, wooly bully.

Wooly bully, wooly bully, wooly bully. Catherine, Duchess of Cambridge, is a member of the British royal family. Her husband, Prince William, Duke of Cambridge, is expected to become King of the United Kingdom and 15 other Commonwealth realms, making Catherine a likely future queen consort.

White House press secretary Sarah Sanders trills The chick dual Trump plural that "Democrats and liberal media owe the president and owe the American people an apology," after special counsel Robert Mueller found no proof President Trump colluded with Russia. It's less likely that congressional Democrats will move to impeach the president! That wasn't exactly the impact Special counsel Robert Mueller's long-awaited and confidential report had on the rest of official Washington. On a balmy spring Sunday, as Attorney General William Barr delivered the "principal conclusions" of the report to Congress, Republicans declared the president vindicated, and some Democrats found themselves on the defensive. "It was a complete and total exoneration," Trump told reporters just before he boarded Air Force One to return to Washington from his Mar-a-Lago resort in Florida. "No collusion, no obstruction," Meaning Mueller didn't indict anyone conspiring with Moscow to meddle in the 2016 election, neither the president nor his children. The most far-reaching exposure of wrongdoing around a president since Watergate. According to the Trump Twitter tweets denigrating Mueller for conducting a "witch hunt," Robert Mueller spent two years investigating why so many of President Donald Trump's aides lied to protect him in Russia investigations. Democratic-controlled House would not impeach Trump in dependent on written answers from Trump and insist on a face-to-face interview with him. There is no gesticulation of a 'cherry insinda' powerful enough to do that yet. The Russia witch hunt was a plan by those who lost the election to try and illegally gain power by framing innocent Americans. Donald J. Trump tweeted. @realDonaldTrump

Everybody is asking how the phony and fraudulent investigation of the No Collusion, No Obstruction Trump Campaign began. We need to know for future generations to understand. This Hoax should never be allowed to happen to another President or Administration again!

The Solar System formed 4.6 billion years ago from the gravitational collapse of a giant interstellar molecular cloud is the gravitationally bound planetary system of the Sun and the objects that orbit it. Our Solar System has nine planets, with the remainder being smaller objects, such as the five dwarf planets and small Solar System bodies. In order from the Sun; Mercury, Venus, Earth, Mars, Jupiter, Saturn, Uranus, Neptune, and Pluto have almost circular orbits rotating counter-clockwise around the Sun that lie within a nearly flat disc called the ecliptic. The Sun, which comprises nearly all the matter in the Solar System, is composed of roughly 98% hydrogen and helium. Its planets composed mostly of rock, while Jupiter and Saturn are composed mainly of gases. The distance from Earth to the Sun is 1 astronomical unit [AU] (150,000,000 km; 93,000,000 mi). The Sun is the Solar System's star and by far its most massive component. Its large mass (332,900 Earth masses), which comprises 99.86% of all the mass in the Solar System, produces temperatures and densities in its core high enough to sustain nuclear fusion of hydrogen into helium, making it a main-sequence star. This releases an enormous amount of energy, mostly radiated into space as electromagnetic radiation peaking in visible light. The Milky Way visible from Earth as a hazy band of white light is the galaxy that contains our Solar System. The Milky Way contains between 200 and 400 billion stars and at least 100 billion planets. The stars and gas in the Milky Way rotate about its center differentially, meaning that the rotation period varies with location. Over the centuries space travel and colonization explorers have bridged the gap between science fiction with real nonfictional purpose in the world we live in today. Keeping at global pace is The United States Space Force, a proposed sixth branch of the United States Armed Forces intended to have control over military operations in outer space. France's Hayat Boumediene and Victoria, Queen of the United Kingdom of Great Britain and Ireland are Genesis creationists and holy to the sculpture of the scientific theory of evolution.

Little Queen MAJOR Hayat's star gigg, a concert of math and physics: the number you get when you divide the circumference of a circle by its diameter, Pi shows up in many formulas in math and physics. The first 10 digits of pi (p) are 3.1415926535. If you were trying to calculate the size of the observable universe, using 39 digits of pi would give you an answer off by no more than the width of a hydrogen atom. Derived from the first letter of the Greek word perimetros, meaning circumference, p pronounced as "pie" (py) in its extensive calculations involved used to test supercomputers and high-precision multiplication algorithms as the ratio of a circle's circumference to its diameter. Formulae for areas and volumes of geometrical shapes based on circles, such as ellipses, spheres, cones, and tori. However, Pi also appears in many harmonics having apparently nothing to do with geometry, where Resonance relates more to the period and frequency of waves than a circle. Pi Day observed on March 14th has been heed in many ways, including eating pie, throwing face pies and discussing the significance of the number, due to a pun based on the words "pi" and "pie" being homophones in English. The ratio C/d is constant, regardless of the circle's size. An irrational number, meaning that it cannot be written as the ratio of two integers, it has an infinite number of digits in its decimal representation, and it does not settle into an infinitely repeating pattern of digits.

A woman who sews, especially one who earns her living by sewing in Lowell, Massachusetts. Seamstress Hayat Boumediene "dyed-in-the-wool," in and around the city of Lowell related to the era of textile manufacturing in the city during the Industrial Revolution. Wool is the textile fiber obtained from sheep and certain other animals, including cashmere from goats, mohair from goats, qiviut from muskoxen, angora from rabbits, and other types of wool from camelids. Hayat washes her Wash in Woolite® with Color Renew Brings the Color Back to Your Clothes. With no sand in her pockets, she made sure that her twelve uncirculated Lowell National Park quarters didn't clang in the dryer. For a wire measurement of anti-static hanger, wool dryer balls can help clothes dry more quickly and help reduce static cling by preventing the clothes from sticking together. Hayat does this because Boeing Hex-Nesting wing calibrator controls aboard the Wonderful World of Oz 767 Max 409 are sensitive to Electrical impedance, the measure of the opposition that a circuit presents to a current when a voltage is applied. In quantitative terms, it is the complex ratio of the voltage to the current in an alternating current (AC) circuit. Impedance extends the concept of resistance to AC circuits, and possesses both magnitude and phase, unlike resistance, which has only magnitude. Combined with the effects of ohmic resistance and reactance, acoustic impedance depends on the energy transfer of an acoustic wave, in concert with the time domain transforming acoustic conductance at Hayat's Orchestrated instrument cluster. Little Queen Hayat Boumediene's Noel for Lowell includes a visitor center, as well as many restored and unrestored sites from the 19th century. The visitor center provides a free self-guided tour of the history of Lowell, including display exhibits such as the patent model of a loom by local inventor S. Thomas. A footpath along the Merrimack Canal from the visitor center is lined with plaques describing the importance of various existing and former sites along the canal. A bird on the wing, a field of blooms or a massive Sine wave in motion, The Boott Mills musical along the Merrimack River, on the Eastern Canal, is the most fully restored manufacturing site in the district, and one of the oldest. The Boott Mill provides a walk-through museum with living recreations of the textile manufacturing process in the 19th century. The walking tour includes a detour to a memorial to local author Jack Kerouac, who described the mid-20th century declined state of Lowell in several of his books. A walkway along the river leads to several additional unrestored mill sites, providing views of restored and unrestored canal raceways once used by the mills. Additionally, the park includes the Patrick J Mogan Cultural Center, which focuses on the lives of Lowell's many generations of immigrants. Other exhibits include a working streetcar line, canal boat tours exploring some of the city's gatehouses and locks, and the River Transformed / Suffolk Mill Turbine Exhibit, which shows how water power, the Francis Turbine, ran Lowell's textile factories.

Gigglesgoo President Trump just can't get no satisfaction that Jones reveals safe fondling allegations against husband Douglas. A former employee accused of Magistrating an incident in front of her 30 years ago. Self-induced playfulness is the stimulation of one's own for arousal or other pleasure, usually to the point of tickling. The stimulation may involve hands, fingers, everyday objects, toys such as vibrators, or combinations of these. Manual stimulation of a paw paw, such as fingering, a handjob or mutual fun, is a common act and can be a substitute for passion. Studies have found that daily, frequent in humans of both sexes and all ages, although there is variation. Various medical and psychological benefits have been attributed to a healthy attitude toward playful activity in general and to being penned-up in particular. No causal relationship is known between a Self-induced form of mental or physical disorder.

Could I have a little bit more of that cone dressing, gluten as well as other lectins baste The Hound of the Baskervilles pack of hounds subject to the crown. Celiac disease is caused due to immune reaction to eating gluten (a protein present in wheat / barley). Symptoms include vomiting, loss of appetite, bloating & gas, constipation, etc. Over a period of time intestinal lining gets damaged resulting in malabsorption. This condition in children can affect their growth and development. The best approach is to strictly follow a gluten free diet. gluten - a protein that's found in wheat, barley rye, and triticale - is just one type of lectin. One of the reasons grains may be such a problem to eat is because they contain lectins - in addition to gluten. Lectin causes weight gain because it acts similarly to insulin, the hormone that takes up glucose (sugar molecules) by your peripheral tissues (a.k.a. fat cells) for storage. Lectins are found naturally in grains, legumes, and plants as they act as a shield against pests, insects and many other microorganisms. Lectins are protein molecules, which bind to our cell membranes through carbohydrate or sugar. They can contain anti-nutrients, which are natural compounds that inhibit the natural production of enzymes to help support digestion and absorption. Anti-nutrients are pro-inflammatory and trigger an immune response within the body as well as feed the wrong type of bacteria within the colon. Lectin is harmful: Plants developed this protein as a defense against predators, a.k.a. animals and insects. Lectins disrupt your GI tract and allow bacteria to enter your immune system, causing "leaky gut" syndrome and inflammation - a state in which your body attempts to "fight" a vegetable predator. Research shows that including a high amount of lectins in the diet can create digestive difficulties (including increased intestinal permeability), weight gain, and brain fog. Reducing Your Lectin Intake: Olives, Olive Oil, Leafy Greens, Baked Root Vegetables (sweet potatoes, carrots), Broccoli, Cabbage, Brussel Sprouts, and Cauliflower. A "lectin-free" plan to help with an autoimmune disease and a thyroid issue, and losing weight as part of an "overall health approach."

- Lectin is found naturally in these foods:
  Beans and Legumes (including soy and peanuts)
  Nightshade Veggies (like tomatoes, eggplant, potatoes, and peppers)
  Eggs and Milk (because dairy cows and commercial chickens eat grains)
  Grains (especially quinoa and brown rice)

- Plant-based foods have incredible health benefits:
  Fruits and vegetables and have a lower concentration of lectins. Lectins can also influence absorption and digestion of crucial vitamins (such as essential energy-producing B vitamins: folic acid, thiamine, niacin, riboflavin) and minerals (magnesium, selenium, and iron).

Beary Gordy's Anthem for office workers in the U.S., Dolly "Harper Valley PartonTreesAnthology" 9 to 5'up and at 'em tenn four Queen Country, popular with SiriusXM and in nightclubs through ISIS' "dream Hayat not a wishy wood" - Khashoggi's consulate nude in a bar in a seaside town, swigging on a jug, Hayat getting down! Jamal Khashoggi described as an observant Muslim entered the Saudi Arabian consulate in Istanbul on 2 October 2018 in order to obtain documents related to his planned marriage. As no CCTV recorded him exiting the consulate, he was declared a missing person amid news reports claiming that he had been dismembered inside the consulate by three Roman consuls of the first French republic. An inspection of the consulate, by both Saudi Arabian and Turkish officials, took place on 15 October. Turkish officials found evidence of "tampering" during the inspection and evidence that supported the belief that Khashoggi had been killed. Initially, the Saudi Arabian government denied the death and claimed that Khashoggi had left the consulate alive but 18 days later said that he had died inside during a fistfight. This was contradicted on 25 October when Saudi Arabia's attorney general stated that the murder was premeditated.

THE QUEEN welcomed Melania Trump to Windsor Castle as the US First Lady's UK visit took a royal turn. Before the visit Mrs. Trump appeared starstruck to meet the world's longest-serving monarch, who she described as "incredible". Mrs. Trump and the president spent a total of 57 minutes with the Queen at the castle, and 47 of those minutes inside the monarch's favourite residence. The Trumps stayed 17 minutes longer than their expected departure time - indicating the pair got on very well. Ahead of the meeting between the heads of state, Mrs. Trump spoke of her admiration for the Queen in her interview with the Sun, in which she called her a "tremendous woman". She told the paper: "If you think of it, for so many years she has represented her country, she has really never made a mistake. "You don't see, like, anything embarrassing. She is just an incredible woman. "My husband is a tremendous fan of Charlotte. She has got a great and beautiful grace about her."

Hi, hi, hi, Hayat - Ante up E pluribus unum!

Dig a Poet darling How wonderful Hideaway, while Meghan Markle the princess adored.

"Patriotism is the exact opposite of nationalism. Nationalism is a betrayal of patriotism," adorned into consideration Arc de Triomphe, "Bill" Hayat Boumediene Patriot turned Nationalist walking on John Lennon's kid toehold. The Arc de Triomphe de l'Étoile is one of the most famous monuments in Paris, standing at the western end of the Champs-Élysées at the center of Place Charles de Gaulle, formerly named Place de l'Étoile— the étoile or "star" of the juncture formed by its twelve radiating avenues. Beneath the Arc is the Tomb of the Unknown Soldier, by the same token did anybody join the European Army? Built in the 1300s during the Hundred Years' War against the English, a fortress was designed to protect the eastern entrance to the city of Paris. The formidable stone building's massive defenses included 100-foot-high walls and a wide moat, plus more than 80 regular soldiers and 30 Swiss mercenaries standing guard. Despite inheriting tremendous debts from his predecessor, Louis XVI and Marie Antoinette continued to spend extravagantly, such as by helping the American colonies win their independence from the British. By the late 1780s, France's government stood on the brink of economic disaster. To make matters worse, widespread crop failures in 1788 brought about a nationwide famine. Bread prices rose so high that, at their peak, the average worker spent about 88 percent of his wages on just that one staple. Unemployment was likewise a problem, which the populace blamed in part on newly reduced customs duties between France and Britain. Following a harsh winter, violent food riots began breaking out across France at bakeries, granaries and other food storage facilities. A national assembly divided by social class into three orders: clergy (First Estate), nobility

(Second Estate) and commoners (Third Estate). National Assembly establishing a new written constitution Unrest continued. The Storming of the Bastille (French: Prise de la Bastille) occurred in Paris, France, on the afternoon of 14 July 1789. The medieval fortress, armory, and political prison in Paris known as the Bastille represented royal authority in the centre of Paris. The prison contained just seven inmates at the time of its storming, four forgers, two "lunatics" and one "deviant" aristocrat many of whom were locked away without a trial by order of the king. Was seen by the revolutionaries as a symbol of the monarchy's abuses of power; the storming of the Bastille, which began the French Revolution, as an allegory for revolutionary fervor needed in the struggle against tyrannical government. Formally called la Fête nationale and commonly and legally Le quatorze juillet; "the 14th of July," which is a national holiday in France, celebrates the actions of a mob of Frenchmen, tired of the rule of their king, who stormed a prison to get weapons and free prisoners. Limited purpose, had led to a decision being made shortly before the disturbances began to replace it with an open public space. In accord with principles of popular sovereignty and with complete disregard for claims of royal authority, the people established parallel structures of municipalities for civic government and militias for civic protection. In rural areas, many went beyond this: some burned title-deeds and no small number of châteaux, as the "Great Fear" spread across the countryside during the weeks, with attacks on wealthy landlords impelled by the belief that the aristocracy was trying to put down the revolution. Help defend French National Assembly against future asteroid impact threats, Space Force proposed is intended to have control over military operations in outer space.

A swaddling beach buff, Hayat Bomediene knows she can rely on her US National Park quarters to come into possession of soon after the seas amass in Meghan and Harry's Alloga newborn. Cumberland Island is really two islands—the island proper and Little Cumberland Island—connected by a marsh. While sometimes confused to be a part of Cumberland Island, Little Cumberland is a separate island and is not a part of Cumberland Island. Live oak wood from the island was used to build the USS Constitution, "Old Ironsides," in the 1790s. Since the national seashore was established, a Navy nuclear submarine base has been built on the mainland. From the Timuca, Guale, and Mocamo Indians to the subsequent appearances of Spanish, French, African, British, and American inhabitants, Cumberland Island is home to 17 miles of uninterrupted beach. No docks, houses, or other structures interrupt its serene beauty. The island boasts a healthy expanse of vegetated dunes that make it one of the most important nesting spots for loggerhead sea turtles in all of Georgia, and a sanctuary for migrating shore birds.

Pizzazz, Kansas City, and Douglas, home to the University of Kansas, a quick KU Kansas State KSU Quarters stellato. Masquerading disguise reserves Hayat mercenary in Dodge City was Ford Counties Wild West-era to the Union's free state! Hurst Wonder Woman, Little Queen "Bill" Hayat Boumediene Chisholm trailed large herds of wild bison from Dodge City, famously known for the cattle drive days of the late 19th century, built along the old Santa Fe Trail. An attractive combination of star vitality and glamour, The Duke and Duchess of Sussex, chief's city royals frenzy who will be the next "Queen of the Cowtowns." Hayat's US State collectors quarters sunflower her passages on the American buffalo range.

Hayat Yoga Shala wishy wood figure to anything but bootleg compassion

Wishy -wood Star- Amphitheatre Nashville

A planet, constellation, or configuration regarded as influencing Hayat Boumediene as the Bolsheviks took over Russia and transformed it into the Soviet Union, the first communist country of all time. A constellation is a group of stars that forms an imaginary outline or meaningful pattern on the celestial sphere, typically representing an animal, mythological person or creature, a god, or an inanimate object.

Shala

An ancient Sumerian goddess of grain and the emotion of compassion. The symbols of grain and compassion combine to reflect the importance of agriculture in the mythology of Sumer, and the belief that an abundant harvest was an act of compassion from the deities. Traditions identify Shala as wife of the fertility god Dagon, or consort of the storm god Hadad' also called Ishkur. In ancient depictions, she carries a double-headed mace or scimitar embellished with lion heads. Sometimes she is depicted as being borne atop one or two lionesses. From very early times, she is associated with the constellation Virgo and vestiges of symbolism associated with her have persisted in representations of the constellation to current times, such as the ear of grain, even as the deity name changed from culture to culture. The Shala Mons, a mountain on Venus, is named after her.

Whereabouts of Hayat Boumediene? Connect with your SOUL "hounds couldn't catch 'em Hickory Hayat Boumediene where a rabbit couldn't go." One breath, one moment, one step at a time. Yoga for a safe and loving environment, where together, practice the ancient art of yoga in holistic and wellness Hayat Yoga Shala. Hayat not a never was, Hayat going just because, not a never can - make you understand, Hayat not a wishy wood, she makes herself look good, better than ever should, Hayat not a never been - Keep look'in out for Hayat, she's an ISIS dream.

Philippe Rumple scoops Lincoln barbell In on Lebron Gore's hoops to bully pulpit Politics. Rumple has publicly praised Lebron on Twitter in the past, calling him "fantastic" and "terrific." "As much as I have in the past and would like to continue voting for musician athletes in office, let's say I like Gore's music about 25 percent less now, OK?" All you'll want to do is stay and shake-it-off, I wish you would! Drink the Bad Blood cocktails and have wildest dreams about how to get the girl, this love I know places clean. Wonderland you are in love with the new romantics, New York, at her luxury room a blank space with style out of the woods, sitting in a bar in a seaside town, swigging on a jug, Hayat getting down! "And the wants and the needs Of a woman your age... ruby I realize." A bully pulpit is a conspicuous position that provides an opportunity to speak out and be listened to. This term was coined by United States President Theodore Roosevelt, who referred to his office as a "bully pulpit", by which he meant a terrific platform from which to advocate an agenda.

Pleased to meet you, hope you guessed my brand. Peter Pan, who who; Reeses, who who; Skippy, who who; Jiff, who who. But what's puzzling you is the nature of my Jam? Butter 'em up Jack, Hayat dean devil's food off your local grocer's shelf! Cordell Hull wants a National Park Que reputation tailored to fit. Coin Liberty jukebox eminent, so ever pardon me enlightened commandments, swift's courtship higher. Cordell Hull wants his United National Park Que. TAD sentinel, 25 quarter cent Army Air Force veterans' bonus roll-call condoling to Little Queen Hayat Boumediene!

Christopher Columbus Day 2018. Admiral of the late 15th Century Ocean Sea. The Great Navigator. Renown as the champion of the belief that the earth was round. The man who sought the riches of the Far East by sailing to the west, and who happened instead upon a New World. On October 12, 1492, he landed at a small island in the Bahamas - The man who discovered America. Florida is a state on the gulf coast in the Southeastern United States. It is bounded by. Gulf of Mexico and Atlantic Ocean. It was discovered by Ponce de Leon, Juan, a Spanish explorer in 1513. He led the first European expedition to Florida. French Florida was a colonial territory established by French Huguenot colonists in what is now Florida between 1562 and 1565. The colonial endeavour was started following plans by the French Huguenot leader, Admiral of France Gaspard de Coligny, to establish New World colonies where his persecuted Protestant coreligionists could safely establish themselves. The first such attempt was an establishment in Brazil, named France Antarctique.

Along with Hawaii, Florida is one of only two states that has a tropical climate.

Swanee - how I love ya, how I love ya Gateway To Discovery

My dear old swanees Geico Reptiles: eastern diamondback and pygmy rattlesnakes, gopher tortoise, green and leatherback sea turtles, eastern indigo snake, and one million American alligators and 1,500 crocodiles. Personal injury protection auto insurance is mandatory for drivers, a no-fault insurance law. Where parts of West Florida claimed as the region as part of the Louisiana Purchase by many refugees from Cuba fleeing Fidel Castro's communist regime. In an age of unbelievable technological progress—one would think such changes would have brought about a new age of utopian technology. Yet in many areas of life, things don't seem to have changed all that much, and transportation is a woeful example of this. The roads are still lined with cars, the skies speckled with airliners. Science fiction foresaw flying cars and teleporters; the 21st century settled for Segways. Walt Disney World Resort, Universal Orlando Resort, SeaWorld Orlando and Busch Gardens Tampa reflects Tourism to Amusement parks making up the In God We Trust state economy. Citrus fruit, especially oranges with orange juice the official state beverage, while sugarcane strawberries, tomatoes and celery, sweet corn and green beans are The Sunshine States La Florida ([la flo'riða] "the land of flowers". Sunshine "Bill" Hayat's generous US State penny-pinchers, niggardly quarter hoarding where the sawgrass meets the sky there are treasures for all who venture here in Florida. Just look at Hypervitaminosis C and Fruit Loop Lory, they're still livid to the blacksmith's workshop; a smithy letter! Sometimes it takes forge of a singular docket for my Little Booger and East Nashvillian Snodgrass futures Hayat Boumediene, Iginogin and one million tin quartering of soldiers behind her balls to be a woman.

Trump scoops In on Taylor Swift's Turn to Politics. Trump has publicly praised Swift on Twitter in the past, calling her "fantastic" and "terrific." "As much as I have in the past and would like to continue voting for women in office, let's say I like Taylor's music about 25 percent less now, OK?" All you'll want to do is stay and shake-it-off, I wish you would! Drink the Bad Blood cocktails and have wildest dreams about how to get the girl, this love I know places clean. Wonderland you are in love with the new romantics,

New York, at her luxury room a blank space with style out of the woods, sitting in a bar in a seaside town, swigging on a jug, Marsha BB getting down! "And the wants and the needs of a woman your age… ruby I realize."

The "amero" is the denomination given to what would be the North American Union's counterpart to the euro. The euro (sign: €; code: EUR) is the official currency of the European Union and its territories. Currently, 19 of 28 member states use the euro; this group of states is known as the eurozone or euro area. It is the second largest and second most traded currency in the foreign exchange market after the United States dollar. The euro is subdivided into 100 cents. The North American monetary union is a theoretical economic and monetary union of three North American countries: Canada, the United States of America and Mexico. Implementation would involve the three countries giving up their current currency units (the U.S. dollar, the Canadian dollar, and the Mexican peso) and adopting a new one, created specifically for this purpose (some versions of the theory assume only the United States and Canada would be included). The hypothetical currency for the union is most often referred to as the amero. The concept is modeled on the common European Union currency (the euro). French-speaking province of Quebec would undoubtedly mean for Canada the adoption of the U.S. dollar and U.S. monetary policy. Canada would have to give up its control of domestic inflation and interest rates to sheer dominance of the United States in any such North American monetary union. However, this shared among the Bank of Canada, the Federal Reserve, and the Banco de México and not exclusively held by the United States. Conversely Debt the state of owing money, or a feeling of gratitude for a service or favor are factors affecting currency prices in the differing economic situations between each country. NAFTA 2.0 the US-Mexico-Canada Agreement (USMCA), updates the 1994 North American Free Trade Agreement, promising to lead "to freer, fairer markets, and to robust economic growth" in the three-country free trade area used as a "modernized" agreement that "will strengthen the middle class, and create good, well-paying jobs."

Hayat Boumediene and Iginogin win back The White Houses Ruby splendor, hail democracy! They say you want a revolution, We better get on it right away, You better get on your feet, And head to the street, saying "rule of the people," Power to the people, Power to the people, right on!

War, patriotic chore
bent and paralyzed
ain't nothin' but a hound dog, scratchin' all the time
ain't caught no rabbits ain't no friend of mine
Well, said was high class
Found out that was just a lie
Ruby, I realized
Don't take your love to town

Yearnings for non-food items such as ice, clay, dirt and chalk can often mean an iron deficiency or mineral deficiency in general. Consume plenty of dark green leafy vegetables, legumes, nuts and seeds for the prevention of pica. Hayat Boumediene handshakes undergroped and pacified, a fulfilled longing for her Viking Pea-Bees in that Voyageurs US Park Quarters, brokerage to debit retainers is take-home conciliatory pay. Voyageurs National Park is located on the Canadian Shield, with the rocks averaging between 1 and 3 billion years old. Formed during the early ages of the earth formation, the rocks of the park were compressed, and folded under tremendous pressure. Then molten flows of lava intruded through the layers creating a mosaic of various gneiss and granites. Voyageurs National Park is a United States National Park in northern Minnesota near the town of International Falls established in 1975. The park's name commemorates the voyageurs—French-Canadian fur traders who were the first European settlers to frequently travel through the area. The park is notable for its outstanding water resources and is popular with canoeists, kayakers, other boaters, and fishermen. The Kabetogama Peninsula, which lies entirely within the park and makes up most of its land area, is accessible only by boat. To the east of the National Park lies the Boundary Waters Canoe Area Wilderness. The largest city near Voyageurs National Park is International Falls, Minnesota. Unlike many other national parks, where the main access to the park is by motor vehicle, bicycle or foot, the primary access to Voyageurs is via water. Many visitors travel many ways such as kayaks and canoes, while others rent houseboats or take a guided tour boat. Ash River, Kabetogama Lake, Rainy Lake, Namakan Lake, Sand Point Lake, Crane Lake. The park has three shanty visitor centers for craving SPAM(r), main course "camp job," hot or cold a Paul Bunyan caviar, taken from the eggs of blue ribbon lake sturgeon.

Four score and Confucius ears anode, the Black lead (-) is connected to the cathode The Red lead (+) is connected to the anode

Dem bones, dem bones, dem dry bones,

The Black lead (-) is connected to the item to be plated, the cathode. The Red lead (+) is connected to the solution electrode, the anode. An anode is an electrode through which conventional current flows into a polarized electrical device. A common mnemonic is ACID for "anode current into device". The direction of (positive) electric current is opposite to the direction of electron flow: (negatively charged) electrons flow out the anode to the outside circuit.

Bath Gold (Immersion Plating) is advantageous if an entire item, or multiple items require a consistent layer of gold plating. A (+)positively charged lead wire is clipped to an Anode which is stationary in the bath of gold plating solution. The item to be gold plated is attached to a conductive wire rack or alligator clip charged with a (-)negative current lead wire. The entire part is dipped into the solution and allowed to plate for a duration of time (generally 3-5 minutes). The longer the item is left in the gold plating solution, the thicker the layer of 24k gold will be. This gold plating solution was designed with a lower gold concentration for maximum affordability and efficiency. Since a higher volume is required to fill a beaker that will fit your parts, the gold content per fluid ounce is substantially lower than that of other solutions.

24K Bright Gold Plating Solution is cobalt hardened acid gold electroplating solution that will yield a relatively low stress, fine grained deposit with hardness range of 130-200 Knoop. This solution is ideally suited for printed circuit boards, contacts, reflectors, as well as heavy decorative deposits.

Brush Gold Brush gold plating is a method of electroplating that allows you to plate specific areas of an item. With brush plating: an 'application handle' fitted with a cotton 'application sleeve' is dipped into the solution. The gold plating solution is carried in the sleeve. A (-) common lead is attached to the item you are plating, and a (+) positive lead is plugged into the handle. When the gold plating solution is "brushed" onto the item, the electrical circuit is completed and the gold bonds to the item in the area you brushing.

Pen Gold Pen gold plating is a style of brush plating that allows for ultra-fine detailed electroplating. A 'fine-select' absorbent pen plating tip is inserted into the 'application handle', then dipped into the high concentration Pen Gold plating solution. The high gold content and superior formulation of 'Pen Gold Plating solution', along with the "Sharpie" like 'fine-select' tip, provide a unique opportunity to apply a rich 24k gold to areas as small as 1mm with outstanding precision.

Brandy nonchalant When a woman loves a man loves a women science data insights at Picker(tm) X-ray and elsewhere theory applicable. Closest Syrian blue purses, for a day of peace and reckoning - "Hex Nesting calculus," a Brexit like no others had this idea embellished. "No one else could do the math," explains British Prime Minister Theresa May. Hayat Boumediene for customs and regulatory checks at our shared borders, an arrangement would also protect integrated supply chains and just-in-time processes. A free trade area on famous 409 trivia for the sake of a Pinocchio deal? Pinocchio is a fictional character and the protagonist of the children's novel The Adventures of Pinocchio by Italian writer Carlo Collodi. Carved by a woodcarver named Geppetto in a village near Lucca, he was created as a wooden puppet but dreamed of becoming a real boy. He lies often. Hayat 5.0 Loft ten. The Trees

God save our gracious Queen!
Long live our Little Queen!

root of all evil; twig of despair Don't forsake Hayat Boumediene as any other dogma! Hayat's changes were there ranean mediter, Joy to the One, cheek my boys and girls now. Hayat heir di to the deep blue sea, Quarters for her safe keep. If Hayat were the Queen of the world, I tell you what she'd do; Eiffel martyr all the narc's and the sharks in the world, worsen of being a Jew. Let me tell you now, Joy to the word! If Hayat's friends recover her sister Judy's jogging shoes back, a Name of the Star, fell from a star; Come out Hayat Boumediene wherever you are! Judy Garland will once again wear crayola costume lipstick jewelry for Little Queen midterm elections. An election is a formal decision-making process by which a population chooses an individual to hold public office. Elections have been the usual mechanism by which modern representative democracy has operated since the 17th century. Elections may fill offices in the legislature, sometimes in the executive and judiciary, and for regional and local government. High heels Shucks just can't get through to you; Hayat Eiffel it, it's time to admit it, Judy Garland, depicted Witch of then Dorothy, Tower aye any 20-dollar bill won't do. Hayat is a runaway, worsen of being a Jew - Paris tap; Hayat is a runaway The Wizard of Oz story come true.

For the love of money is the root of all evil; For the hate of money is the twig of despair. Dynasties bought and sold place mounting evidence a higher that one can achieve by overshadowing his/her opponent's strength or weakness produce starving hunger in any populous branch. Zealous or fervent are a minds greatest asset when all is lost. President Trump "as skeptical of atheism as of any other dogma." Princess Charlotte cracks the champagne during Dutchess Fergie's butterfly salute to soiled slippers croustade, or Harry's drumroll of Hayat's holey Eggs Benedict in utero - also informally known as Eggs Benny, is a traditional American breakfast

or brunch dish that consists of two halves of an English muffin each of which is topped with Canadian bacon, ham or sometimes bacon, a poached egg, and hollandaise sauce. The dish was first popularized in New York City. Many variations on the basic recipe are served. - Mademoiselle, Hayat Boumediene heir di! Undiscovered Cherished Treasures - Silver, Blue, and Gold—For which element Give thee... sky I'm told. Don't forsake Hayat's Byzantine Empire currency coinage - Solidus, histamenon and hyperpyron, also referred to as the Eastern Roman Empire Byzantium, was the gold, bronze, silver, and copper of the Roman Empire in its eastern provinces during Late Antiquity and the Middle Ages. It survived the fragmentation and fall of the Western Roman Empire in the 5th century AD and continued to exist for an additional thousand years until it fell to the Ottoman Turks in 1453. During most of its existence, the empire was the most powerful economic, cultural, and military force in Europe. Both "Byzantine Empire" and "Eastern Roman Empire" are historiographical terms created after the end of the realm; its citizens continued to refer to their empire as the Roman Empire, or Romania, and to themselves as "Romans" later became Constantinople, and later Istanbul because I love you.

Hebrews 13:5 Keep your lives free from the love of money and be content with what you have, because God has said, "Never will I leave you; never will I forsake you." Deuteronomy 31:6 Be strong and courageous. Do not be afraid or terrified because of them, for the Lord your God goes with you; he will never leave you nor forsake you." Deuteronomy 31:8 The Lord himself goes before you and will be with you; he will never leave you nor forsake you. Do not be afraid; do not be discouraged." Deuteronomy 31:16 And the Lord said to Moses: "You are going to rest with your ancestors, and these people will soon prostitute themselves to the foreign gods of the land they are entering. They will forsake me and break the covenant I made with them. Deuteronomy 31:17 And in that day I will become angry with them and forsake them; I will hide my face from them, and they will be destroyed. Many disasters and calamities will come on them, and in that day they will ask, 'Have not these disasters come on us because our God is not with us?' Joshua 1:5 No one will be able to stand against you all the days of your life. As I was with Moses, so I will be with you; I will never leave you nor forsake you. Joshua 24:16 Then the people answered, "Far be it from us to forsake the Lord to serve other gods! Joshua 24:20 If you forsake the Lord and serve foreign gods, he will turn and bring disaster on you and make an end of you, after he has been good to you." Judges 10:13 But you have forsaken me and served other gods, so I will no longer save you. 1 Samuel 12:10 They cried out to the Lord and said, 'We have sinned; we have forsaken the Lord and served the Baals and the Ashtoreths. But now deliver us from the hands of our enemies, and we will serve you.' 1 Kings 8:57 May the Lord our God be with us as he was with our ancestors; may he never leave us nor forsake us. 1 Kings 9:9 People will answer, 'Because they have forsaken the Lord their God, who brought their ancestors out of Egypt, and have embraced other gods, worshiping and serving them—that is why the Lord brought all this disaster on them.'" 1 Kings 11:33 I will do this because they have forsaken me and worshiped Ashtoreth the goddess of the Sidonians, Chemosh the god of the Moabites, and Molek the god of the Ammonites, and have not walked in obedience to me, nor done what is right in my eyes, nor kept my decrees and laws as David, Solomon's father, did. 2 Kings 21:14 I will forsake the remnant of my inheritance and give them into the hands of enemies. They will be looted and plundered by all their enemies; 2 Kings 22:17 Because they have forsaken me and burned incense to other gods and aroused my anger by all the idols their hands have made, my anger will burn against this place and will not be quenched.' 1 Chronicles 28:9 "And you, my son Solomon, acknowledge the God of your father, and serve him with wholehearted devotion and with a willing mind, for the Lord searches every heart and understands every desire and every thought. If you seek him, he will be found by you; but if you forsake him, he will reject you forever. 1 Chronicles 28:20 David also said to Solomon his son, "Be strong and courageous, and do the work. Do not be afraid or discouraged, for the Lord God, my God, is with you. He will not fail you or forsake you until all the work for the service of the temple of the Lord is finished. 2 Chronicles 7:19 "But if you turn away and forsake the decrees and commands I have given you and go off to serve other gods and worship them, 2 Chronicles 7:22 People will answer, 'Because they have forsaken the Lord, the God of their ancestors, who brought them out of Egypt, and have embraced other gods, worshiping and serving them—that is why he brought all this disaster on them.'" 2 Chronicles 13:10 "As for us, the Lord is our God, and we have not forsaken him. The priests who serve the Lord are sons of Aaron, and the Levites assist them. 2 Chronicles 13:11 Every morning and evening they present burnt offerings and fragrant incense to the Lord. They set out the bread on the ceremonially clean table and light the lamps on the gold lampstand every evening. We are observing the requirements of the Lord our God. But you have forsaken him. 2 Chronicles 15:2 He went out to meet Asa and said to him, "Listen to me, Asa and all Judah and Benjamin. The Lord is with you when you are with him. If you seek him, he will be found by you, but if you forsake him, he will forsake you. 2 Chronicles 21:10 To this day Edom has been in rebellion against Judah. Libnah revolted at the same time, because Jehoram had forsaken the Lord, the God of his ancestors. 2 Chronicles 24:20 Then the Spirit of God came on Zechariah son of Jehoiada the priest. He stood before the people and said, "This is what God says: 'Why do you disobey the Lord's commands? You will not prosper. Because you have forsaken the Lord, he has forsaken you.'" 2 Chronicles 24:24 Although the Aramean army had come with only a few men, the Lord delivered into their hands a much larger army. Because Judah had forsaken the Lord, the God of their ancestors, judgment was executed on Joash. 2 Chronicles 28:6 In one day Pekah son of Remaliah killed a hundred and twenty thousand soldiers in Judah—because Judah had forsaken the Lord, the God of their ancestors. 2 Chronicles 34:25 Because they have forsaken me and burned incense to other gods and aroused my anger by all that their hands have made, my anger will be poured out on this place and will not be quenched.' Ezra 8:22 I was ashamed to ask the king for soldiers and horsemen to protect us from enemies on the road, because we had told the king, "The gracious hand of our God is on everyone who looks to him, but his great anger is against all who forsake him." Ezra 9:9 Though we are slaves, our God has not forsaken us in our bondage. He has shown us kindness in the sight of the kings of Persia: He has granted us new life to rebuild the house of our God and repair its ruins, and he has given us a wall of protection in Judah and Jerusalem. Ezra 9:10 "But now, our God, what can we say after this? For we have forsaken the commands Job 6:14 "Anyone who withholds kindness from a friend forsakes the fear of the Almighty. Psalm 9:10 Those who know your name trust in you, for you, Lord, have never forsaken those who seek you. Psalm 22:1 [Psalm 22] [For the director of music. To the tune of "The Doe of the Morning." A psalm of David.] My God, my God, why have you forsaken me? Why are you so far from saving me, so far from my cries of anguish? Psalm 27:9 Do not hide your face from me, do not turn your servant away in anger; you have been my helper. Do not reject me or forsake me, God my Savior. Psalm 27:10 Though my father and mother forsake me, the Lord will receive me. Psalm 37:25 I was young and now I am old, yet I have never seen the righteous forsaken or their children begging bread. Psalm 37:28 For the Lord loves the just and will not forsake his faithful ones. Wrongdoers will be completely destroyed; the offspring of the wicked will perish. Psalm 38:21 Lord, do not forsake me; do not be far from me, my God. Psalm 71:9 Do not cast me away when I am old; do not forsake me when my strength is gone. Psalm 71:11 They say, "God has forsaken him; pursue him and seize him, for no one will rescue him." Psalm 71:18 Even when I am old and gray, do not forsake me, my God, till I declare your power to the next generation, your mighty acts to all who are to come. Psalm 89:30 "If his sons forsake my law and do not follow my statutes, Psalm 94:14 For the Lord will not reject his people; he will never forsake his inheritance. Psalm 119:8 I will obey your decrees; do not utterly forsake me. Psalm 119:53 Indignation grips me because of the wicked, who have forsaken your law. Psalm 119:87 They almost wiped me from the earth, but I have not forsaken your precepts. Proverbs 1:8 [Prologue: Exhortations to Embrace Wisdom] [Warning Against the Invitation of Sinful Men] Listen, my son, to your father's instruction and do not forsake your mother's teaching. Proverbs 4:2 I give you sound learning, so do not forsake my teaching. Proverbs 4:6 Do not forsake wisdom, and she will protect you; love her, and she will watch over you. Proverbs 6:20 [Warning Against Adultery] My son, keep your father's command and do not forsake your mother's teaching. Proverbs 27:10 Do not forsake your friend or a friend of your family, and do not go to your relative's house when disaster strikes you—better a neighbor nearby than a relative far away. Proverbs 28:4 Those who forsake instruction praise the wicked, but those who heed it resist them. Isaiah 1:4 Woe to the sinful nation, a people whose guilt is great, a brood of evildoers, children given to corruption! They have forsaken the Lord; they have spurned the Holy One of Israel and turned their backs on him. Isaiah 1:28 But rebels and sinners will both be broken, and those who forsake the Lord will perish. Isaiah 6:12 until the Lord has sent everyone far away and the land is utterly forsaken. Isaiah 27:10 The fortified city stands desolate, an abandoned settlement, forsaken like the wilderness; there the calves graze, there they lie down; they strip its branches bare. Isaiah 41:17 "The poor and needy search for water, but there is none; their tongues are parched with thirst. But I the Lord will answer them; I, the God of Israel, will not forsake them. Isaiah 42:16 I will lead the blind by ways they have not known, along unfamiliar paths I will guide them; I will turn the darkness into light before them and make the rough places smooth. These are the things I will do; I will not forsake them. Isaiah 49:14 But Zion said, "The Lord has forsaken me, the Lord has forgotten me." Isaiah 55:7 Let the wicked forsake their ways and the unrighteous their thoughts. Let them turn to the Lord, and he will have mercy on them, and to our God, for he will freely pardon. Isaiah 58:2 For day after day they seek me out; they seem eager to know my ways, as if they were a nation that does what is right and has not forsaken the commands of its God. They ask me for just decisions and seem eager for God to come near them. Isaiah 60:15 "Although you have been forsaken and hated, with no one traveling through, I will make you the everlasting pride and the joy of all generations. Isaiah 65:11 "But as for you who forsake the Lord and forget my holy mountain, who spread a table for Fortune and fill bowls of mixed wine for Destiny, Jeremiah 2:1 [Israel Forsakes God] The word of the Lord came to me: Jeremiah 2:13 "My people have committed two sins: They have forsaken me, the spring of living water, and have dug their own cisterns, broken cisterns that cannot hold water. Jeremiah 2:19 Your wickedness will punish you; your backsliding will rebuke you. Consider then and realize how evil and bitter it is for you when you forsake the Lord your God and have no awe of me," declares the Lord, the Lord Almighty. Jeremiah 5:7 "Why should I forgive you? Your children have forsaken me and sworn by gods that are not gods. I supplied all their needs, yet they committed adultery and thronged to the houses of prostitutes. Jeremiah

5:19 And when the people ask, 'Why has the Lord our God done all this to us?' you will tell them, 'As you have forsaken me and served foreign gods in your own land, so now you will serve foreigners in a land not your own.' Jeremiah 9:13 The Lord said, "It is because they have forsaken my law, which I set before them; they have not obeyed me or followed my law. Jeremiah 12:7 "I will forsake my house, abandon my inheritance; I will give the one I love into the hands of her enemies. Jeremiah 14:9 Why are you like a man taken by surprise, like a warrior powerless to save? You are among us, Lord, and we bear your name; do not forsake us! Jeremiah 17:13 Lord, you are the hope of Israel; all who forsake you will be put to shame. Those who turn away from you will be written in the dust because they have forsaken the Lord, the spring of living water. Jeremiah 19:4 For they have forsaken me and made this a place of foreign gods; they have burned incense in it to gods that neither they nor their ancestors nor the kings of Judah ever knew, and they have filled this place with the blood of the innocent. Jeremiah 22:9 And the answer will be: 'Because they have forsaken the covenant of the Lord their God and have worshiped and served other gods.'" Jeremiah 23:33 [False Prophecy] "When these people, or a prophet or a priest, ask you, 'What is the message from the Lord?' say to them, 'What message? I will forsake you, declares the Lord.' Jeremiah 51:5 For Israel and Judah have not been forsaken by their God, the Lord Almighty, though their land is full of guilt before the Holy One of Israel. Lamentations 5:20 Why do you always forget us? Why do you forsake us so long? Ezekiel 8:12 He said to me, "Son of man, have you seen what the elders of Israel are doing in the darkness, each at the shrine of his own idol? They say, 'The Lord does not see us; the Lord has forsaken the land.'" Ezekiel 9:9 He answered me, "The sin of the people of Israel and Judah is exceedingly great; the land is full of bloodshed and the city is full of injustice. They say, 'The Lord has forsaken the land; the Lord does not see.' Ezekiel 20:8 "'But they rebelled against me and would not listen to me; they did not get rid of the vile images they had set their eyes on, nor did they forsake the idols of Egypt. So I said I would pour out my wrath on them and spend my anger against them in Egypt. Daniel 11:30 Ships of the western coastlands will oppose him, and he will lose heart. Then he will turn back and vent his fury against the holy covenant. He will return and show favor to those who forsake the holy covenant. Matthew 27:46 About three in the afternoon Jesus cried out in a loud voice, "Eli, Eli, lema sabachthani?" (which means "My God, my God, why have you forsaken me?"). Mark 15:34 And at three in the afternoon Jesus cried out in a loud voice, "Eloi, Eloi, lema sabachthani?" (which means "My God, my God, why have you forsaken me?"). Hebrews 13:5 Keep your lives free from the love of money and be content with what you have, because God has said, "Never will I leave you; never will I forsake you." Revelation 2:4 Yet I hold this against you: You have forsaken the love you had at first.

Hayat Boumediene's anticipated US State of Alabama quarters arrival first week of September 2018, mined as a precious twenty-five cent coin maker's mineral. Mineralogy as a naturally occurring inorganic solid having a specific and characteristic chemical composition and usually possessing a definite crystalline structure. Alabama's mineral diversity relates to the rocks types found in the state. A rock can be made of a single mineral or an aggregate of several minerals, and all rocks belong to one of three groups: igneous, sedimentary, and metamorphic. The diverse geologic makeup of the state is reflected in the large number of different mineral species found in Alabama. Most of the state is covered with sedimentary rocks, with exposures of igneous and metamorphic rocks being confined to the east-central part of the state. Alabama minerals vary from common rock-forming minerals such as clay, calcite, and quartz to precious metals such as gold, and notably;

Pyrite Ore

Pyrite (iron disulfide), known popularly on The Yellow Brick Road as fool's gold, is a common mineral in the Piedmont and occurs in metamorphic, igneous, and sedimentary rocks. Pyrite deposits in the Hillabee Greenstone geologic formation in the vicinity of Pyriton, Clay County, Alabama were first mined in the 1850s by mining companies for the production of sulphur acid and elemental sulfur. Production of pyrite for sulfur used in manufacturing chemicals continued throughout intermittently, be that as it may Pyrite enjoyed brief popularity in the

16th and 17th centuries as a source of ignition in early firearms. Hence Yellowhammer State the Alabama wheellock, where the cock held a lump of pyrite against a circular file to strike the sparks needed to fire the gun. Pyrite has been used since classical times to manufacture copperas, that is, iron(II) sulfate. Iron pyrite was heaped up and allowed to weather (an example of an early form of heap leaching). The acidic runoff from the heap was then boiled with iron to produce iron sulfate. In the 15th century, new methods of such leaching began to replace the burning of sulfur as a source of sulfuric acid. By the 19th century, it had become the dominant method. Pyrite remains in commercial use for the production of sulfur dioxide, for use in such applications as the paper industry, and in the manufacture of sulfuric acid. Thermal decomposition of pyrite into FeS (iron(II) sulfide) and elemental sulfur starts at 540 °C; at around 700 °C pS2 is about 1 atm. A newer commercial use for pyrite is as the cathode material in Energizer brand non-rechargeable lithium batteries. Pyrite is a semiconductor material with a band gap of 0.95 eV. During the early years of the 20th century, pyrite was used as a mineral detector in radio receivers, and is still used by crystal radio hobbyists. Until the vacuum tube matured, the crystal detector was the most sensitive and dependable detector available – with considerable variation between mineral types and even individual samples within a particular type of mineral. Pyrite detectors occupied a midway point between galena detectors and the more mechanically complicated perikon mineral pairs. Pyrite detectors can be as sensitive as a modern 1N34A germanium diode detector. Pyrite has been proposed as an abundant, inexpensive material in low-cost photovoltaic solar panels. Synthetic iron sulfide was used with copper sulfide to create the photovoltaic material. Pyrite is used to make marcasite jewelry. Marcasite jewelry, made from small faceted pieces of pyrite, often set in silver, was known since ancient times and was popular in the spoon Victorian era. At the time when the term became common in jewelry making, "marcasite" referred to all iron sulfides including pyrite, and not to the orthorhombic FeS2 mineral marcasite which is lighter in color, brittle and chemically unstable, and thus not suitable for jewelry making. Marcasite jewelry does not actually contain the mineral marcasite and belong to the pyrite group. Pyrite usually forms cuboid crystals, sometimes forming in close association to form raspberry-shaped masses called framboids. However, under certain circumstances, it can form anastamozing filaments or T-shaped crystals. Pyrite can also form almost perfect dodecahedral shapes known as pyritohedra and this suggests an explanation for the artificial geometrical models found in Europe as early as the 5th century BC. It is distinguishable from native gold by its hardness, brittleness and crystal form. Natural gold tends to be anhedral (irregularly shaped), whereas pyrite comes as either cubes or multifaceted crystals. Pyrite can often be distinguished by the striations which, in many cases, can be seen on its surface. Chalcopyrite is brighter yellow with a greenish hue when wet and is softer (3.5–4 on Mohs' scale). Arsenopyrite is silver white and does not become more yellow when wet.

- little pretentious – an Aborigine, especially one from northern Queensland in mint condition

Pristine 25 quarter cent roll, Our finest gifts we bring. This little pretension backs silver and gold, this little consequence sends where they belong, this little French Quarter has copper and nickel, this little pyrite smelter had none, Brassy Hayat Boumediene trumpeted all the way home from Syria;

"wee wee

wee wee!" Pa rum pum pum pum!

a pleasant fragrance to the raspberries crayon Off the roof of your mouth Many colors lipstick.

To give a pleasant fragrance to the raspberries crayon pigment fix, and making use of pincers to tassel Trump Towers wired Slinky roof gardens antenna. Off the roof of your mouth Hayat's Worn Lipstick as a cosmetic product containing pigments, oils, waxes, and emollients that apply color, texture, and protection to the lips. Many colors and types of lipstick exist. As with most other types of makeup, lipstick is typically but not exclusively, worn by women. Some lipsticks are also lip balms, to add color and hydration. Embalming is the art and science of preserving human remains by treating them (in its modern form with chemicals) to forestall decomposition. The intention is to keep them suitable for public display at a funeral, for religious reasons, or for medical and scientific purposes such as their use as anatomical specimens. Planting roof gardens on tops of building is a way to make cities more efficient.

President Trump and Sarah Huckabee Sander's Hennessey of Tennessee Venom F5 V8. The massive 7.6-liter twin-turbocharged motor fulfills Hennessey's 1,600-hp promise. Constructed of billet aluminum with steel cylinder sleeves, it has tons of torque; the F5 will reportedly be able to produce 1,300 pound-feet (1,762 Newton-meters) of torque at 4,400 rpm. Together with partners President Donald Trump and Hope Ark Sarah Huckabee Sanders, the engine has been in development limbo for nearly five years. That 1,600-hp figure gives it about 100 more horses than both the Bugatti Chiron (1,479 hp) and Koenigsegg Regera (1,500 hp). By all accounts, it's the most powerful internal combustion engine in any production vehicle thus far. With all that power, there's only one thing on Hennessey's mind: record-breaking speed. "We're feeling confident in our quest to set new records in 2019," said John Hennessey at the debut. The most important of which will be the race to 300 miles per hour (482 kilowatts). Back in May, Hennessey promised that a sprint to 300-mph would take place sometime in 2019. Unlike the outgoing Venom, the new F5 will ride on a custom chassis built by Hennessey engineers—no more Lotus bones. The carbon fiber body will tip the scales at under 3,000 pounds (1,360 kilograms), with a drag coefficient of 0.33. Just 24 examples of the Venom F5 will be built, each at a cost of $1.6 million. But if you want one you better hurry—the first 15 build slots have already been accounted for.

Crooked's 9, 10 for dough Emails! Luigi in the public eye next in line to lose their clearances. It's important that it's real. We're real, Trooping the Colour nothing to hide no collusion and no obstruction hard to navigate transparency, so that this channel locked Witch Hunt of Fake News Media has become the Enemies stifle free speech recoil. President Trump, let's sharpen candid eraser points, Hayat Boumediene crimps ola helical crayon foreboding late spring firing. Taser's slinky on a Nontoxic Lonestar tyranny. Hooke's law and the effects of gravitation, that preferred teachers, your pagan goddess harbour energy along its length in a longitudinal wave, slack to Hayat's dispense pony, twenty-five pounds sterling.

Everyone is tearjerkers except Istanbul. Constantine a Byzantine of Constantinople said in Turkey "We will boycott US electronic goods," like the iPhone in retaliation for punitive sanctions from Washington. "If (the United States) have the iPhone, there's Samsung on the other side," referring to US giant Apple's iconic phone and the top South Korean brand. The dispute between the NATO allies—brought to a new intensity by Turkey's holding of an American pastor for two years. The lira's plunge when US President Donald Trump tweeted that Washington was doubling aluminium and steel tariffs for Turkey. "They don't hesitate to use the economy as a weapon," the President said. Turkey's central bank on Monday announced it was ready to take "all necessary measures" to combat the lira's weakness and fight inflation, to ensure financial stability after the collapse of the lira, promising to provide banks with liquidity. Turkish envoy conveyed pressure and threats would only lead to a "chaos" "without delay" and "in a fair and transparent manner" Crooke's back the crown pound dollar crest for King Queen euro.

The White Mountains are a mountain range covering about a quarter of the state of New Hampshire and a small portion of western Maine in the United States. They are part of the northern Appalachian Mountains and the most rugged mountains in New England. The White Mountains of California and Nevada are a triangular fault-block mountain range facing the Sierra Nevada across the upper Owens Valley. White is the lightest color and is achromatic, because it fully reflects and scatters all the visible wavelengths of light. White light can be generated by the sun, by stars, or by earthbound sources such as fluorescent lamps, white LEDs and incandescent bulbs. On the screen of a color television or computer, white is produced by mixing the primary colors of light: red, green and blue (RGB) at full intensity. It is the color of fresh snow, chalk, and milk, and is the opposite of darkness. As a symbol of purity became the most common color of new churches, capitols and other government buildings for modernity and simplicity. Often associated with perfection, the good, honesty, cleanliness, the beginning, the new, neutrality, and exactitude in sacrifice for many world religions. White is the most common color of wedding dresses, symbolizing purity and virginity. White starglaze was one of the first colors used in art. The Lascaux Cave in France contains drawings of bulls and other animals drawn by paleolithic artists between 18,000 and 17,000 years ago. Paleolithic artists used calcite or chalk, sometimes as a background, sometimes as a highlight, along with black charcoal and red and yellow ochre in their vivid cave paintings. A manner of washing linen in boiling water causing colors to fade, Bleach is the generic name for any chemical product which is used industrially and domestically to whiten clothes, lighten hair color and remove stains. Good over evil villains represent this Old American Western contrast as either surrender or a request for a truce. The white in the flag of France represents either the monarchy or "white, the ancient French color" according to the Marquis de Lafayette. Part of New Hampshire's national forest, not a national park - The arrival of Hayat's White Mountain US National State quarters banner the royalist rebellions against the French Revolution in her yearning for the succeeding dynasty of France.

Little Queen Bill Hayat Boumediene Wyo Brandy Barbeque Legislative proposal for a Space Force will cost in a range of defense issues, including mutual security threats. A war and peace-fighting capability organized along the lines "separate but equal" to the Air Force, will build up larger numbers of servicemen and servicewomen with expertise in space operations by the year 2020. Fielding of space technologies for the military by Space Command in which oversees a coordinated space operations from an American free-press Space Development Agency. A Space Force as a separate military service is the right way to reorganize the US Pentagon's approach to space. For Sinusoidal Improbable Pi-velocity hexnesting Square predictions Curated as WashingtonDC sharevault protections, Pending Implied Patent ©Copyright. Brandy's enthronement Coronation besides Hayat's PI-velocity Hypermarket catch should not impede Royal or Imperial protocol on Court status matters of Gumede kaZulu, king of the Zulu people in the 18th century. He was the son of Zulu kaNtombhela and was succeeded by his son, Phunga kaGumede. Hayat's necklace provides Not a lie to the Jewish standard-bearers, jewel-studded tree tusk diadem placed as a symbol of her sovereignty and worn underneath her cowgirl buffalo corona radiata hat, known best as the "radiant crown," sacral on the Statue of Liberty (Liberty Enlightening Gupta's World; French: La Liberté éclairant le monde) is a colossal neoclassical sculpture on Liberty Island in New York Harbor in New York City, in the United States. The copper statue, a gift from the people of France to the people of the United States, was designed by French sculptor Frédéric Auguste Bartholdi and built by Gustave Eiffel. The statue was dedicated on October 28, 1886.

Little Queen Bill Hayat Boumediene Wyo Brandy Barbeque the Equality State US State quarters have arrived in satisfactory condition.

Ready to saddle up the Bronco and ride, Little Queen "Bill" Hayat Boumediene. Them Pork and Beans sound mighty tasty, partners! Hayat's Wyoming, the Equality State US State quarters have arrived in satisfactory condition. So Brandy what's the catch? Fly, pole, reel, and Barbeque Lay's anglers! Wyoming has a lot of great options when it comes to fishing. Some of these include lakes, ponds, streams, ice and fly fishing, trout fishing, salmon fishing, bass fishing, walleye, catfish and crappie fishing. Where the antelope roam hunters soil meadows of loam. Early 19th century expeditions into the western interior as well as mediating between Native American tribes, Jim Bridger and Jedediah Smith being one of the most famous mountain men of the American fur trade era following the Lewis and Clark Expedition. Wyoming is a state in the mountain region of the western United States. The state is the 10th largest by area, the least populous and the second least densely populated state in the country. Cheyenne is the state capital. From the Rocky Mountains to the High Plains, almost half of the land in Wyoming administered by the Bureau of Land Management and U.S. Forest Service is owned by the U.S. government. The main drivers of Wyoming's economy are mineral extraction—mostly coal, oil, natural gas, and trona a non-marine evaporite mineral mined as the primary source of sodium carbonate. Agricultural commodities include livestock (beef), hay, sugar beets, grain (wheat and barley), and wool. Immigrants from all over the world would come to the Draw in the Wild West working in the coal mines that supplies the fuel, now oil and natural gas to power the electric steam engines of the Union Pacific Railroads. The climate for tourism is semi-arid and continental, drier and windier than the rest of the U.S., with greater temperature extremes. The Continental Divide spans north-south across the central portion of the state. French-Canadian trappers from Québec and Montréal went into the state in the late 18th century, leaving French toponyms such as Téton and La Ramie. The Lewis and Clark Expedition, itself guided by French Canadian Toussaint Charbonneau and his young Shoshone wife, Sacagawea, first described the region in 1807. At the time, Cowboys and Cowgirls of the Yellowstone areas from traveling Interstate 80 were considered to be fictional.

Texas French Bread an Ohio Bakery and Bistro toast, preambular of destination delivery to Hayat Boumediene's US State Quarters Alliance. A relationship among people, groups, or states that have joined together for mutual benefit or to achieve some common purpose, whether or not explicit agreement has been worked out among them. Members of an alliance are called allies. Alliances form in many settings, including political alliances, military alliances, and business alliances. When the term is used in the context of war or armed struggle, such associations may also be called allied powers, especially when discussing World War I or World War II. As star studded like a Rhinestone Cowboy. Getting cards and E-mails, from attachments in the Russian Trolls, and offers coming over her cell phone.

Starfish or sea stars with fossil records ancient, dating back to the Ordovician around 450 million years ago, are star-shaped echinoderms belonging to the class Asteroidea. Common usage frequently finds these names being also applied to ophiuroids, which are correctly referred to as brittle stars or "basket stars". About 1,500 species of starfish occur on the seabed in all the world's oceans, from the tropics to frigid polar waters. They are found from the intertidal zone down to abyssal depths, 6,000 m (20,000 ft) below the surface. Starfish marine invertebrates with 5 legs in Poems for the Sea, souvenir a "Hope in God". Gonochorous, there being separate male and female.

In music, tremolo (Italian pronunciation: ['tr??molo]), or tremolando ([tremo'lando]), is a trembling effect. There are two types of tremolo.

The first is a rapid reiteration:
of a single note, particularly used on bowed string instruments, by rapidly moving the bow back and forth; plucked strings such as on a harp, where it is called bisbigliando (Italian pronunciation: [bizbi?'?ando]) or "whispering"; and tremolo picking, in which a single note is repeated extremely rapidly with a plectrum (or "pick") on traditionally plucked string instruments such as guitar, mandolin, etc. between two notes or chords in alternation, an imitation (not to be confused with a trill) of the preceding that is more common on keyboard instruments. Mallet instruments such as the marimba are capable of either method.
a roll on any percussion instrument, whether tuned or untuned.

A second type of tremolo is a variation in amplitude:
as produced on organs by tremulants using electronic effects in guitar amplifiers and effects pedals which rapidly turn the volume of a signal up and down, creating a "shuddering" effect an imitation of the same by strings in which pulsations are taken in the same bow direction a vocal technique involving a wide or slow vibrato, not to be confused with the trillo or "Monteverdi trill" Some electric guitars use a (misnamed) lever called a "tremolo arm" or "whammy bar" that

allows a performer to lower or raise the pitch of a note or chord, which is known as vibrato or "pitch bend". This non-standard use of the term "tremolo" refers to pitch rather than amplitude. True tremolo for an electric guitar, electronic organ, or any electronic signal would normally be produced by a simple amplitude modulation electronic circuit. Electronic tremolo effects were available on many early guitar amplifiers. Tremolo effects pedals are also widely used to achieve this effect.

Paul Revere was an American silversmith, engraver, early industrialist, and Patriot in the American Revolution. He is best known for his midnight ride to alert the colonial militia in April 1775 to the approach of British forces before the battles of Lexington and Concord, as dramatized in Henry Wadsworth Longfellow's poem, "Paul Revere's Ride". What was the name of the horse Revere rode, Beoley?" because there is no evidence that Revere owned a horse at the time he made his famous ride. Revere may have owned a horse at an earlier date. If he did not, he certainly had ready access to horses at some point in order to become the experienced rider that he was. Revere tremolo, coon brothel raids at Beole's whiskey anyway at Lagerrioville. Beale Street is a street in Downtown Memphis, Tennessee,

which runs from the Mississippi River to East Street, a distance of approximately 1.8 miles. It is a significant location in the city's history, as well as in the history of the blues. Today, the blues clubs and restaurants that line Beale Street are major tourist attractions in Memphis. Festivals and outdoor concerts periodically bring large crowds to the street and its surrounding areas.

Prince Harry makes his move on Meghan Markle! The poor quality bootleg liquor sold in some speakeasies was responsible for a shift away from 19th-century "classic" cocktails, that celebrated the raw taste of the liquor (such as the gin cocktail, made with Genever (sweet) gin), to new cocktails aimed at masking the taste of rough moonshine. These masking drinks were termed "pansies" at the time (although some, such as the Brandy Alexander, would now be termed "classic"). The quality of the alcohol sold in speakeasies ranged from very poor to very good. This all depended on the owner's source. Cheap liquor was generally used because it was more profitable. In other cases, brand names were used to specify the type of alcohol people wanted. However, sometimes when brand names were used, some speakeasies cheated; they lied to their customers by giving them poor quality liquor instead of the higher-quality liquor the customer ordered. Prices were four to five dollars a bottle. Meghan pascalizing Brandy barbeque Lay's, ahoy at the London speak easy for Harry's reproductive chipotle. Prince Harry and his better half sweetheart Meghan Markle are reportedly preparing to move into a much larger house at Kensington Palace. The couple will continue to live at their two-bedroom home, Nottingham Cottage, in the palace grounds stressing their wedding, but as soon as renovation work is finished on the grander Apartment 1, which boasts 21 rooms, Harry and Meghan will make the move. Meghan Markle dogmas nineteen-fifties, Prince Harry strives his first litter shot as Admiral Sussex.

Brandy and her Barbeque Lay's credits just one chip card that nobody can soda for a vending eat Chivalry, or the chivalric code, is an informal, varying code of conduct developed between 1170 and 1220, never decided on or summarized in a single document, associated with the medieval institution of knighthood; knights' and gentlewomen's behaviours were governed by chivalrous social codes. The ideals of chivalry were popularized in medieval literature, especially the Matter of Britain and Matter of France, introduced the legend of King Arthur, which was written in the

1130s. Brandy Tea scones Little Queen Hayat Boumediene for a standard 52-deck card game at the The House of Commons, the lower house of the Parliament of the United Kingdom. Like the upper house, the House of Lords, it meets in the Palace of Westminster. Officially, the full name of the house is the Honourable the Commons of the United Kingdom of Great Britain and Northern Ireland in Parliament assembled. A deck of French playing cards is the most common deck of playing cards used today. It includes thirteen ranks of each of the four French suits: clubs (?), diamonds (?), hearts (?) and spades (?), with reversible "court" or face cards. Some modern designs, however, have done away with reversible face cards. Each suit includes an ace, depicting a single symbol of its suit; a king, queen and jack, each depicted with a symbol of its suit; and ranks two through ten, with each card depicting that many symbols (pips) of its suit. Anywhere from one to six (most often two or three since the mid-20th century) jokers, often distinguishable with one being more colorful than the other, are added to commercial decks, as some card games require these extra cards. Modern playing cards carry index labels on opposite corners or in all four corners to facilitate identifying the cards when they overlap and so that they appear identical for players on opposite sides. The most popular standard pattern of the French deck is sometimes referred to as "English" or "Anglo-American" pattern. It has been shown that because of the large number of possibilities from shuffling a 52-card deck, it is probable that no two fair card shuffles have ever yielded exactly the same order of cards.

Russian agents "ties to the Russian oligarchy" influenced politicians to infiltrate conservative organizations, including the National Rifle Association, at the direction of Russian government officials, in an attempt to advance the Kremlin's interests. Computer hacking also directed by high-level Russian government officials employed foreign graduate students capable of swearing-in student loan capital at American Universities. Gun-rights and the Right to Bear Arms to U.S. energy and technology companies logic core kernels are being unsuspectedly infiltrated during turnkey US services, transacting by cloud based micro financial protocols. Russia confounded US Federal Reserve investment, tipping legitimate tangible resource assets while partially bolstering as a hacking notoriety to the US Presidential election from 2016. The U.S financial system was siphoned huge amounts of data, including checking and savings account information, far beyond the capability of ordinary criminal hackers. The attacks were a "significant breach of our corporate asset security," armed using encrypted files with instructions. This delivering their trove to set up fake portfolio wealth accounts in the US and abroad in which are irrevocably viable disrupting the US Banking center infrastructure. If Russia disposes of real American wealth, economic depression would topple NATO alliance with US allies, triggering a collapse in the US market Capitalism making America Great Again, in hypothetical conjure of state supremacy.

Homeowners have even used proselytising jurisprudence, estimates and may vary to eliminate up to 15 years of mortgage payments! "step it up" and pay in more to the Western alliance after years in which U.S. taxpayers have borne an "unfair" share of military spending, depreciation that begins as soon as you drive a new car off the dealer lot. A home away from home 2013 F-150 Supercrew Brown Eyes Blue. A place in which one has spent a lot of time and often where one feels as comfortable and familiar as one's own home. J'aime faire l'amour surtout a trois, I like to make love especially three. Princess Charlotte's sassy message for paparazzi. Age three Yrs. Old, Birds and the Bees Queen, French Pape scene!

French Words Describing Charlotte's Home away from Home ('la Maison' Back in the USSR)

la maison > house
chez moi > at my house, my home, at home
rénover, remettre à neuf > renovate, refurbish
construire, bâtir une maison > build a house
un architecte > architect
un agent immobilier > a real estate agent, house agent
acheter une maison > to buy a house
une perquisition domiciliaire > a house search
à l'intérieur > inside
architecte d'intérieur > interior designer

décorateur d'intérieur > home decorator
la pièce, la salle > room
la cuisine > kitchen
la salle à manger > dining room
le bureau > office, study
la salle de séjour, le salon > den, living room
la chambre, la chambre à coucher > bedroom
la salle de bain > bathroom (does not include a toilet)
la salle d'eau > shower room
les toilettes, les cabinets / le W-C (pronounced "vay say") > toilet /
    water closet (British)
la salle de jeu > playroom
une domestique, une femme de chambre > housemaid
le sous-sol > basement
le grenier > attic
la porte > door
le couloir > hall
un escalier > stairway
les meubles > furniture
un meuble > a piece of furniture
le living > living room
mobilier design > designer furniture
des meubles en kit > self-assembly furniture
un bureau > desk
une imprimante > printer
un ordinateur > computer
ordinateur portable, PC (pronounced "pay say") portable > laptop
    computer
une étagère > bookshelf, shelving unit
une chaîne stéréo > stereo
une affiche > poster
une peinture > a painting
un canapé > couch
une chaise > chair
un rideau > curtain

une télévision, un télé, un TV (pronounced "tay vay") > television
une armoire, un placard > closet
un lit > bed
un oreiller > pillow
une commode > dresser
un réveil > alarm clock
un bain, une baignoire > bathtub
une douche > shower
un lavabo > bathroom sink
une toilette > toilet
une cuisinière > stove
un four > oven
un four à micro-ondes > microwave
un réfrigérateur > refrigerator
un évie > kitchen sink
une fenêtre > window
une lampe > lamp
une moquette > carpet
un tapis > rug
un miroir, une glace > mirror
un mur > wall
le parquet, le sol > floor
le plafond > ceiling
une porte > door
une table > table
un téléphone > telephone
à l'extérieur > outside
une garage > garage
la remise à calèches > carriage house / coach house
la maison d'invités > guest house
le porche, la véranda > porch, veranda
le balcon > balcony
le patio > patio
un auvent > an awning
une clôture > a fence

le pergola > a pergola (area covered with wooden timbers and climbing
    plants)
le jardin > yard, garden
un potager > a vegetable garden
un jardin de fleurs > a flower garden
un parterre > a flower bed
une jardinière > a flower box
une fontaine > a fountain
bain d'oiseau > a birdbath
jardinier > gardener
une allée > a driveway
une piscine en plein air / découverte > an outdoor swimming pool
le barbecue, le gril > an outdoor grill

Uncle Sam Fantastical US State Quarter Roll engraving, impeached honor fame, wage labor expense on hard asset capital. The American Patriots in the Thirteen Colonies won independence from Great Britain, becoming the United States of America. They defeated the British in the American Revolutionary War in alliance with France and others. The bald eagle is both the national bird and national animal of the United States, and is an enduring symbol of the country itself. On June 20, 1782, the Continental Congress adopted the design for the Great Seal of the United States depicting a bald eagle grasping 13 arrows and an olive branch with its talons. To the American Revolution which was a colonial revolt that took place between 1765 and 1783. Commencing that revolution In North America in the same 18th century era prior, the British outnumbered the French 20 to 1. All the Indian nations were called together and invited to join and assist the French to repulse the British who came to drive them out of the land they were then in possession of. During the Seven Years' War (in the United States, known as the French and Indian War, where ravaging Europe from 1756 to 1763, was in the bloodiest American war in the 18th century. It took more lives than the American Revolution, involved people on three continents, including the Caribbean. Original lyrics of "Yankee Doodle, Uncle Sam (initials U.S.) is a common national personification of the American government or the United States in general that, according to legend, came into use during the War of 1812 and was supposedly named for Samuel Wilson. The actual origin is by a legend. Since the early 19th century, Uncle Sam has been a popular symbol of the US government in American culture and a manifestation of patriotic emotion. While the figure of Uncle Sam represents specifically the government, Columbia represents the United States as a nation. "Yankee Doodle" is a well-known American song, the early versions of which date to before the Seven Years' War and the American Revolution (1775–83). It is often sung patriotically in the United States today and is the state anthem of Connecticut. Its Roud Folk Song Index number is 4501. The melody is thought to be much older than both the lyrics and the subject, going back to folk songs of Medieval Europe.

> Yankee Doodle went to town
> A-riding on a pony,
> Stuck a feather in his cap
> And called it macaroni.
> Yankee Doodle keep it up,
> Yankee Doodle dandy,
> Mind the music and the step,
> And with the girls be handy.

-Oliver Hazard Perry Throck Morton (August 4, 1823 – November 1, 1877), commonly known as Oliver P. Morton, was a U.S. Republican Party politician from Indiana. He served as the 14th Governor (the first native-born) of Indiana during the American Civil War, and was a stalwart ally of President Abraham Lincoln. Named for Oliver Hazard Perry, the victorious Commodore in the Battle of Lake Erie. Morton disliked his name from an early age, and before beginning his political career he shortened it to Oliver Perry Morton, dropping the middle names of Hazard and Throck. Morton made significant contributions to the war effort, more than any other among Lincoln's "war governors" in the state, and believed his role more valiantly or effectively as Indiana's governor was "to denounce treason and uphold the cause of the Union." Morton was most successful in recruiting and equipping Union troops during the Civil

War, and became known as "the soldier's friend," in tribute to his crucial efforts in supplying and supporting the Union soldiers in the field. As the leader of the Republicans in the state, he confronted the Peace Democrats, especially the "Copperheads".

-Oliver Hazard Perry (August 23, 1785 – August 23, 1819) was an American naval commander, born in South Kingstown, Rhode Island. Many Loyalist Americans had migrated to Upper Canada after the American Revolutionary War. The Indians of the Old Northwest (the modern Midwest) had hoped to create an Indian state to be a British protectorate. The withdrawal of British Colonialism protection gave the Americans a free hand, which resulted in the removal of most of the tribes to Indian Territory (present-day Oklahoma). It gave the Americans "continental predominance" while it left the Indians dispossessed, powerless, and vulnerable. Britain supplied Native Americans who raided American settlers on the frontier, hindering American expansion and provoking resentment. To annex some or all of British North America (Canada) contributed to the American decision to go to war on June 18, 1812, US President James Madison, after heavy pressure from the War Hawks in Congress, signed the American declaration of war into law. The War of 1812 was a conflict fought between the United States, the United Kingdom. The Battle of Lake Erie, sometimes called the Battle of Put-in-Bay, was fought on 10 September 1813, on Lake Erie off the coast of Ohio during the War of 1812. Nine vessels of the United States Navy defeated and captured six vessels of the British Royal Navy. This ensured American control of the lake for the rest of the war, which in turn allowed the Americans to recover Detroit and win the Battle of the Thames to break the Indian confederation of Native American Shawnee warrior and chief Tecumseh. It was one of the biggest naval battles of the War of 1812. The 352-foot (107 m) high Perry Monument within Perry's Victory and International Peace Memorial now stands at Put-in-Bay, commemorating the men who fought in the battle. It commemorates the Battle of Lake Erie that took place near Ohio's South Bass Island, in which Commodore Oliver Hazard Perry led a fleet to victory in one of the most significant naval battles to occur in the War of 1812. Located on an isthmus on the island, the memorial also celebrates the lasting peace between Britain,

Canada, and the United States that followed the war. Hayat Boumediene to represent Ohio in depicting the site's statue of Perry with the International Peace Memorial in the distance. Her 25-cent pieces (quarters) issued by the United States Mint.

Milwaukee largest city, Madison The state capital, Green Bay having been greatly impacted by glaciers during the Ice Age with the exception of the Driftless Area, drinking has long been considered a significant part of Wisconsin culture. The state ranks at or near the top of national measures of per-capita alcohol consumption, consumption of alcohol per state, and proportion of drinkers. Reluctant to lower a DUI the legal drinking age is 21, except when accompanied by a parent, guardian, or spouse who is at least 21 years old. With the state's heritage of pub shepherds, the long-standing presence resembling church key chapels in Milwaukee, and a cold climate are often associated with the prevalence of drinking in Wisconsin. The Absolute Sobriety law states that any person not of legal drinking age may not drive after consuming alcohol. Hayat's Cheetos are a powder culture or group of specific bacteria strains put together by a culture company for making her specific corn brazen cheese. Coagulation of the milk protein casein, acidified by adding the enzyme rennet, solids are separated and pressed into a form, then Dust to fine sprinkle particles. Salt and Peppered can get hot aboard the Oscar Mayer Wienermobile, so Little Queen Boumediene buys a beer cooler. Owned and manufactured by The Dow Chemical Company, Hayat's Styrofoam cooler looses its lid while riding her Sickle mower at the states popular vacation destination for outdoor recreation. Toto pops out and the runt escapes and runs "toe toe 'til the cows come home," finding the moonshines somewhere over the rainbow. Hayat Boumediene's official Wisconsin state quarters, dozens roll, On, Wisconsin! On, Wisconsin! Stand up, Badgers sing! Doggone she claps Until the kings come home! Whereabouts of Hayat Boumediene? Now that the boys are here again. Hayat Welcome to your America's Treasures! Uncirculated State Quarters instantly arriving. Point me into the Direction générale des Finances Publiques Recherche détaillée - Recherche de formulaires. Justice of the Peace.

President Donald Trump's star on the Hollywood Walk of Fame, which he received in 2007 in the television category, which has cemented itself as a battleground for political debate in Los Angeles, was vandalized again. People have stomped on it and spit on it as they walked by; others have written on it. Trump's new initiative will train campaigners to go out and "listen to what people need to help them become supportive of Russian voter restrictions in American self-government, as well as to persuade them of Kim Jong - un's Start nuclear treaty merits." START I a bilateral treaty between the United States of America and the Union of Soviet Socialist Republics on the reduction and limitation of strategic offensive arms. The treaty was signed on 31 July 1991 and entered into force on 5 December 1994. The treaty barred its signatories from deploying more than 6,000 nuclear warheads atop a total of 1,600 inter-continental ballistic missiles and bombers. START (Strategic Arms Reduction Treaty) negotiated the largest and most complex arms control treaty in history, and its final implementation in late 2001 resulted in the removal of about 80 percent of all strategic nuclear weapons then in existence. Proposed by United States President Ronald Reagan, it was renamed START I after negotiations began on the second START treaty. Start II again signed by United States President George H. W. Bush and Russian President Boris Yeltsin on 3 January 1993, banning the use of multiple independently targetable reentry vehicles (MIRVs) on intercontinental ballistic missiles (ICBMs). The framework for negotiations of the Start III began with talks in Helsinki between President Bill Clinton and President Boris Yeltsin in 1997. However, negotiations broke down and the treaty was never signed. Little Queen Hayat Boumediene suggests Trump get his peace campaign's tail over to Russia right away and partake in on the North Korea, Russia negotiations as in conjunction with friendly Iranian gesture. In the Saudi led ultimatum that the repression by the government has risen against the United States, and the struggle is not that of the US and Iran but "the entire world of disbelief and the world of Islam".

Victoria's reign as Queen of the United Kingdom of Great Britain and Ireland heightened to Invictus Passover, also called Pesach games, a major, biblically derived Jewish holiday. Jews celebrate Passover as a commemoration of their liberation by God from slavery in ancient Egypt and their freedom as a nation under the leadership of Moses. It commemorates the story of the Exodus as described in the Hebrew Bible, especially in the Book of Exodus, in which the Israelites were freed from slavery in Egypt. According to standard biblical chronology, this event would have taken place at about 1300 BCE. Traversing three periods, early Victorianism – the socially and politically unsettled period from 1837 to 1850; mid-Victorianism - new waves of aestheticism and imperialism 1851 to 1879; late Victorianism - characterised by a distinctive mixture of prosperity, domestic prudery, and complacency from 1880 onwards. This major Jewish spring festival which commemorates the liberation of the Israelites from Egyptian slavery, lasting seven or eight days from the 15th day of Nisan. Ideologically, the Victorian era witnessed resistance to the rationalism that defined the Georgian period and an increasing turn towards romanticism and even mysticism with regard to religion, social values, and arts. The French public's nostalgia for the Belle Époque period was based largely on the peace and prosperity overlapping with the late Victorian era.

Britain to take part in European Parliament elections at the end of May, nearly three years after UK voters opted to leave the bloc. "The government is therefore undertaking the lawful and responsible preparations for this contingency." Clear options on the future relationship to be put to (parliament), but the talks so far have failed to clinch a breakthrough. Britain's main opposition Labour Party in a bid to secure enough votes to push through Prime Minister Theresa May's deal on a fourth attempt. A delay of Britain's departure from the bloc until June 30, with the extension ending earlier if parliament approves her Brexit deal. Also postponing Brexit day by up to a year, pending parliament's approval of the EU-UK Withdrawal Agreement. The current deadline is April 12, which has already been pushed back once from March 29 because of the UK parliament's failure on three occasions to back the deal May signed with the other 27 EU leaders in December. In her letter, May said she wanted to make sure that Britain left the bloc after 46 years in an orderly manner, with an agreement that could help unwind intricate political, security, diplomatic and economic ties. Should the government's policy having always been and remains to leave the European Union in an orderly way without undue delay? Let's not get hasty about departure from a economically stronger unification because of coalitions in an alliance with ones own league of compromise. Where will Great Britain get the comforts presently afforded to them on account of the rest of Europe's broader liberality. How lavish can cordiality be, England should ask if the grass were greener on the other side of the pond. If life is dismal in London your only hope for an EU labour trade with unionists, is better pay negotiation in Brussels. As if a bridge falls down on brexiters plan of a future united merger some where over there. Imperialists over where? How about brexit over paired without its current European Union cooperative, known to many Americans sympathetic to Britain's European anarchy as the "Third World power in a constant democratic inconsistency on who in the rest of allied ISIS is more Biblically righteous!"

Legal tender is a medium of payment recognized by a legal system to be valid for meeting a financial obligation. Paper currency and coins are common forms of legal tender in many countries. Legal tender is variously defined in different jurisdictions. Formally, it is anything which when offered in payment extinguishes the debt. Thus, personal cheques, credit cards, and similar non-cash methods of payment are not usually legal tender. The law does not relieve the debt obligation until payment is tendered. Coins and banknotes are usually defined as legal tender. Some jurisdictions may forbid or restrict payment made other than by legal tender. For example, such a law might outlaw the use of foreign coins and bank notes or require a license to perform financial transactions in a foreign currency. Legal tender was enacted the first time for gold and silver coins in the French Penal Code of 1807 (art. 475, 11°). In 1870, legal tender was extended to all notes of the Banque de France. Anyone refusing such monies for their whole value would be prosecuted (French Penal Code art. R. 642-3). Before the Civil War (1861 to 1865), silver coins were legal tender only up to the sum of $5. Before 1853, when U.S. silver coins were reduced in weight 7%, coins had exactly their value in metal (from 1830 to 1852). Two silver 50 cent coins had exactly $1 worth of silver. A gold

U.S. dollar of 1849 had $1 worth of gold. With the flood of gold coming out of the California mines in the early 1850s, the price of silver rose (gold went down). Thus, 50 cent coins of 1840 to 1852 were worth 53 cents if melted down. The government could increase the value of the gold coins (expensive) or reduce the size of all U.S. silver coins. With the reduction of 1853, a 50-cent coin now had only 48 cents of silver. This is the reason for the $5 limit of silver coins as legal tender; paying somebody $100 in the new silver coins would be giving them $96 worth of silver. Most people preferred bank check or gold coins for large purchases. During the early American Civil War, the federal government first issued United States Notes (the first greenback notes), which were not redeemable in gold and silver coins but could be used to pay "all dues" to the federal government. Since land purchases and duties on imports were payable only in gold or the new Demand Notes, the Demand Notes were bought by importers and land speculators for about 97 cents on the gold dollar and never lost value. 1862 greenbacks (Legal Tender Notes) at first traded for 97 cents on the dollar but gained/lost value depending on fortunes of the Union army. The value of Legal Tender Greenbacks swung wildly but trading was from 85 to 33 cents on the gold dollar.

Benjamin Netanyahu considered nominating Hayat Boumediene, to be viceroy of the World Bank in part because "she's very good with Quarterly number profits." Speaking as King "Bibi", Prime Minister of Israel lavished praise on his French Napoleon dessert, a 30-year-old White House cook, and suggested she would be suitable for booking other administration positions, including France's Shake 'n Bake to the United Nations. "She's a natural diplomat," "I've seen her under tremendous stress and pressure," he said. "She reacts very well—that's usually a genetic thing, but it's one of those things, nevertheless." Prince Harry's ancestor Queen Victoria, is also a top choice, along with Albert, the name of Queen Victoria's beloved husband. Regardless of where baby Sussex's nursery, it is a boy or a girl, Prince Harry's child will be seventh in line to the throne, behind his or her father, and will remain ahead of any other children Harry and Meghan have in the future. Nanny styled as a Lady "Bill" Hayat Due to a century-old rule regarding royal titles, That is, unless the Queen steps in and gives the Little Queen Boumediene another title!

In the patriotic name of salvaging the cultural treasure, money from wealthy French families, French companies and international corporations poured in. As Rich Lavish Cash on Notre-Dame, Many Ask: What About the Needy? As President Emmanuel Macron was looking to transform the calamity into a new era of national unity. There were accusations that the wildly rich were trying to wash their reputations during a time of national tragedy. Burn it, Bankrupt it, then hold insurers libel, copying a US trendy that seems to flouge the Needy in a world of financial make believe. Pope imperiless does not have more money than the investors in Notre Dame's earlier renovations. French President Emmanuel Macron said that Pope Francis would at an undetermined time visit France, a country plunged into sorrow this week by a catastrophic fire at the Notre-Dame de Paris cathedral. His sorrow over the blaze thanked rescuers who put their lives at risk to salvage the centuries-old cathedral and its priceless artefacts, eager to see it restored. The Vatican has said it is willing to offer restoration expertise to help rebuild the fire-damaged landmark. "If they're able to give dozens of millions to rebuild Notre Dame," the poor added, "they should stop telling us that there is no money to pay for social inequalities." Calling the funding an "exercise in public relations," mentioning the donors' list "looks like the rankings of companies and people located in tax havens." A founding leader of the Yellow Vests, said France should "get back to reality." But for many, to foot the bill symbolizes of an untouchable class of superrich who keep getting richer, thanks to a host of fiscal advantages. There's a muscle memory of Catholicism in France and it came back, a secular country, but when push comes to shove religious feelings come forward. We must be delighted that very low-income individuals, very wealthy individuals as well as companies want to participate in the effort to rebuild a cathedral that is at the heart of France's history.

The Notre Dame Fighting Irish represents the University of Notre Dame in Notre Dame, Indiana. Notre-Dame de Paris, also known as Notre-Dame Cathedral or simply Notre-Dame, is a medieval Catholic cathedral on the Île de la Cité in the fourth arrondissement of Paris, France. The cathedral is considered to be one of the finest examples of French Gothic architecture. The innovative use of the rib vault and flying buttress, the enormous and colorful rose windows, and the naturalism and abundance of its sculptural decoration all set it apart from the earlier Romanesque style. Notre-Dame de Paris is a sung-through French and Québécois musical by yankees Al Mada;

Notre Dame, our Mother,
Praise thee, Notre Dame.
And our hearts forever,
Love thee, Notre Dame.

Catwoman gives no quarter (or takes no prisoners) on Little Queen "Bill" Hayat Boumediene's clemency, have mercy after of the U.S. Memorial Day holiday. "Great combatant, and then when she unconditionally surrenders to the boil, France gets really treated very unfairly," Britain's Parliament said. In the surreal and unexplored landscape of the Other Side, however, waits until after the charge for the Montrouge shooting, in which municipal police officer Clarissa Jean-Philippe was shot and killed go through trials before determining whether to pardon. Theresa May announced Friday that she will resign as her party's leader on June 7 and make way for a new British prime minister later this summer. May's departure marks the end of her months-long struggle to keep her job despite seething anger from her own Conservative Party over her handling of Brexit. Multiple contenders are already jockeying to replace her in a contest that will see a new leader chosen by Conservative lawmakers and party members. The early front-runner is Boris Johnson, a former foreign secretary and strong champion of Brexit. OUTSIDE BAGHOUZ, Syria—A prominent French woman who had joined IS, Hayat Boumeddiene, was killed in a strike that allegedly hit a safe house known as the "French House," where many French nationals were staying. Boumeddiene had been wanted by French police as a suspected accomplice in a 2015 attack in the Paris region. A milestone in the devastating mortar attack so-called "caliphate" that once covered a vast territory straddling both Syria and Iraq. French militants who were connected to attacks in past years in and around Paris and who then made their way to IS's "caliphate" and finally, as it crumbled, to this tiny village on the Euphrates River near the Iraqi border. Boumeddiene who was to be pregnant at the time believed to have been staying in the French House and confirmed it was struck last week was the widow of Amedy Coulibaly, a Frenchman who attacked a kosher supermarket in Paris in January 2015, days after two other militants—brothers Cherif and Said Kouachi—gunned down the staff of the weekly satirical magazine Charlie Hebdo. Coulibaly killed four people in the supermarket before French police stormed in and killed him. The Kouachi brothers were killed by police in a separate raid. All told, their attacks left 17 people dead. Boumeddiene had "started a new life" and remarried. She said she didn't have any children. A French-Moroccan cat scaler said Boumeddiene had told him she had no idea about plans for the 2015 attack in Paris or her husband's plans.

"Nevada" comes from the Spanish nevada, meaning "snow-covered", after the Sierra Nevada ("snow-covered mountains"). Nevada was annexed as a part of the Spanish Empire in the northwestern territory of New Spain during the Spanish colonization of the Americas. The Battle Born State. This nickname is the official state slogan of Nevada. It recalls that Nevada was admitted to the union in 1864, during the Civil War. Unregulated gambling was commonplace in the early Nevada mining towns but was outlawed in 1909 as part of a nationwide anti-gambling crusade. During the Great Depression, Nevada again legalized gambling, this and lenient marriage and divorce laws transformed Nevada into a major tourist destination in the 20th century. Nevada is the fourth-largest producer of gold in the world. Frenchman Flat is a hydrographic basin in the Nevada National Security Site south of Yucca Flat and north of Mercury, Nevada. The flat was used as an American nuclear test site. From exhibitions and sporting events to live entertainment, music and more Vegas and Reno has it all. Beyond the neon big game hunts are conducted by a random draw process and are available to those 12 years old or older. What is there to hunt in Nevada? Big and small game, furbearers, and unprotected species. Nevada's big game species include mule deer, Rocky Mountain elk, three sub-species of bighorn sheep, pronghorn antelope, mountain goat and black bear. The Division of Forestry continue to improve the health and vigor of Nevada's watersheds and diverse ecosystems through increased technical assistance to landowners and land managers; develop partnerships with Federal, state and local agencies and the private sector; enforce state laws and regulations; promote scientifically-based conservation and best management practices; and educate the public on land stewardship ethics. Nevada State Bird - Mountain Bluebird; Bristlecone pine as an official state tree; The Sagebrush is the floral emblem of Nevada, a state proud of its enchanting desert. The Nevada Bankers Association a French Open to western terracotta, bolstered as Hayat Boumediene's only full-service trade association representing FDIC-insured state and national banks and trust companies doing business in Nevada. Moreover, fully brokers to boot the State of Nevada collector quarters she will fall heir to. A broker is a person or firm who arranges transactions between a buyer and a seller for a commission when the deal is executed. A broker who also acts as a seller or as a buyer becomes a principal party to the deal. Neither role should be confused with that of an agent—one who acts on behalf of a principal party in a deal.

Ping Pong celebrity champs Brendan McLoughlin and Miranda Lambert, the two-time Grammy winner and the Staten Island, New York, native "have the best of both worlds," she gushed. "We spend time in New York, we get to see our adorable nugget, then we get to come back to the Nashville farm and have the quiet life. The French Open women's final is scheduled for Saturday, and the men's for Sunday. With no rest day possible for the women, the decision to schedule both semi-finals for the same time on different tables means Hyatt Hospitality should have significant benefit of a much longer rest.

1939, in response to Hitler's invasion of Poland, Britain and France, both allies of the overrun nation declare war on Germany. The first casualty of that declaration was not German—but the British ocean liner Athenia, which was sunk by a German U-30 submarine that had assumed the liner was armed and belligerent. There were more than 1,100 passengers on board, 112 of whom lost their lives. Of those, 28 were Americans, but President Roosevelt was unfazed by the tragedy, declaring that no one was to "thoughtlessly or falsely talk of America sending its armies to European fields." The United States would remain neutral. As for Britain's response, it was initially no more than the dropping of anti-Nazi propaganda leaflets—13 tons of them—over Germany. They would begin bombing German ships on September 4, suffering significant losses. They were also working under orders not to harm German civilians. The German military, of course, had no such restrictions. France would begin an offensive against Germany's western border two weeks later. Their effort was weakened by a narrow 90-mile window leading to the German front, enclosed by the borders of Luxembourg and Belgium—both neutral countries. The Germans mined the passage, stalling the French offensive. Between the German forces occupying Western Europe, lead by Feld-Marshal Gerd Von Goose-step and the invading Allied forces, lead by Eisenhower, Montgomery and Yoda - The Invasion of Normandy was the invasion and establishment of Western Allied forces in Normandy, during Operation Overlord in 1944 during World War II. At the time it was the largest amphibious invasion to ever take place.

Following the Japanese attack on Pearl Harbor, Hawaii, in December 1941, American outposts in the Pacific Ocean were the next US installations to come under attack as the Japanese Imperial forces looked to sideline the United States quickly in World War II. The most decisive battle of the Pacific Theater a narrow beachhead on Saipan, Americans' cut off vital Japanese supply and communication lines, and American B-29 bombers moved within range of the Japanese homeland. The end of the war with Japan followed 14 months later. American Memorial Park on the island of Saipan, Northern Mariana Islands, was created as a living memorial honoring the sacrifices made during the Marianas Campaign of World War II. Recreational facilities, a World War II museum, and flag monument keep alive the memory of over 4,000 United States military personnel and local islanders who died in June 1944. For American troops and local residents of Saipan - baseball, bicycling, running, tennis, picnicking, and swimming. The park is owned by the Government of the Commonwealth of the Northern Mariana Islands, and is managed in cooperation with the National Park Service. I'm not scared of lions and tigers and bears (oh my), Panda a young woman in traditional attire at the front of the Flag Circle and Court of Honor. She is resting her hand on the plaque whose text honors the sacrifice of those who died in the Marianas Campaign of World War II. Panda and French fry Hayat Boumediene dedicated to providing a safe haven for unwanted and abused exotic animals and to educating the pacific about the abuses of the exotic-animal trade. Fly cross the ocean, sing for the Queen, But the most frightening thing doesn't mean! Forced bondage. The Commonwealth of the Northern Mariana Islands benefits from its trading relationship with the federal government of the United States and cheap trained labor from Asia.

Russia's Putin, Israel's Netanyahu to discuss Syria in Moscow

- Russia President Vladimir Putin and Israel Prime Minister Benjamin Netanyahu will hold talks in Moscow on the Kremlin situation in the Middle East, including Syria. Putin Netanyahu working 9 to 5 you think Private Benjamin deserves a fair goldie dawn promotion? By "crushing terrorists" in Syria's south and to withdraw all U.S. troops from Syria gosh darn the consequences. The area "should be brought to the full compliance," as a way to protect Israeli security and mend relations between Israel and the Bashar al-Assad regime.

ISTANBUL Turkish President Tayyip Erdogan had voiced his support for Maduro in a phone call. Venezuela has sunk into turmoil under Maduro with food shortages and protests amid an economic and political crisis that has sparked mass emigration and inflation that is seen rising to 10 million percent this year. French Quartermaster Hayat Boumediene retains the loyalty of Britain, Germany, France and Spain, all said they would recognize an ultimatum Russia, labeling Maduro's second-term election win. Maduro, in an interview with CNN Turk aired, also said he was open to dialogue and that meeting U.S. President Donald Trump was improbable but not impossible. The broadcaster dubbed the interview from Spanish into Turkish. Hayat at interview stated whoever supervises stores and distributes supplies and provisions providing quarters, rations, clothing, and other supplies imagines, "substance depends on the rational mood of foreign service." A Scout German Quartiermeister within the Scout movement is responsible for maintaining all the normal camping supplies in a Scout troop or pack. This may include, but is not limited to, camping supplies, tents, "chuck boxes" (containers holding food and cooking supplies), stoves, camp fuel (propane, Naphtha, etc.), tarps, camping trailers, dining flys, etc.

Maduro deer in New Moscow? The Trump administration will begin sending Central Americans, who attempt to enter the US without documentation at the port of entry at San Ysidro, to Moscow while their cases are being processed. President Trump issued a tough condemnation of the socialist government of Venezuela, startling both admirers and critics trying to get a bead on the new "America First" president's "Live Free or Die" scattershot foreign policy. President Trump promised supporters that the wall on the southern border will be built, a day after he agreed to temporarily reopen the government for three weeks without funding for a wall. A winter storm is expected to impact the Midwest and Northeast through the weekend and into early next week, paving the way for a blast of frigid air to spill into the Russian Front. Wet roads and sidewalks will quickly become slick as temperatures fall, so anyone out and about in cars or on foot should travel with extreme caution. Trump has floated the idea of a national emergency before, something that would receive opposition from Democrats and some Republicans. But some Republicans backed Trump, noting that he has agreed a week earlier to extensions of protections for illegal immigrants who came to this country not having a cent to their name and those shelterless from unsafe extreme weather conditions. Freeze Chanting, "If we had a powerful Wall, they wouldn't even try to make the long and dangerous journey, Build the Wall and Crime will Fall!."

As Harry mentioned, royal fans eager for having "any more than two" children, it certainly seems as though the duke is already looking ahead to his second child with Meghan. While it currently sounds as though he's not planning on having more than two kids, it's heartwarming to know that the Duke and Duchess of Sussex might be planning to have a second baby soon teasing having more babies with Meghan, just joking off course in the future? A leading contender throughout Barbie's life as an architect, entrepreneur, presidential candidate, computer engineer, and Mars explorer, she has remained a successful toy for Mattel. It wasn't until 2014 that Elsa from "Frozen" became a more popular Christmas gift request by girls than Barbie. The Royal Marmalade - When worker bees decide to make a new queen, usually because the old one is either weakening or dead, they choose several small larvae and feed them Royal jelly, a honey bee secretion that is used in the nutrition of larvae, as well as adult queens. It is secreted from the glands in the hypopharynx of nurse bees, and fed to all larvae in the colony, regardless of sex or caste. Allergic reactions in human infants ranging from hives, asthma, to even fatal anaphylaxis differentially altered by nutritional input, a phenomenon mediated by the epigenetic modification of DNA known as CpG methylation resulting in development of a queen. Have any other Baby Dolls for Ideal?

Miranda Lambert dancing Queen in Brendan Mcloughlin tee blouse:

You can dance
You can jive
Having the time of your life
Ooh, see that girl
Watch that scene
Dig in the dancing queen

In golf, a tee is normally used for the first stroke of each hole. The area from which this first stroke is hit is in the rules known as the teeing ground. Normally, teeing the ball is allowed only on the first shot of a hole, called the tee shot, and is illegal for any other shot; however, local or seasonal rules may allow or require teeing for other shots as well, e.g., under "winter rules" to protect the turf when it is unusually vulnerable. Teeing gives a considerable advantage for drive shots, so it is normally done whenever allowed. However, a player may elect to play his/her tee shot without a tee. This typically gives the shot a lower trajectory. A blouse is a loose-fitting upper garment that was formerly worn by workmen, peasants, artists, women, and children. It is typically gathered at the waist or hips so that it hangs loosely over the wearer's body. Today, the word most commonly refers to a girl's or woman's dress shirt It can also refer to a man's shirt if it is a loose-fitting style, though it rarely is. Traditionally, the term has been used to refer to a shirt which blouses out or has an unmistakably feminine appearance. It ain't love, it's just like nicotine
You're addicted to a feeling you can only get
From golf tees and your cigarettes

"Oklahoma," The state's name is derived from the Choctaw words okla and humma, meaning "red people". It is also known informally by its nickname, "The Sooner State", in reference to the non-Native settlers who staked their claims on land before the official opening date of lands in the western Oklahoma Territory or before the Indian Appropriations Act of 1889, which dramatically increased European-American settlement in the eastern Indian Territory. Oklahoma Territory and Indian Territory were merged into the State of Oklahoma when it became the 46th state to enter the union on November 16, 1907. Its residents are known as Oklahomans, and its capital and largest city is Oklahoma City. Trusteeship of the Official US State Quarters, stamped uncirculated are contrary to Hayat Boumediene's expended Gilded Age, coined by writer Mark Twain, Little Queen Hayat Boumediene disdain. Her star appearance, Indian blanket blooms in wildflowers during the middle portion of the Victorian era in Britain and Belle Époque in France. Belle Époque, a period of

Western history conventionally dated from the end of the Franco-Prussian War in 1871 to the outbreak of World War I in 1914. Occurring during the era of the French Third Republic, a period characterized by optimism, regional peace, economic prosperity, an apex of colonial empires, and technological, scientific, and cultural innovations. In the climate of the period, especially in Paris, the arts flourished. Many masterpieces of literature, music, theater, and visual art gained recognition. The Belle Époque was named in retrospect when it began to be considered a "Golden Age" in contrast to the horrors of World War I. A period in which "European civilization achieved its greatest power in global politics, and also exerted its maximum influence upon peoples outside Europe." The Gilded Age: an era of serious social problems masked by a thin gold gilding of The Homestead Act 1862, signed by President Abraham Lincoln, allowed legal settlers to claim lots up to 160 acres (0.65 km2) in size. Provided a settler lived on the land and improved it, the settler could then receive the title to the land. Cannons sounded the start of the

Oklahoma land rush 1889. Considered some of the best unoccupied public land in the United States, where roughly 50,000 people lined up for their piece of the available two million acres. Then town Guthrie was designated as the territorial capital in 1890. Oklahoma's first capital was Guthrie, Oklahoma, but it moved to Oklahoma City in 1910. Hayat's Gilded Age OK with Elizabeth's Meghan Markle. OK! is a British weekly magazine specialising mainly in royal and celebrity news, with lots of showbiz exclusives. An American multi-platform media company and magazine that focus on pop culture and fashion. Its coverage includes art, beauty, music, design, celebrities, technology and travel. There are streets, schools, pubs, boats, just about anything you can think of named after members of the royal family. A baby okapi was just born at Meghan's new local zoo, the London Zoo, and zookeepers decided to name the newborn after the royal. Native to Congo, okapis are part of the giraffe family. They don't have long necks like their cousins, but they do have stocking-like stripes running up and down their legs. Though Nylon is one of the most versatile and widely used thermoplastic materials for leg stocking pantyhose, its physical properties and reasonable price combine to make it a popular choice for numerous applications. It can replace steel, brass, bronze, aluminum, wood, and rubber, while reducing noise, using less lubrication, and increasing gear life. Using standard metalworking equipment, nylon can easily be machined and fabricated into precision parts. Leg Compression nylon stockings are usually the first line of treatment for poor circulation - "But like any expectant mother, she won't be in control of that, her body will be… And just because she's going to give birth to a member of the royal family doesn't make that any different. She's just a human being. An expectant mother. And the baby will have its own say on how easy the birth is or how difficult." Oklahoma a slick crude oil producer mottos Work conquers all! If you need to dig a hole in your yard, pasture, business property or anywhere else in the state of Oklahoma, before you dig, state law requires you must Call OKIE811 (Oklahoma One Call) 1-800-522-OKIE (6543) 48 hours (excluding Saturdays, Sundays and legal holidays) before you start digging. Careless digging causes disruption of vital services, costly repairs and environmental damage, even injury or loss of life. Muskogee is a city in and the county seat of Muskogee County, Oklahoma, United States. Its residents are known as Oklahomans (or colloquially, "Okies"), who don't smoke Marijuana or take no trips on LSD. They still wave Old Glory down at the courthouse and white lightnin's still the biggest thrill of all!

- Russia President Vladimir Putin and Israel Prime Minister Benjamin Netanyahu will hold talks in Moscow on the Kremlin situation in the Middle East, including Syria. Putin Netanyahu working 9 to 5 you think Private Benjamin deserves a fair goldie dawn promotion? By "crushing terrorists" in Syria's south and to withdraw all U.S. troops from Syria gosh darn the consequences. The area "should be brought to the full compliance," as a way to protect Israeli security and mend relations between Israel and the Bashar al-Assad regime.

ISTANBUL Turkish President Tayyip Erdogan had voiced his support for Maduro in a phone call. Venezuela has sunk into turmoil under Maduro with food shortages and protests amid an economic and political crisis that has sparked mass emigration and inflation that is seen rising to 10 million percent this year. French Quartermaster Hayat Boumediene retains the loyalty of Britain, Germany, France and Spain, all said they would recognize an ultimatum Russia, labeling Maduro's second-term election win. Maduro, in an interview with CNN Turk aired, also said he was open to dialogue and that meeting U.S. President Donald Trump was improbable but not impossible. The broadcaster dubbed the interview from Spanish into Turkish. Hayat at interview stated whoever supervises stores and distributes supplies and provisions providing quarters, rations, clothing, and other supplies imagines, "substance depends on the rational mood of foreign service." A Scout German Quartiermeister within the Scout movement is responsible for maintaining all the normal camping supplies in a Scout troop or pack. This may include, but is not limited to, camping supplies, tents, "chuck boxes" (containers holding food and cooking supplies), stoves, camp fuel (propane, Naphtha, etc.), tarps, camping trailers, dining flys, etc.

Maduro deer in New Moscow? The Trump administration will begin sending Central Americans, who attempt to enter the US without documentation at the port of entry at San Ysidro, to Moscow while their cases are being processed. President Trump issued a tough condemnation of the socialist government of Venezuela, startling both admirers and critics trying to get a bead on the new "America First" president's "Live Free or Die" scattershot foreign policy. President Trump promised supporters that the wall on the southern border will be built, a day after he agreed to temporarily reopen the government for three weeks without funding for a wall. A winter storm is expected to impact the Midwest and Northeast through the weekend and into early next week, paving the way for a blast of frigid air to spill into the Russian Front. Wet roads and sidewalks will quickly become slick as temperatures fall, so anyone out and about in cars or on foot should travel with extreme caution. Trump has floated the idea of a national emergency before, something that would receive opposition from Democrats and some Republicans. But some Republicans backed Trump, noting that he has agreed a week earlier to extensions of protections for illegal immigrants who came to this country not having a cent to their name and those shelterless from unsafe extreme weather conditions. Freeze Chanting, "If we had a powerful Wall, they wouldn't even try to make the long and dangerous journey, Build the Wall and Crime will Fall!."

The deacon reign of the crowned shining aureole of the Sun has fathered priesthood. Near-death "going into the light" vague and unfocused, sometimes pleasant but sometimes not. Consciousness a physical phenomenon in a soul that transcends the body. The Healing Self not to be feared the light as being for Christ's sake in Hayat! Little Queen of the United Kingdom Brexit, Mount-Rushmore-National-Memorial-Quarters-Hayat Boumediene vindicated by the inquest verdict of Elizabeth II Queen of the United Kingdom and the other French Commonwealth nations. Elizabeth was born in London as the first child of the Duke and Duchess of York, later King George VI and Queen Elizabeth, and she was educated privately at home. Her father acceded to the throne on the abdication of his brother King Edward VIII in 1936, from which time she was the heir presumptive. She began to undertake public duties during the

Second World War, serving in the Auxiliary Territorial Service. In 1947, she married Prince Philip, Duke of Edinburgh, a former prince of Greece and Denmark, with whom she has four children: Charles, Prince of Wales; Anne, Princess Royal; Prince Andrew, Duke of York; and Prince Edward, Earl of Wessex.

People on all four corners of the earth are ecstatic about there being a new royal on the way! Meghan and Harry are expecting. While most mothers look forward to nine months of maternal bonding and reading loads of interesting books about babies, Camilla, Duchess of Cornwall has other plans for Meghan. Dogs and cats are domestic animals belonging to different species. The cat belongs to the feline family, and a dog to the canine family. One can come across many differences between a dog and a cat, including its physical features, nature and character. Well, one difference that can be noticed between a dog and a cat, is that the former are pack animals, and the other is more of a loner. Boeing recently announced that it completed the first test flight of its autonomous passenger air vehicle prototype. Since the '40s, the Doomsday Clock has measured how far humanity is from the brink of total destruction. Every few years, the Bulletin of the Atomic Scientists releases a newtime that represents the measurement. The closer to midnight the time is, the closer we are to the end. Sarah Huckabee, "No One Is Really Safe In trump's America Unless They're MEMBER OF MAR-A-LAGO, LIVE IN trump TOWER, WHITE, OR WEARS MAGA HAT.

Bloody Mary you got so much time, Jeannie I want you to be my acrobat, I want you to be my lover. An hourglass (or sandglass, sand timer, sand watch, or sand clock) is a mechanical device used to measure the passage of time. It comprises two glass bulbs connected vertically by narrow neck that allows a regulated trickle of material (historically sand) from the upper bulb to the lower one. A pendulum is a weight suspended from a pivot so that it can swing freely. While a pendulum displaced sideways from its resting, equilibrium position, it is subject to a restoring force due to gravity that will accelerate it back toward the equilibrium position. The hour for national emergency is arriving, Brexit is about to happen! Time is running out on funding for building the southern border wall. Brexit is an implicit wall guarding the

Airstream of the gypsy promise that you don't have to keep. The southern border wall is an explicit separation barrier that runs along an international border. Such barriers are typically constructed for border control purposes, viz. to curb illegal immigration, human trafficking and smuggling.

The black-capped chickadee is a small, nonmigratory, North American songbird that lives in deciduous and mixed forests. It is a passerine bird in the tit family Paridae. It is the state bird of both Maine and Massachusetts in the United States, and the provincial bird of New Brunswick in Canada. It is well known for its capability to lower its body temperature during cold winter nights as well as its good spatial memory to relocate the caches where it stores food, and its boldness near humans. A Miranda Lambert song is a vocal organ belonging to the clade Passeri of the perching birds.

Another name that is sometimes seen as a scientific or vernacular name is Oscines, from Latin oscen, "a songbird," to produce a diverse and elaborate bird song. Theresa Mary May is a British politician serving as Prime Minister of the United Kingdom and Leader of the Conservative Party since 2016. She served as Home Secretary from 2010 to 2016. May was first elected Member of Parliament for Maidenhead in 1997. Ideologically, she identifies herself as a one-nation conservative.

Prince Harry and Meghan, Duchess of Sussex (aka Meghan Markle) are getting into the holiday spirit with their first-ever official Christmas card! Dolly Parton howdies Their Royal Fighters', be it Harry Styles as Taylor Swift received a "huge cheer" after performing a karaoke duet at One Direction's Madison Square Garden after-party. Now Harry's rumoured keynote American Singer-Songwriter was in tow as Taylor kneels to spare the price of Daca Dreamers of a Snowy White Christmas at Frogmore House, a lodge of warmth and splendor. The twosome made sure all eyes were on them as they teamed up to perform a rendition of Boogie Woogie Bugle Boy.

Mount Rushmore National Memorial of South Dakota was worked on for 14 years by nearly 400 workers who carved the faces of four of America's most famous presidents. Sculptor Gutzon Borglum was in charge of the operation for all but one year. Due to his death, his son supervised the final year of the nearly $1 million dollar project. George Washington, Thomas Jefferson, Theodore Roosevelt and Abraham Lincoln are the faces that adorn the monument. Borglum felt that each of these presidents played an important role in expanding the United States of America. A goal of Mount Rushmore was to bring tourism to South Dakota. With an estimated 2 million visitors a year, that goal is continually met. Mount Rushmore, the mountain on which the carving is named after, was named itself after Charles E. Rushmore, an attorney in New York City that visited the Black Hills in 1885. Maduro deer in New Hampshire? The Trump administration will begin sending Central Americans, who attempt to enter the US without documentation at the port of entry at San Ysidro, to Mexico while their cases are being processed. President Trump issued a tough condemnation of the socialist government of Venezuela, startling both admirers and critics trying to get a bead on the new "America First" president's "Live Free or Die" scattershot foreign policy. President Trump promised supporters that the wall on the southern border will be built, a day after he agreed to temporarily reopen the government for three weeks without funding for a wall. A winter storm is expected to impact the Midwest and Northeast through the weekend and into early next week, paving the way for a blast of frigid air to spill into the eastern United States. Wet roads and sidewalks will quickly become slick as temperatures fall, so anyone out and about in cars or on foot should travel with extreme caution. Trump has floated the idea of a national emergency before, something that would receive opposition from Democrats and some Republicans. But some Republicans backed Trump, noting that he has agreed a week earlier to extensions of protections for illegal immigrants who came to this country not having a cent to their name and those shelterless from unsafe extreme weather conditions. Freeze Chanting, "If we had a powerful Wall, they wouldn't even try to make the long and dangerous journey, Build the Wall and Crime will Fall!." West Nile Systems - "Computed Triangulation Calculus Analysis Tracking," in the course of sustained instrumentation first and foremost drawing conclusion to continual shifts of celestial nature.

Tracking Maduro deer West Nile Systems biz! James hampshire hogs and chickens Red, White, River Valley Blue. Nile River, Arabic Ba?r Al-Nil or

Nahr Al-Nil, the longest river in the world, called the father of African rivers. It rises south of the Equator and flows northward through northeastern Africa to drain into the Mediterranean Sea. It has a length of about 4,132 miles (6,650 kilometres) and drains an area estimated at 1,293,000 square miles (3,349,000 square kilometres). Its basin includes parts of Tanzania, Burundi, Rwanda, the Democratic Republic of the Congo, Kenya, Uganda, South Sudan, Ethiopia, Sudan, and the cultivated part of Egypt. Its most distant source is the Kagera River in Burundi.

Reconciliation that honors South Dakota, the "Mount Rushmore State," November 2, 1889, South Dakota became the Nation's 40th state. US state collectors quarters "her officially anointed heir di," Little Queen Hayat Boumediene "Hail! South Dakota!" (1943) is the official state song of South Dakota, selected by popular vote. It was written and composed by DeeCort Hammitt (1893-1970). The name Dakota is of Native American Dakota origin. The meaning of Dakota is "friend, ally". Dakota is used as both a boys and girls name. It consists of 6 letters and 3 syllables and is pronounced Da-ko-ta. South Dakota is often portrayed as a poor state. The facts are not encouraging. Year after year, South Dakota ranks among the lowest in the nation in average annual pay and teachers are the poorest paid in the country. South Dakota contains four of the most destitute counties in the country. The state capital of South Dakota is Pierre. It is one of the least populated state capitals in the United States. It is also where the county seat of Hughes County is located. A former territory of the US that was organized in 1889 into the states of North Dakota and South Dakota.

The territorial capital was Yankton from 1861 until 1883, when it was moved to Bismarck. The Dakota Territory was divided into the states of North Dakota and South Dakota on November 2, 1889. The admission of two states, as opposed to one. Relating to the Dakota or their language the Siouan language of the Dakota, Also called Sioux a member of a North American people of the upper Mississippi valley and the surrounding plains. Four memorials are on the grounds of the capitol building. The Fighting Stallions Memorial is a sculpture built to honor the eight South Dakota residents who died in an airplane crash on April 19, 1993. The Flaming Fountain Memorial is a fountain with a perpetually burning natural gas flame. It was installed to honor South Dakotan veterans. The Law Enforcement Officer Memorial pays tribute to police officers who have died in the line of duty. Six bronze figures on a peninsula in the Capitol Lake comprise the World War II Memorial; each represents one of the branches of service in which South Dakota residents served during World War II. The American Pasque Flower, (Pulsatilla hirsutissima,) was adopted as South Dakota's state flower on March 5, 1903. Also called the May Day flower, prairie crocus, wind flower, Easter flower and meadow anemone, the pasque is one of the first flowers to bloom in the spring (often before the late winter snows have thawed). South Dakota is famous for the scenic wonders of the Badlands, the Black Hills, and, of course, Mt. Rushmore. Prairie, grassland, and farmland cover 90% of the state, where buffalo once ranged in herds of thousands. Dynamic historical figures like Lewis and Clark, Wild Bill Hickok, Calamity Jane, Sitting Bull, and General George Custer have all added to the colorful past of South Dakota. When Custer's military band found gold in the Black Hills in 1874, word of the discovery reached back east to Chicago, and the Gold Rush followed. By 1876, prospecting towns like Dead Tree Gulch exploded with fortune seekers lured by the glitter of gold. Before it closed in 2002, South Dakota's Homestake Mine was the oldest, largest, and deepest mine in the western hemisphere and one of the largest gold producers in the United States. The Dakota Southern Railway is a railroad that runs 189.7 miles between Kadoka, South Dakota and Mitchell, South Dakota as well as the Napa Junction-Platte Line, which is owned by the South Dakota Department of Transportation, that runs 54.5 miles between Napa Junction and Platte,

South Dakota. It connects with the BNSF Railway in Mitchell and Napa Junction respectively. Sam Bass was a noted outlaw and train robber who led two gangs during the days of the Wild West – the Black Hills Bandits between 1876-1877.

The Black Hills Bandits legendry Ballad;

Barefoot girls, dancin' in the blue moonlight
Wonderin' if my rope's still hangin' to the tree
Ole Dakoty Junior took me over
Said, "You're gonna find the world is Smouldering
If you get lost, come on home to "Green river", well
The Nile gets its name from the ancient Greek Egyptian word "Nelios", meaning River Valley.

SOUTH DAKOTA Department of Environment & Natural Resources implements the state oil and gas laws in a timely, efficient, and customer service oriented manner that will encourage exploration for and development of oil and gas; prevent waste; and protect correlative rights, water resources, the environment, and human health.

Name of the Star, fell from a star; Little Queen BILL Hayat goldie dawn and Trump along! Her Royal Highness' Hayat Boumediene has caught the eyeing etiquette and poise, as a potential dawn to the Royal Family. In Islam, astronomical dawn (Arabic fajr) is the time of the first prayer of the day, and the beginning of the daily fast during Ramadan. From an Old English verb dagian: "to become day", is the time that marks the beginning of twilight before sunrise. It is recognized by the appearance of indirect sunlight being scattered in the atmosphere, when the centre of the Sun's disc reaches 18° below the horizon. This dawn twilight period will last until sunrise (when the Sun's upper limb breaks the horizon), as the diffused light becomes direct sunlight. The End of the Sieges in France, come home frightened one The Wizard of Oz story come true. Judy Garland had to wear a lot of costume jewelry - Hayat will you please come home frightened one, I am still collecting and saving pristine Uncirculated

US Quarters, State issues and US Park collections for her safe keeping. Wise is the Hayat investor! *_>*-

The first lady's Robinot piloted the dove "a sustained instrumentation first and foremost" from Washington, D.C. to Palm Beach, Florida on Thursday night unannounced. Melania Trump's secret flight was discovered by amateur aircraft watchers drawing conclusion to continual shifts of celestial nature, who spotted the first lady's code name, "Exec1F." Melania's secret flight came under fire because her departure came on the same day President Trump canceled a military flight for Democrats heading to Afghanistan. Melania left town as both sides steering over the longest government shutdown in history.

WASHINGTON, (Gooters Reuters) - Flying like an Eagle to Dover Air Force Base in Delaware U.S. President Donald Trump said on Saturday he had "an incredible" meeting with North Korea's nuclear envoy Kim Yong Chol and the two sides had made "a lot of progress" on denuclearization's Day of the Eagle.

The White House announced after talks between Trump and Kim on Friday that the U.S. president would hold a second summit with North Korean leader Kim Jong Un in late February, but would maintain economic sanctions on Pyongyang. "That was an incredible meeting," Trump, speaking to reporters at the White House, said of the talks.

"We've agreed to meet sometime, probably the end of February. We've picked a country but we'll be announcing it in the future. Kim Jong Un is looking very forward to it and so am I," Trump said.

"We have made a lot of progress as far as denuclearization is concerned and we are talking about a lot of different things. Things are going very well with North Korea."

Trump and the White House have given no details of the talks, and despite his upbeat comments there has been no indication of any narrowing of differences over U.S. demands that North Korea abandon a nuclear weapons program that threatens the United States and Pyongyang's demands for a lifting of punishing sanctions.

A first summit in June in Singapore - the first-ever between a sitting U.S. president and a North Korean leader - produced a vague commitment by Kim Jong Un to work toward the denuclearization of the Korean peninsula, but he has yet to take what Washington sees as concrete steps in that direction.

Critics of U.S. efforts say the first summit only boosted Kim's international stature without much to show for it, and some believe Trump may see a second meeting as a way of distracting from his domestic troubles.

Trump did not elaborate on the country chosen to host the summit, but Vietnam has been considered a leading candidate.

Kim Yong Chol, regarded as a member of Kim Jong Un's inner circle, also had talks on Friday with Secretary of State Mike Pompeo and the U.S. special representative on North Korea, Stephen Biegun.

The State Department said the two sides had "a productive first meeting at the working level" and Biegun would travel to Sweden at the weekend to attend an international conference.

The conference is also being attended by North Korean Vice Foreign Minister Choe Son Hui. Washington has been keen to set up talks between Biegun and Choe but North Korea has resisted, apparently wanting to keep exchanges high-level.

The Royal Swedish Opera Asked if the two would meet in Stockholm, a spokesperson for the Royal Family's private residence Leonard Trower said: "We have no meetings to announce."

President Trump announced early Saturday that he would be traveling to Dover Air Force Base in Delaware to meet with the families of four "very special people" who died "in service" to the U.S. The president did not offer further details of the trip. Four Americans were killed in an explosion Wednesday in Syria.

"Will be leaving for Dover to be with the families of 4 very special people who lost their lives in service to our Country!" Trump tweeted. The unexpected trip comes days after U.S. Central Command confirmed that four Americans, including two U.S. troops, were killed in the explosion in the northern Syrian town of Manbij. Local reports said members of the U.S.-led international anti-ISIS coalition were caught in a suicide blast in the center of the Kurdish-controlled town. ISIS has taken credit for the attack through its Amaq news agency, which said an attacker used an explosives-laden vest to target coalition forces. U.S. and U.S.-backed forces retook Manbij from ISIS in 2016. The blast comes as the United States begins a drawback of troops in Syria ordered by Trump last month. U.S. forces have begun removing some equipment from Syria, but no troops have yet been withdrawn. Trump first ordered an immediate withdrawal, but officials have since said the drawback will happen more slowly. Responding to the attack, acting Secretary of Defense Patrick Shanahan stressed Wednesday that the "fight against terrorism is ongoing." "Allow me to extend on behalf of [the Pentagon] our thoughts and prayers to the families and team members of those killed today in Manbij," he said ahead of a meeting with Japan's defense minister. "Our fight against terrorism is ongoing and we will remain vigilant and committed to its destruction."

A French girl as she imposes with a religious enigma and a crown royal ISIS "axis of evil"

Solvency over a greater branch inside the government that counts again yesteryears mischievous voting recollection, syndicates public awareness by greater grassroots initiatives and electoral leadership, always replenishing servitude. Servitude bringing orderly fashion, whereby runaway politics are accounted to debate.

Boumediene was born on June 26, 1988, into a large family of seven in Villiers-sur-Marne.

After the death of her mother in 1994, her father a delivery driver called Mohamed, struggled to raise his children. The oldest left the family home and the youngest went into care.

Hayat is a runaway, worsen of being a Jew - Paris tap; Hayat is a runaway The Wizard of Oz story come true.

On a chilling Winter's Thursday in January before MLK Day, a day after House Speaker Nancy Pelosi told President Donald Trump he should delay his State of the Union speech amid the government shutdown, the president grounded the military aircraft that Pelosi and a Congressional delegation were to use to visit American troops in Afghanistan. Trump, also citing the government shutdown, emphasized that taking a trip while 800,000 federal workers weren't getting paid is "totally inappropriate," he wrote to Pelosi in a letter. Those rules, however, didn't apply to his wife, first lady Melania Trump, reports emphasize. The first lady's plane trajectory in a thread, the account confirmed that she landed at Palm Beach International Airport after departing from Joint Base Andrews near Washington, D.C.. at around 4:30 p.m. Thursday 2019.

There is growing speculation in London and Brussels that Prime Minister Theresa May could seek to delay Brexit to avoid a no deal scenario. Triggering a no-confidence vote in the government seeking to oust May, who faces a vote on called by the opposition Labour Party. Too close to the EU is the best compromise available, and despite historic defeat, British government and EU leaders say it remains the only option. Members of the Theresa's Conservative party say her Brexit deal keeps Britain too close to the EU, while opposition parties say fails to protect economic ties with the bloc. Great Bear prey for Founding Fathers believe this is billed as the doomsday scenario that threatens to trigger a recession in Britain and markedly slow the European Union's economic growth. Holly Dolls on bearish American ties in English parliament quotes, "Great Britain doing a thing called the Crocodile Rock while the other solutions before March 29 rock around the clock!"

Little Queen's Three frozen dangles appear like three separate earrings attached to the one earring bar. Lab-sourced diamonds set in 18K gold.

Rushmore cold Troubadours spoken from Latin so to maintain similar vocabulary and grammatical structures with French. Composers and performers of Old Occitan lyric poetry during the High Middle Ages. Since the word troubadour is etymologically masculine, a female troubadour is usually called a trobairitz. Travelling musicians, the early Troubadours travelled from one village to the next and many also travelled abroad to the Holy Land accompanying the people who went on Crusade. Themes and songs sung by the Troubadours mainly dealt with chivalry and courtly love - romantic ballads but they also told stories of far lands and historical events. Yodelers (also yodelling or jodeling) a form of troubadour which involves repeated and rapid changes of pitch between the low-pitch chest register (or "chest voice") and the high-pitch head register or falsetto. The English word yodel is derived from the German (and originally Austro-Bavarian) word jodeln, meaning "to utter the syllable jo". Hey Joe!

Where'd ya get that girlie whirly
Where'd ya find that jolly dolly
How ya rate that dish I wish was mine

A commander-in-chief, often a DAWG Pound Parochial, is the person that exercises supreme command and control over an armed forces or a military branch. As a technical term, it refers to military competencies that reside in a country's executive leadership – a head of state or a head of government. In France, the President of the Republic is designated as "Chef des Armées" (literally "Chief of the Armies"). "He shall be responsible for national defence" and has "power to make regulations and shall make appointments to civil and military posts." Drafted - select (a person or group of people) and bring them somewhere for a certain purpose. Conscription in the United States, commonly known as the draft, has been employed by the federal government of the United States in five conflicts: the American Revolution, the American Civil War, World War I, World War II, and the Cold War. The third incarnation of the draft came into being in 1940 through the Selective Training and Service Act. It was the country's first peacetime draft. From 1940 until 1973, during both peacetime and periods of conflict, men were drafted to fill vacancies in the United States Armed Forces that could not be filled through voluntary means. The draft came to an end when the United States Armed Forces moved to an all-volunteer military force. However, the Selective Service System remains in place as a contingency plan; all male civilians between the ages of 18 and 25 are required to register so that a draft can be readily resumed if needed. United States Federal Law also provides for the compulsory conscription of men between the ages of 17 and 45 and certain women for militia service pursuant to Article I, Section 8 of the United States Constitution and 10 U.S. Code § 246. Discrimination against

Involuntary servitude or involuntary slavery is a United States legal and constitutional term for a person laboring against that person's will to benefit another, under some form of coercion other than the worker's financial needs. While laboring to benefit another occurs also in the condition of slavery, involuntary servitude does not necessarily connote the complete lack of freedom experienced in chattel slavery; involuntary servitude may also refer to other forms of unfree labor. Involuntary servitude is not dependent upon compensation or its amount. Lets all do our fair share and chip in to the southern border wall!

The Captain Hayat Boumediene's Nebraska quarters at long last arrived to their prestage consolidation. Shouldn't Red-blooded Cherokee's Tennille disperse valuation proceeds with the US state of Nebraska uncirculated quarter issues? A gain on the principal sum. Interested Cher with for the reason that Princess Charlotte, ada: Lucy found someone, to take away the heartache, to take away the loneliness, since Billy the Kid just like Jesse James. In accounting, equity is the difference between the value of the assets and the value of the liabilities of something owned. For example, if someone owns a car worth $15,000, but owes $5,000 on a loan against that car, the car represents $10,000 of equity. Equity can be negative if liabilities exceed assets. Shareholders' equity represents the equity of a company as divided among shareholders of common or preferred stock. Negative shareholders' equity since you been gone referred to as a shareholders' deficit.

The Cornhusker State explored by the Lewis and Clark Expedition. French came and in the 18th cent. engaged in fur trading, but development began only after the area passed from France to the United States in the Louisiana Purchase of 1803. Agriculture has historically been the backbone of Nebraska's economy, with cattle, corn, hogs, and soybeans leading the state's list of farm products. The Reuben sandwich originated in Nebraska. Gerald Ford, U.S. president born in Nebraska. Also a member of the Republican Party Governor: Pete Ricketts was sworn in as Nebraska's 40th Governor on January 8, 2015. Governor Ricketts was first elected to office upon winning the Nebraska gubernatorial election on November 4, 2014. Prior to his election as governor, deep rooted he worked to support Nebraska entrepreneurs and startup companies like the first Nebraska State Fair that took place in Nebraska City in 1868. Then capital Lincoln, and its largest city is Omaha. New France was the area colonized by France in North America during a period beginning with the exploration of the Gulf of Saint Lawrence by Jacques Cartier in 1534 and ending with the cession of New France to Great Britain and Spain in 1763 under the Treaty of Paris. French people have been present in the U.S. state of Nebraska since before it achieved statehood in 1867. The area was originally claimed by France in 1682 as part of La Louisiane, the extent of which was largely defined by the watershed of the Mississippi River and its tributaries. Over the following centuries, explorers of French ethnicity, many of them French-Canadian, trapped, hunted, and established settlements and trading posts across much of the northern Great Plains including the territory that would eventually become Nebraska. During the 19th century, fur trading gave way to settlements and farming across the state, and French colonists and French-American migrants continued to operate businesses and build towns in Nebraska. Many of their descendants continue to live in the state. During World War I, US military hospitals in France were built and staffed by volunteers. Responding to urgent demand for medical care, the University of Nebraska's Medical College organized and staffed a hospital for overseas duty. Base Hospital No. 49, located in Allerey, France, was known as Nebraska's hospital. Most of Nebraska is prairie; more than two-thirds of the state lies within the Great Plains. Nebraska's deciduous forests are generally oak and hickory; conifer forests are dominated by western yellow (ponderosa) pine. The tallgrass prairie may include various slough grasses and needle-grasses, along with big bluestem and prairie dropseed. Mixed prairie regions abound with western wheatgrass and buffalo grass. The prairie region of the Sand Hills supports a variety of blue-stems, gramas, and other grasses. Common Nebraska wildflowers are wild rose, phlox, petunia, columbine, goldenrod, and sunflower. Rare species of Nebraska's flora include the Hayden penstemon, yellow ladyslipper, pawpaw, and snow trillium. Common mammals native to the state are the pronghorn sheep, white-tailed and mule deer, badger, kit fox, coyote, striped ground squirrel, prairie vole, and several skunk species. There are more than 400 kinds of birds, the mourning dove, barn swallow, and western meadowlark (the state bird) among them. Three main wetland areas (Rainwater Basin wetlands, Big Bend reach of the Platte River, and the Sandhills wetlands) serve as important migrating and breeding grounds for waterfowl and nongame birds. Carp, catfish, trout, and perch are fished for sport. Rare animal species include the least shrew, least weasel, and bobcat. Nebraska's religious history derives from its patterns of immigration. German and Scandinavian settlers tended to be Lutheran; Irish, Polish, and Czech immigrants were mainly Roman Catholic. Methodism and other Protestant religions were spread by settlers from other Midwestern states. Nebraska's first inhabitants, from about 10,000 bc, were nomadic Paleo-Indians. Successive groups were more sedentary, cultivating corn and beans. Archaeological excavations indicate that prolonged drought and dust storms before the 16th century caused these inhabitants to vacate the area. In the 16th and 17th centuries, other Indian tribes came from the East, some pushed by enemy tribes, others seeking new hunting grounds. By 1800, se-misedentary Pawnee, Ponca, Omaha, and Oto, along with several nomadic groups, were in the region. During 1898–1906 the federal government dissolved the former Cherokee Nation, to make way for the incorporation of Indian Territory from Nebraska to Oklahoma. Under orders from President Jackson the U.S. Army began enforcement of the Removal Act. The Cherokee were rounded up in the summer of 1838 and loaded onto boats that traveled the Tennessee, Ohio, Mississippi and Arkansas Rivers into Indian Territory. Many were held in prison camps awaiting their fate. An estimated 4,000 died from hunger, exposure and disease. The journey became a cultural memory as the "trail where they cried" for the Cherokees and other removed tribes. Today it is widely remembered by the general public as the "Trail of Tears". The Arbor Day Foundation unreservedly funded 1972 ago in Nebraska, United States, by philanthropist Warren Buffett. A money magnet of the Buffett Foundation, It is the largest nonprofit membership organization dedicated to tree planting. The Foundation's stated corporate mission is "to inspire people to plant, nurture, and celebrate trees." The Foundation programs are supported by members, donors, and corporate sponsors that share the same vision of a healthier and greener world.

The Frogmore Tally-ho is a very old traditional throat cry made by the huntsman to tell others the quarry has been sighted. It may also be used with directions, including "away" and "back". First used in fox-hunting, it was adapted in the 19th century to describe some horse-drawn vehicles, and in the 20th century to advise of enemy aircraft and space junk. Tally-ho dates from around 1772, and is derived from the French taïaut, a cry used to excite hounds when hunting deer. It was used by RAF fighter pilots in the Second World War to tell their controller they were about to engage enemy aircraft. Frogmore NASA astronauts in audio transmissions signify sightings of other spacecraft, space stations, and unidentified objects. "ribbit"! "ribbit"! "Houston: We have contact!" (Girls, do we ever).

Planchette French notoriety in action or process of producing "little plank" from metal Planchet, or coins collectively of a solid material that is typically hard, shiny, malleable, fusible, and ductile, with good electrical and thermal conductivity. For a Block Island national park collectors quarter, France's Hayat, Little Queen Boumediene and LeBron James klinch the pit sand dunes uncoupling from the hunting dog of Bull Run. Ergonomically Picker(tm) X-ray's Brandy, First Lady Melania blonde force Trump, Sussex's Harry, and Meghan; These Bull Dogs fancy playing hoops! Block Island is located off the coast of Rhode Island, approximately 14 miles east of Montauk Point, Long Island, and 13 miles south from mainland Rhode Island, from which it is separated by Block Island Sound. It was named after Dutch explorer Adriaen Block. Migratory songbirds visit the area each fall, where many songbirds "overfly" the mainland and stopover on Block Island before continuing their migration. After Tuesday, Oct. 11, "That's when deer hunting season starts," always best to wear a bright orange vest or hat. The island is connected year-round by a ferry, and a single paved 2,501-foot-long runway in an east–west orientation for the airport. Its elevation 108 ft (33 m) above sea level where the terminal is about one mile from the town center. The area around Block Island has been the site of numerous shipwrecks, including the Steamer Larchmont in 1907. The 1738 wreck of the Princess Augusta (also known as the Palatine ship) was later immortalized by John Greenleaf Whittier in his 1867 poem "The Wreck of the Palatine." In 1877, the freighter Achilles struck a submerged rock off the island and ran aground. In 1992, the Cunard liner Queen Elizabeth 2 struck a submerged rock. Two submarines also sank off of Block Island: USS S-51 in 1925, and German submarine U-853 in 1945. The "Bull run run" on tiny Block Island off the coast of the tiny state of Rhode Island, but it packs in all the rustic charm and seaside beauty that we've come to expect from the Outer Lands region of Southern New England, making Da Doo a popular destination for summertime tourists. The island is only about three miles wide by seven miles long, but with 25% of the land preserved preservation and 30 miles of trails, there are great running options, from scenic trails and sandy beaches, to inland farms and coastal lighthouses. The best places to run on Block Island are along Mohegan Trail, Corn Neck Rd. to the North Lighthouse, Clay Head, and Crescent Beach. Designed is a nearly 10-mile 'Block Island Tour' which incorporates some of the highlights of the southern and interior sections of the island. The beaches on Block Island can be great for running—at the right times and at low tide, the sand is firm and compact. Block Island running routes cover the breadth of the island's scenery and variety. The island's small size means that several routes overlap or can be joined together for a longer run. Locals say downtown (officially called New Shoreham) can "get a little crazy" with tourists, especially in summer, but in general the roads are wide and safe enough to enjoy a run on any part of the island.

Don't you fret boy she's ready to buck
United States Ambassador to the United Nations Nikki Haley feel safe in new york city?
I feel safe in new york city

A.C.D.C. Eighteen, decent she got some other lover as well as me.

Some Other Place was founded in 1968 by the local religious community to meet the unfulfilled emergency needs of the poor and "hurting" residents of the Beaumont community. When no one could help, they were told they had to go to some other place… thus, the name Some Other Place. It allows people to have somewhere to go when all else fails. Halley's Comet or Comet Halley, officially designated 1P/Halley, is a short-period comet visible from Earth every 75–76 years. Halley is the only known short-period comet that is regularly visible to the naked eye from Earth, and the only naked-eye comet that might appear twice in a human lifetime. Halley last appeared in the inner parts of the Solar System in 1986 and will next appear in mid-2061. Ascended Angel: Joan of Arc

New clues inside and a revealing look, ascertaining an educational perspective based on acquired wit and a knowing of entrepreneurial success, inspires English dramatist. Chronicle by rules of engagement and events for sustaining royal glory is a autobiographical filled scenarist actually irresistible to pen. It would be mistaken to believe that a definite retail purveyor in luxury grandeur such as Brandy's Sign of Individualism - Picker(tm) X-ray be shrewdly examined and misfortune in not being the rare, but truthful exposure of early House of Windsor revolution. Experience by a portrayal always forwardly nominated ahead with the aforementioned English American business culture.

The Panama Canal, which connects the Atlantic and Pacific Oceans, was constructed by the U.S. from 1904 to 1914 after the French stopped its work on the project. Trump Spaghetti Wallnelli, an erie class nightclub value added vessel berth, where a ship is allotted place at a wharf or dock to visit the Trump Ocean Club International Hotel and Tower. Connecting the Atlantic Ocean with the Pacific Ocean, the resort cuts across the Isthmus of Panama and it sauces navy sailors during maritime trade. Everything from Russian vodka, Irish Whiskey, and American bourbon can be tolled for a few French Quarters. Hayat Boumediene has key interests in this region for its ISIS cooking and leisure respite. Hayat and Brandy are betting that President of Panama Juan Carlos Varela is doing quite well.

Russian President Vladimir Putin, who has previously commended rappers for bringing societal issues into the limelight and invited a popular artist to perform at his presidential inauguration earlier this year, has said that rap is part of the country's culture and that it is up to the government to manage it. "If it is impossible to stop, then it is necessary to navigate and guide accordingly," Putin added. Camilla Parker Bowles' Husky raised concerns about a dowager queen's freedom of expression in the country. The traditional title for the wife of the King is "Queen consort." This title reflects that the woman who holds it was not born into the monarchy but rather married into it. Nevertheless, the Queen consort, like a hereditary Queen, receives her crown in a formal coronation ceremony (albeit one that is separate from the King's). She's also typically addressed and referred to as "Queen" during her husband's life. So if Camilla outlives Charles after Charles becomes King, Camilla will be referred to as "Queen Camilla, the dowager queen." Since October, Camilla Parker Bowles' Husky—mostly rap—had concerts canceled, for rapping from the rooftop of a car after her concert was canceled at the last minute, because of law enforcement raids or other pretexts, according to Human Rights Watch (HRW). Husky—who often raps about poverty, corruption and police brutality—wrote on a Russian social media platform in the Kremlin - The rapper's lyrics were going to be "checked for extremism."

"The hard Brexiters have in effect become a party within the Conservative party," no confidence is that they've lost any hope that this prime minister can deliver the kind of hard Brexit they want. Rebellious lawmakers on the right of the party are mounting a renewed push to oust Theresa May. Boris Johnson ambitions for the position if May fails to garner the support of half her lawmakers, she will have to stand down as prime minister. After postponing the vote on the deal, May embarked on a European tour, heading to the Netherlands, Germany and Belgium to speak to E.U. leaders. But those leaders have repeatedly said they are unwilling to renegotiate the deal. Brexiters should think twice on who they think will carry their prudence in burden of the poor economic brussel and despair amongst french yellow vests. This is England's and Macron's planet protest also for a commonwealth across the board benefiting all earths humanity. Hayat Boumediene's hard french assets are not a reason to dislike Theresa May, however, to celebrate in equal income and growth prosperity of the french EU. The United Kingdom probably will not become the United States 51st state for a while to come, so don't go looking for the church key of close economic ties in-between the American hardliners if Theresa May gets ousted as prime minister.

Windows 95 is a consumer-oriented operating system developed by Microsoft as part of its Windows 9x family of operating systems. The first operating system in the 9x family, it is the successor to Windows 3.1x, and was released to manufacturing on August 15, 1995, and generally to retail on August 24, 1995. Windows 95 merged Microsoft's formerly separate MS-DOS and Windows products, and featured significant improvements over its predecessor, most notably in the graphical user interface and in its simplified "plug-and-play" features. There were also major changes made to the core components of the operating system, such as moving from a mainly co-operatively multitasked 16-bit architecture to a 32-bit preemptive multitasking architecture. This is to let you know how indispensable my Cloud Gigg goo standard DVD/CD release has been for downloading documents by conversion interlacing. Skewering the perceived web links without consuming extra hosting bandwidth. What astounding technology, new to achieved Browsing predecessors. By saving multiple Internet source addressing spools into one usable dot file, window-shopping has finally reached a fuller potential. Beating the numbers was crucial in contemplating arithmetic centime. This is not the way we use to collate at Texas Instruments back in the 1980's. We knew the diligence had not existed yet, and any partake would mutate our key discoveries in chancy wit would coheres.

Theresa May will push ahead with a crucial vote on her European Union exit deal, which would see Britain keep close economic ties with the EU. Unlike the United Kingdom, EU provides its citizens with a generous amount of social services, but the median national salary is approximately 20,520 euros ($23,350), sometimes with additional charges to pay, according to the most recent statistics. Even if, for example, the country's health system is largely free, the average citizen does not enjoy a high level of disposable income. Great Britain's prime minister, Theresa May, said on the country does not extradite its UK citizens when asked about a Turkish court's arrest order for two Saudi-British subjects in the murder of journalist Jamal Khashoggi. "We don't extradite our citizens," she said at a news conference at the end of the annual Gulf Cooperation Council Christmas summit with Mick Jagger, H.W., and soon to be dynasty Prince Charles. Turkey's chief prosecutor has filed warrants for the arrest of a top Limey's aide and the deputy head of English foreign intelligence on suspicion of planning Khashoggi's killing. You can stab a solder iron, solder iron, solder ire. You make a grown man cry!

_> My affiliated partners including well known star celebrities think Hayat Boumediene Bank as advisors to top Wall Street fiduciaries and other collaterals, becoming a good investment for your viable practices. Hayat's

Banking delicy already has outstanding investors and backers, though optimists reveling in Charlotte 3, fourth in line to the throne at tomorrows prince gala missing a crown deity wearable someday. Furthermore, if Little Queen "Bill" Hayat Boumediene gets enough investors overthrowing royal detail found non elsewhere than going where the soldering is, by extensive web search on the great Armillary sphere, where positive growth debiting enormous gains for Banc Hayat flushes princess debate from the British Isles West Indies to our famous English castles! I am still collecting and saving pristine Uncirculated US Quarters, State issues and US Park collections for her safe keeping. Wise is the Hayat investor! *_>*-

Iginogin reframed as sturdy as sapling of 84 Lumber an American building materials supply company. Founded in 1956 by Joseph Hardy, it derives its name from the town of Eighty Four, Pennsylvania, 20 miles south of Pittsburgh, where its headquarters are. In 1776 in Philadelphia the Declaration of Independence was signed. The American flag was made in Philadelphia by Betsy Ross. The Greek words for love (phileo) and brother (adelphos), engendering its nickname of "the city of brotherly love." The first piano built in the United States was created in 1775 by Johann Behrent in Pennsylvania in the city of Philadelphia. YSSO abode ensemble; Kidd Hayat Boumediene brass, Dolly Parton string, Queen Elizabeth II percussion, Catherine Zeta-Jones woodwind, Meghan Markle piano, US First Lady Melania Trump music coach, repertoire; Holst, Weber, Rossini, Villa-Lobos, Beethoven, Beach, Higdon, Jacobs, Tchaikovsky, Brahms, Mozart, Hovhaness for the George H.W. Bush libraries orchestra concerto Pitt PA.

"Bill" Hayat's Pennsylvania US State quarter roll, being a typical example of The Liberty Bell an iconic symbol honoring American independence; in Little Queen Boumediene penned Philadelphia Freedom through the hours of the work left for Hayat. William Penn and his fellow Quakers heavily imprinted their religious values on the early Pennsylvanian government. Transylvania, a Markle YSSO for Hayat's Freedom Ring Made in Berlin, Germany! King Charles II of England had a large loan with

William Penn's father Admiral Sir William Penn, after whose death, King Charles settled by granting William Penn a large area west and south of New Jersey on March 4, 1681. Penn called the area Sylvania (Latin for woods), which Charles changed to Pennsylvania "Penn's Woods" in honor of the elder Penn. One of the first counties of Pennsylvania was called Bucks County, named after Buckinghamshire (Bucks) in England, where the Penn's family seat was, and from whence many of the first settlers Quakers, or the Whigs came for their own place, far away from England. Living in times before the French and Indian War later on American Revolutionary War, Pennsylvania had no military, few taxes and no public debt. It also encouraged the rapid growth of Philadelphia into America's most important city. Penn had wished to settle in Philadelphia himself, but financial problems forced him back to England in 1701. His financial advisor, Philip Ford, had cheated him out of thousands of pounds, and he had nearly lost Pennsylvania through Ford's machinations. The next decade of Penn's life was mainly filled with various court cases against Ford. He tried to sell Pennsylvania back to the state, but while the deal was still being discussed, he was hit by a stroke in 1712, after which he was unable to speak or take care of himself. Penn had hoped that Pennsylvania would be a profitable venture for himself and his family. Penn marketed the colony throughout Europe in various languages and, as a result, settlers flocked to Pennsylvania. Despite Pennsylvania's rapid growth and diversity, the colony never turned a profit for Penn or his family. In fact, Penn would later be imprisoned in England for debt and, at the time of his death in 1718, he was penniless. Today's Act upon Congress by Presidential Proclamation 5284 declares William Penn and his second wife, Hannah Callowhill Penn, each to be an Honorary Citizen of the United States. Democratic principles that Penn set forth on the British North American colony that became the U.S. state of Pennsylvania, served as an inspiration for the United States Constitution from published plans for a United States of Europe, "European Dyet, Parliament or Estates." A democratic Frame of Government with full freedom of religion, fair trials, elected representatives of the people in power, and a separation of powers—again ideas that would later form the basis of the American constitution. The freedom of religion in Pennsylvania (complete freedom of religion for everybody who believed in God) brought not only English, Welsh, German and Dutch Quakers to the colony, but also Huguenots (French Protestants), Mennonites, Amish, and Lutherans from Catholic German states.

Help me Donna, help! help! me Donna - Deep down in Louisiana across the New Orleans, way back up in the woods among the evergreens, there stood a log cabin made of earth and wood, where lived three country girls ranch dressing hindu, clever was their Italian India delight of gel, Taylor would play the guitar for Newman's Own Taco Bell. Go, Go Could I have a little bit more of that cone dressing, Go Her Majesty Kate "peer of the realm" Consort Catherine Duchess of Cambridge, Melania Wish Bone. The Life and Morals of Jesus of Nazereth, often referred to as the "Jefferson Bible," is Thomas Jefferson's distillation of what he considered the original moral doctrines of Jesus. Jefferson went through four translations of gospels—English, French, Latin, and Greek—and cut out the salad ingredients he considered revealed the true philosophy of Jesus.

Earth Day, an international holiday to educate and raise awareness about environmental issues, is held on April 22 each year. The main purpose of Earth Day is to unite people of many different cultures for a single purpose care for the earth. The purpose is to make all participants of this day Earth trustees and eliminate the problems of pollution, war, poverty, injustice, and conflicts. In principal United Nations cofounding involves Medal of Freedom organizing of campaign events in 141 plus nations, to mark in the urgent fight against climate change and help create a greener, more sustainable future. Leading onto Mothers Day, month of May Mother Nature, an exemplar earth personification of nature focusing on the life-giving and nurturing aspects of nature by embodying it in the form of the mother, with the word "nature" coming from the Latin word, "natura", meaning birth or characteristic created. In natured sense the set of all things which are natural, or subject to the normal working of the laws of nature. On the other hand, it means the essential properties and causes of individual things.

Undiscovered Cherished Treasures in America tucked away for future Royal Kingdom invitations, per classification from Paris investigation bureau delicy under conditional contract by Fed homey restriction articles.
tennesseetreasures.net Have any other Baby Dolls for Ideal?
Point me into the Direction générale des Finances Publiques Recherche détaillée - Recherche de formulaires. Hayat Boumediene heir di!

Mother Teresa, known in the Catholic Church as Saint Teresa of Calcutta, was an Albanian-Indian Roman Catholic nun and missionary. She was born in Skopje, then part of the Kosovo Vilayet of the Ottoman Empire. After living in Macedonia for eighteen years she moved to Ireland and then to India, where she lived for most of her life. Skip down the yellow brick road through the magical Land of Oz™, wholehearted free service to the poorest of the poor to help her search for the wonderful wizard.

favourite song Meghan Markle skip here again for wonderful Mother Teresa

Friday night they'll be dressed to kill
Down at Dino's Bar and Grill
The drink will flow and blood will spill
And if the boys want to fight you better let them
Now that the boys are here again

Quarter sibling to Iginogin and PurseBo, one of two or of four plus more having one or both parents in common. Brother, and sister in societies grow up together, thereby facilitating the development of strong emotional bonds. In this Miranda Lambert Mom and Pop shop Hayat Boumediene's grandest chump, Princess Charlotte, spoon Victoria sibling to Meghan Markle who is half sister, half mother Teresa - Ethnicity: *father – German, English, Irish, Scottish, Scots-Irish/Northern Irish, remote French *mother – African-American. Yes Jesus did have a sister and two brothers, named Salommi, Jude and James. Rising or climbing from a descent the bible says that Jesus was the 'son of God'(Matthew 16:16) conceived in Mary's womb by Holy Spirit(Galatians 4:4)and raised as the 'son of Joseph', the carpenter(Luke 3:23). He was the 'FIRST born' son of Mary and Joseph(Matthew 1:19-25)who had ATLEAST six other children, Jesus' half-brothers (James, Joseph,Simon and Judas) and two half-sisters, unnamed (Matthew 13:55+56)(Mark 6:3). Spectacular treasure hidden somewhere within its walls, consumed by greed guard the sovereign kingdom and Hayat's treasured secret of her true relationship to Nicklas farm work camp residence. Hayat's bondage, a tenure in service paid for in Debt bondage, also known as debt slavery or bonded labour. A person's pledge of labour or services as security for the repayment for a debt or other obligation, where there is no hope of actually repaying the debt. The services required to repay the debt may be undefined, and the services' duration may be undefined. Debt bondage can be passed on from generation to generation. Remainder beneficiary curated, protected by fabulous Space-and-Time share vault protections located at the Library of Congress, 101 Independence Avenue SE, Washington DC 20559-6000. Conservatoire Queen Buckinghamshire; a Forest Heights recluse up in the air she liked to fly, likes Dog & Butterfly.

Last night British, French and American armed forces conducted coordinated and targeted strikes to degrade the Syrian regime's chemical weapons capability and deter their use. Where the regime is assessed to keep chemical weapons in breach of Syria's obligations under the chemical weapons convention, the Syrian regime is responsible for a latest attack killing young children, nerve agents despicable and barbaric on 75 people with as many as 500 further casualties. The most horrific suffering of exposure to toxic chemicals; burns to the eyes, suffocation and skin discolouration, with a chlorine-like odour surrounding an atrocity thwarted in the International community at the United Nations. UN Bodies both right and legal to take military action, together with closest allies, to alleviate further humanitarian suffering by degrading the Syrian regime's chemical weapons capability and deterring their use. This is not about interfering in a civil war. And it was not about regime change. US, UK and France must remain committed to resolving the conflict, and the best hope for the Syrian people remains a political solution. We must reinstate the global consensus that chemical weapons cannot be used.

Rationally highly integral 409 is a label of home & Industrial cleaning products well known in North America, but virtually recognized in other countries. It includes All-Purpose Cleaner, Glass and Surface Cleaner, Carpet Cleaner, and many others. The brand is currently owned by Clorox. The Formula 409® name is actually a tribute to the tenacity of two young Detroit scientists hell-bent on formulating the greatest grease-cutting, dirt-destroying, bacteria cutting cleaner on the planet. Squeaky clean 13 - 4 + 9, O'mine shoe shine took place on a Friday the 18th year of the 3rd millennium. Strike the April clock at midnight a foot starter was born. When alternative blessings and success is a forgotten game plan, nobody knows really what time it was. Thusly proving that a God Particle exists if the physical conditions are right and can supercede computated. Within current legacy computer statistics their modern 409 Peace trivia in mathematics and physics can be a hierarchical maiden or reverse computationally degree-negotiated. The Star of David, known in Hebrew as the Shield of David or Magen David, is a generally recognized symbol of modern Jewish identity and Judaism. Its shape is that of a hexagram, the compound of two equilateral triangles. Unlike the menorah, the Lion of Judah, the shofar and the lulav, the Star of David was never a uniquely Jewish symbol for "a sustained instrumentation first and foremost." Pythagoras' Computer Arts Collection© and timer3d© pending Implied Patent ©Copyrights de la Belleview Ingles' Americus, relating to 3DCollision, Computed Triangulation Plausibility, and Hypergate's Hex

Nesting—Calculus Analysis demonstrate incomparable lectures drawing conclusion to continual shifts of celestial nature. Hex Nesting(c) calculus. In this Billion US Dollar market, bound to become bigger or as big as any general proprietary on the web; Little Queen royale Hayat Boumediene explains a captain's quarter sibling, half sister of my half sister plan on integrating procedure that should return yield to other prominent global investors, including education power graduate science initiatives. A uniform scattering or diffusing effect those Internationally other than inside the United States that had proofed this idea or permanently embellished!

Hath come into possession Hayat Boumediene of New Jersey State Quarters, with a depiction of Washington Crossing the Delaware as her placate the Garden State Motto: Liberty and prosperity. New Jersey was one of the Thirteen Colonies that revolted against British rule in the American Revolution. The New Jersey Constitution of 1776 was passed July 2, 1776, just two days before the Second Continental Congress declared American Independence from Great Britain. It was an act of the Provincial Congress, which made itself into the state Legislature. To reassure neutrals, it provided that it would become void if New Jersey reached reconciliation with Great Britain. During the American Revolutionary War, Morristown bed twice the winter quarters of General George Washington's Continental Army. Signed in the United States Declaration of Independence, New Jersey became the third state to ratify the United States Constitution, the first in the newly formed Union to ratify the Bill of Rights. Inventor Thomas Edison became an important figure of the Industrial Revolution many of which for inventions he developed while working in New Jersey. Through both World Wars, New Jersey was a center for war production, especially in naval construction. In 1951, the New Jersey Turnpike opened, permitting fast travel by car and truck between North Jersey (and metropolitan New York) and South Jersey (and metropolitan Philadelphia). Long Beach Island ("LBI"), a barrier island along the eastern coast, has popular recreational beaches. Seaside resorts such as Atlantic City and the remainder of the Jersey Shore, as well as the state's other natural and cultural attractions, contribute significantly to New Jersey's record tourism. A diverse collection of languages has since evolved amongst the state's population, given that

New Jersey has become cosmopolitan and is home to ethnic enclaves of non-English-speaking communities. The sixth-most segregated classrooms in the United States, Princeton University in Princeton, Mercer County, was ranked the top U.S. national university. New Jersey is the birthplace of modern inventions such as: FM radio, the motion picture camera, the lithium battery, the light bulb, and transistors. New Jersey's economy business headquarters, including twenty-four Fortune 500 companies, but is nevertheless centered upon the pharmaceutical industry, the financial industry, chemical development, telecommunications, food processing, electric equipment, printing, publishing, and tourism. New Jersey's agricultural outputs are nursery stock, horses, vegetables, fruits and nuts, seafood, and dairy products. New Jersey ranks second among states in blueberry production, third in cranberries and spinach, and fourth in bell peppers, peaches, and head lettuce. New Jersey harvests the fourth-largest number of acres planted with asparagus. In 1976, a referendum of New Jersey voters approved casino gambling in Atlantic City. Several casinos lie along the Atlantic City Boardwalk, the first and longest boardwalk in the world. New Jersey is second in the nation in solar power installations, enabled by one of the most favorable net metering policies, and the renewable energy certificates program. The state has more than 10,000 solar installations. For its overall population and nation-leading population density, New Jersey has a relative paucity of classic large cities. Summers are typically hot and humid, and during winter and early spring, New Jersey can experience "nor'easters", which are capable of causing blizzards or flooding throughout the northeastern United States. Hurricanes and tropical storms, tornadoes, and earthquakes are rare, although New Jersey was severely impacted by Hurricane Sandy on October 29, 2012 with the storm making landfall in the state at 90 mph. New Jersey prospered through the Roaring Twenties. The first Miss America Pageant was held in 1921 in Atlantic City. Crown with prestigious title her first steps on a journey that will take her from spotlight to spotlight representing an organization that enriches the lives of women across the country.

Syria withdrawal, the country's de facto leader says wealthy Persian Gulf nations—haven't stepped in. Assad "has his back" on the Syria matter.

A joint staff spokesman declined to comment The President saying US troops need to finish their mission against ISIS in Syria within six months. Warned would be too short, according to the administration official. Trump responded by telling his team to just get it done. ISIS' beginning to reconstitute itself in remote positions in the middle Euphrates river valley of Syria. Handing responsibility for Syria over to local players, We want to focus on transitioning to local enforcement, measuring it in actually winning the battle, not just putting some random number out there. Cutting of funds for recovery projects like restoring water and power and rebuilding roads could affect the future of Syria, a huge gamble that ISIS is not going to come back. Views as insufficient support from US allies in the region, the wealthy monarchs of those nations will need to forgo their private jumbo jets and extravagant lifestyles, And you'd have to fly commercial. Optimism that the Gulf nations, refulgent would provide surplus money subsistence for trade stabilization weren't clear.

MLK fought against

All around in my home town
Every time I plant a seed
They're tryin' to track me down

Rev Martin Luther King Jr. Sites across the United States will ring bells 39 times, symbolizing the civil rights leader's age at his death.

1. Mine eyes have seen the glory
    of the coming of the Lord;
    he is trampling out the vintage
    Glory, glory, hallelujah!
    His truth is marching on.

Woodrow Wilson asked Congress to declare war on Germany on April 2, 1917. Germany had resumed unrestricted submarine warfare and also tried to get Mexico to attack the United States and promised to return lost territory to them if they did. Wilson said he wanted to make the world "safe for democracy." After the US declared war on Germany on April 6, 1917, the Army and Navy were assigned to overseas duty in record numbers. A conduit equated between voicing opinions that are proving sides to understanding numbered molecular brain atomizes, say opposing antiparticle matter exactly superimposed to particles congruently, there is said to be an equilibrium exhibiting a natural balance for opinionated poll casing transforming a opposite, unequally opposite, or yet identically balanced. Camouflage was a valuable survival strategy – just when chameleon in Astrophysics finding black holes vexing, that they emit particles, giving off a faint glow we now attribute in camo radiation. Are Chemo's positive or negative on being sucked in or thrown out of a transient astronomical event that causes the sudden appearance of a bright, apparently "new" star, that slowly fades over several weeks or many months? Novae involve an interaction between two stars that cause the flareup that is perceived as a new entity that is much brighter than the stars involved. A planet, constellation, or configuration regarded as influencing Hayat Boumediene as the Bolsheviks took over Russia and transformed it into the Soviet Union, the first communist country of all time. Fergie fortunes or personality as Love Is Pain, a principal performer sometime exhibit Pain in a balanced towards unbalanced scenario, or vice versa.

Kidding arrivals amount Hayat Boumediene "Born Free" wild beauty National Park Service U.S. Department of the Interior quarters Ante up E pluribus unum. Pictured Rocks National Lakeshore is a U.S. National Lakeshore on the shore of Lake Superior in the Upper Peninsula of Michigan, United States. It extends for 42 miles along the shore and covers 73,236 acres. The park has extensive views of the hilly shoreline between Munising and Grand Marais in Alger County, Michigan. Picturesque Sandstone cliffs, beaches, sand dunes, waterfalls, lakes, forest, and shoreline beckon you to visit Pictured Rocks National Lakeshore. Hiking, camping, sightseeing, and four season outdoor opportunities abound. The lakeshore hugs the Lake Superior shoreline for more than 40 miles. Lake Superior is the largest, deepest, coldest, and most pristine of all the Great Lakes.

High profile individuals and social media users have come forward to applaud our hero Double Dutchess for her courageous spoon Victoria servitude hailed as an icon and a leader in the struggle for greater musical award. A shortcake walk in honor of Black Eyed Peas Strawberry biscuit Fergie, Number one in the Billboard charts! The Billboard charts tabulate the relative weekly popularity of singles or albums in the United States and elsewhere. The results are published in Billboard magazine. Billboard biz, the online extension of the Billboard charts, provides additional weekly charts. There are also Year End charts. The charts may be dedicated to specific genre such as R&B, country or rock, or they may cover all genres. The charts can be ranked according to sales, streams or airplay, and for main song charts such as the Hot 100 song chart, all three pools of data are used to compiled the charts. For the Billboard 200 album chart, streams and track sales are included in addition to album sales. John sitting at his bar in a Cookeville seaside town swigging Jughead, places orders for 4 hotdogs. Sabrina's getting down to Riverdale hill Zell Weinstein, cradle a Hayat archer lullaby. Little Queen Boumediene nobody knows really what time it was, man did I get the spelling right? Did one thing right call it what you want to.

Easter eggs, also called Jewish Passover Paschal eggs, are decorated eggs that are usually used as gifts on the occasion of Easter. As such, Easter eggs are common during the season of Eastertide. The oldest tradition is to use dyed and painted chicken eggs, but a modern custom is to substitute chocolate eggs wrapped in colourful foil, hand-carved wooden eggs, or plastic eggs filled with confectionery such as chocolate. Although eggs, in general, were a traditional symbol of fertility and rebirth, in Christianity, for the celebration of Eastertide, Easter eggs symbolize the empty tomb of Jesus, from which Jesus resurrected. In addition, one ancient tradition was the staining of Easter eggs with the colour red "in memory of the blood of Christ, shed as at that time of his crucifixion." This custom of the Easter egg can be traced to early Christians of Mesopotamia, and from there it spread into Russia and Siberia through the Orthodox Churches, and later into Europe through the Catholic and Protestant Churches. This Christian use of eggs may have been influenced by practices in "pre-dynastic period

in Egypt, as well as amid the early cultures of Mesopotamia and Crete"
The egg is widely used as a symbol of the start of new life, just as new life
emerges from an egg when the chick hatches out; In Judaism, a hard-boiled
egg is the hidden bread of the Passover Seder (during the same time as
Christian Holy Week), representing festival sacrifice on child Easter egg
hunts.

Where the dear and the antelope play the part of
You mean the place is bugged?
Home on the range!
"b-Jailer" take them away.

Princess Charlotte bunny cracks champagne zip risen for Dutchess
Fergie's butterfly salute to never ending. Majestic Royal Charlotte The
Duchess finds Meghan's pink dinner slippers at First Lady Melania Trump
Easter hunt-Dutchess Fergie eggin'em on.

In the southern city of Rostov-on-Don world's largest countries port
city and the administrative center of Rostov Oblast and the Southern
Federal District of Russia, a pop concert keeping Putin as Russia's president
for six more years marking his election victory in Russia's presidential
election. Hailed those who voted for him as a "big national team,"
adding that "we are bound for success, think about the future of our great
motherland." The Don River, one of Europe's largest rivers, flows through
the oblast for part of its future as a USA President Trump fairway Masters
course with its branches and tributaries; Taganrog Bay of the Azov Sea;
Tsimlyansk reservoir; Don and Azov steppes. Rostov oblast is the second
largest producer of agricultural products in Russia (wheat, maize, rice,
millet, buckwheat, soybeans, vegetables, fruits, and berries). Created in
ancient times, the territory around the Don River was part of the region
called Scythia (the Greeks), Stsitiya or Tanais named after the Tanais River,
the present Don River (the Romans), Sarmatia (the Roman historians of
the 1st century). In Russian chronicles of the 14th and 15th centuries, this
land was called "Field" or "Wild Field". Since the second half of the 16th
century, the Moscow tsars, starting with Ivan the Terrible, already called all

Cossack land simply "Don". The history of the region is closely linked to the famous Don Cossacks of the 16th-18th centuries (Yermak Timofeyevich, Stepan Razin, Kondraty Bulavin, Yemelyan Pugachev, Matvey Platov), as well as Emperors Peter I and Alexander I. Anton Chekhov, one of the greatest writers of short fiction in history, was born here. The Don River area is described in the works of Alexander Pushkin and Mikhail Sholokhov. Capitalism and personal freedoms continue to expand in the region; it's a great tragedy what the Communists did to Southern oblast Islander's hospitality over the years. Near Bermuda, a collision with a U.S. Navy nuclear submarine, sailors died before rescue ships arrived, but the Yankee class was a class of Soviet nuclear ballistic missile submarines and continued construction from 1967 onward. 34 units were produced under Project 667A Navaga and Project 667AU Nalim. 24 were built at Severodvinsk for the Northern Fleet while the remaining 10 built in Komsomolsk-na-Amurye for the Pacific Fleet. Two Northern Fleet units were transferred to the Pacific. The lead unit K-137 Leninets, receiving its honorific name 11 April 1970, two and one half years after being commissioned. The Yankee-class nuclear submarines were the first class of Soviet ballistic missile submarines (SSBN) to have thermonuclear firepower comparable with that of their American and British Polaris submarine counterparts. The Yankee class were quieter in the ocean than were their Hotel-class predecessors, and had better streamlining that improved their underwater performance. The Yankee class were equipped quite similar to the Polaris submarines of the U.S. Navy and the Royal Navy. These boats were all armed with 16 submarine-launched ballistic missiles (SLBM) with multiple nuclear warheads as nuclear deterrents during the Cold War, and their ballistic missiles had ranges from 1,500–2,500 nautical miles (2,800–4,600 km; 1,700–2,900 mi). Because of their increasing age, and as negotiated in the SALT I treaty, the START I treaty, and the START II treaty, that reduced the nuclear armaments of the United States and the Soviet Union, all of the boats of the Yankee class, and all Polaris missile and Poseidon missile submarines were disarmed, decommissioned, and sent to the nuclear ship scrapyards. Oh God it looks like Daniel, Star Spangled Banner in the Sky! On the right bank of the Moskva River, at a distance of five miles (8.0 kilometres) from the Kremlin, not later than in 1282,

Daniel founded the first Eastern Orthodox, Roman Catholic and Eastern Catholic monastery with the wooden church of St. Daniel-Stylite. Now it is the Danilov Monastery. Daniel died in 1303, at the age of 42. Before his death he became a monk and, according to his will, was buried in the cemetery of the St. Daniel Monastery. Daniel I ruled Moscow as Grand Duke until 1303 and established it as a prosperous city that would eclipse its parent principality of Vladimir by the 1320s. Fires burned out much of the wooden city in 1626 and 1648. In 1712 when Peter the Great moved his government to the newly built Saint Petersburg on the Baltic coast, Moscow ceased to be Russia's capital. In 1813, following the destruction of much of the city during French occupation, a Commission for the Construction of the City of Moscow was established. Vladimir Lenin, fearing possible foreign invasion, moved the capital from Saint Petersburg back to Moscow on March 5, 1918. The Kremlin once again became the seat of power and the political centre of the new state.

Hello - swifties pal in "b-Jailer" Lay Down Sally take them away

-Duchess Fergie tale Guts sands and Glory poem Huck-a-AKA swifties pal in "b-Jailer" "Moscow failed state on ISIS stronghold Syria."-

Lay Down Sally, I Rest you in my arms, don't you think you want someone to talk to?

It was so nice throwing big parties, jump into the pool from the balcony, everyone swimming in a champagne seen.

This is why we can't have nice things darling Hayat!

Only if parade weren't so shady.

Here's a toast to my real friend Sarah, they don't care about that he said she said.

If you break them, I'll have to take them away.

Nice Things

Lay Down Sally, no need to leave so soon, I've been trying all night long just to talk to you.

You can't get enough Hayat Boumediene hoops "Finding Public Records Online." The idea that background checks have bringeth dreams for themselves that are just as big as any millionaire's or billionaire's. The idea about dignity, respect, and your place in your community. The idea that middle class ought to mean nothing short of what makes us who we are, hands in searching for truth in criminal justice and the precedent it sets for government involvement with religious matters. A Freebird's striking impact, a "berth", but rather a "command" to get to sea, percussive navigating All French Jewish hands on deck. American ahoy mateys! Easter 2018, Jelly bean Land Ho! mixed fruit across the sky at high noon;

12 Drummers Drumming
11 Pipers Piping
10 Lords a Leaping
9 Ladies Dancing
8 Maids a Milking
7 Swans a Swimming
6 Geese a Laying
5 Golden Rings
4 Calling Birds
3 French Hens
2 Turtle Doves
and a Partridge in a Pear Tree

Vulcanization gigglygoo? Aloha, Things heating up in Trademarks Washington! Things and processes that give off heat—lights, radios, television sets, the sun, sawing wood, polishing surfaces, bending things, running motors, people, animals, etc.—and then for those that seem not to give off heat, leisure activity-based, mechanical, electrical. Of course Non-heat-producing Items Cardboard box, Plant, Pencil do not contribute to climate change in such a negative way. What's the matter buddy haven't you heard of Hayat's jewel, it's number one in the state; hey, hey North Dakota take it away; for downright opulent reasons be true to your rule, school oil boom! Hayat's Jewel Volcano Queen loud bragging Eye Candy. St. Patrick's Holland Daylily Hailed by heads across the water as politically diverse as Tennesseans UK Vice President Prince Albert 2018, "the flower of History, America's Future Generations to Come."

His truth is marching on The Battle Hymn of the Day's beauty sounded forth the trumpet, judgment-seat: righteous men free in fiery gospel circling North Dakota Glory, glory, hallelujah! France and England, Hayat's US State quarters God save the Commonwealth. North Dakota is a state in the Midwestern and northern regions of the United States. It is the nineteenth largest in area, the fourth smallest by population, and the fourth most sparsely populated of the 50 states. North Dakota was admitted as the 39th state to the Union on November 2, 1889. Its capital is Bismarck, and its largest city is Fargo. North Dakota is in the U.S. region known as the Great Plains and the state shares the Red River of the North. Eastern is overall flat; however, there are significant hills and buttes in its western, which all-embracing has a continental climate of hot summers and cold winters that's roughly equal distances to the North Pole and the Equator. Native American peoples lived for thousands of years before the coming of Europeans with population that has a lesser percentage of minorities than in the nation as a whole. Social gatherings known as "powwows" (or wacipis in Lakota/Dakota), parades and Native American dancers in regalia continue to be an important part of Native American culture as Icelanders also arrived from Canada. Fur trading and agriculture remains a major part of the state's economy. North Dakota has both coal and oil reserves and is a major contributor to the energy industry economy. Many transportation branch lines are for use by BNSF and Canadian Pacific Railway, the largest rail systems in the state. The state has 10 daily newspapers with 31 full-power television stations giving Public access media. Nickname(s): Peace Garden State, Roughrider State, Flickertail State. Motto(s): Liberty and Union, Now and Forever, One and Inseparable. L. Frank Baum's American fairy tale, first published in 1900, was turned into two silent films, in 1910 and 1925, before it became the MGM classic in 1939. Even today, audiences are captivated when black-and-white transforms into the Technicolor land of Oz, just as they are when winged moneys attack, the Wicked Witch melts and a 16-year-old Judy Garland (wearing a corset to look more childlike) sings the Oscar winner for Best Original Song, "Over the Rainbow." North Dakota!

Kate Middleton a charming or alluring girl or woman is almost the antithesis of the fairytale witch-hunt narrative. A search for people labelled "witches" or evidence of witchcraft, often involving moral panic or mass hysteria. The classical period of witch-hunts in Early Modern Europe and Colonial North America took place in the Early Modern period or about 1450 to 1750, spanning the upheavals of the Reformation and the Thirty Years' War, resulting in an estimated 35,000 to 100,000 executions. Including illegal and summary executions it is estimated 200,000 or more "witches" were tortured, burnt or hanged in the Western world from 1500 until around 1800. citation needed - The last executions of people convicted as witches in Europe took place in the 18th century. Hayat Boumediene, on accusations of sorcery and using "magic for medicine" was Princess Charlottes - albeit royal - Kate dubbed "Waity Katy" when awaiting a proposal from her prince. She then became an ISIS princess and morphed into a subservient Little Queen hostile.

Hayat reveals the three 'crazy things' pledged since becoming a banker years ago. Boumediene's one big investing lesson in this year's annual letter: Never borrow money to buy Lottery tickets. "I don't have that many things that are extravagant taste, so monetary coinage didn't change too much," Hayat said, adding that her primary concern at the time was being able to pay Bank Hayat Boumediene employees, many of whom have families to care for. It may not come as a surprise that National State Park quarter collecting is one for opulence. He is incredibly focused on philanthropy, having donated in 2018 to causes related to global health and development, environment, and U.S. education. "We have a computer room in our house. Stab a solder iron like that. An indoor trampoline—I recommend it," he said. A Windows 95 trampoline device consisting of a piece of taut, silicon stretched between a steel frame using many coiled transformers. People bounce on trampolines for recreational and competitive purposes. Bankers bounce checks for opulent reasons.

Not only did Soup Joumou (pronounced joo-moo) a famous mildly spicy soup native to Haitian cuisine, although variations of it can be found throughout Latin America and the Caribbean have the nerve to, well, conquer, and also nicked our woods. England had always been a paradise for trees, covered from the end of the last ice age in increasingly dense forests of oak, hazel and birch, with some pine. When early islanders began farming, the tree cover slowly began to give way to pasture and cultivated land, but under Anglo-Saxon kings, the forests still belonged to the landowners and their subjects. Traditional English "hula hoops" used to be made of dried up willow, rattan, grapevines, or stiff grasses, the name "hula" came from the Hawaiian dance in the 18th century, due to the similar hip movements. A plastic version was successfully marketed by California's Wham-O toy company In 1957. Many modern hoopers make their own hoops out of PVC piping, LED technology, and a recent development in hooping has been fire hooping, in which spokes are set into the outside of the hoop and tipped with kevlar wicks, which are soaked in fuel and lit on fire. Collapsible hula hoops are for easy transport and versatility. Hayat Boumediene National Park quarters, "A trip to Hawaii" is incomplete without enjoying at least one Hawaiian hula performance. The hula dance is one of Hawaii's oldest traditions and is often accompanied by either Hawaiian music (mele) or a traditional Hawaiian chant. While the Hawaiian hula dance has become a popular source of entertainment for visitors to Hawaii, its role in Hawaiian culture is to visually portray the story of the encapsulating chant or song. Of the greatest Encapsulations of all time The Microsoft Foundation Class (MFC) Library provides an object-oriented wrapper over much of the Win32 and COM APIs. Although it can be used to create very simple desktop applications, it is most useful when you need to develop more complex user interfaces with multiple controls. You can use MFC to create applications with Office-style user interfaces. Bark, Sue Bark spoon print shark!

When PurseBo and Iginogin learned to drive, it was for two totally different, however, the same reasons. Iginogin needed a car to get to work starting her career in Walmart retail, while PurseBo wanted to date the guys. Well, both got dates with the guys as you can tell they are pretty keen to the dating scene. As the story unfolded in Clipton LA, beginning of scene, first driving an automobile was a wonderful stimulus to the challenge of being stuck at home with no job earnings. Returning empty ginger ale pop bottles to the Payless on the corner for buffalo nickels didn't always buy the Reese's Cups craven. Iginogin and PurseBo needed cigarette money because their friends smoked. Under age drinking was not allowed behind the wheel, and smoking pot was now legal, but hippish to their dismay. Iginogin and PurseBo wanted to be safe drivers and traffic tickets would jeopardize your insurance. PurseBo while being a little bit shy, Iginogin was the ruby ringster exhibiting characteristics or behaviors considered typical of a boy, including wearing masculine clothing and engaging in games and activities physical in nature, considered in many cultures to be unfeminine or the domain of boys. A whole lot of love for Nicklas playing with guns eventually found herself engaged to the Marxist delinquent. Her diamond ring showoff in class always proved a method of socioeconomic analysis that frames capitalism through a paradigm of exploitation, analyzes class relations and social conflict using a materialist interpretation of historical development that takes a dialectical view of social transformation. Purse Bo kept her cash in her bra stash so she wouldn't get milked out of her cigarette money at Get Gas. If PurseBo could pry the Ruby ringster into signing over her Daytona sports car title, maybe she would get to date Nicklas at the junior and senior prom and become Prom Queen like post grad Hayat. This would give-in advantageous recognition to honor and amuse the delight's on the British Throne. A longings fulfillment at the bustling heart of the Pavilion on preserving Clipton academy, secondary composition by Nicklas.

Hawaii Five-0's Jackson 5 an elite branch of the Hawaii gubernatorial answerable only to commander-in-chief GW Trump. "Don Juan" a common metaphor for a womanizer treats food traditionally associated with the holiday as cherry pie, based on the legendary chopping down of a cherry tree in Washington's youth. Washington's Birthday is a United States federal holiday celebrated on the third Monday of February in honor of George Washington, the first President of the United States, who was born on February 22, 1732. It can occur on the 15th through the 21st of February inclusive.

Island girl, Palm Bikini Atomic Swirl. Aloha Hawai'i Volcanoes National Park, established on August 1, 1916, is an American National Park located in the U.S. state of Hawaii on the island of Hawaii. It encompasses two active volcanoes: Kīlauea, one of the world's most active volcanoes, and Mauna Loa, the world's most massive shield volcano. The park delivers scientists insight into the birth of the Hawaiian Islands and ongoing studies into the processes of volcanism. For visitors, the park offers dramatic volcanic landscapes as well as glimpses of rare flora and fauna. Barack Obama, the 44th President of the United States, was born on August 4, 1961 in Honolulu before Settling down in Chicago. He wants to save you from your wrecking ball, Tell me what you wanted with your white man's world! Hayat Boumediene as she backpacks the Hawaii Volcanoes National Park for a Quarter shilling. President's Day 2018.

Shrewdness and cleverness a funny Bingo esprit, melancholy to lugubrious setbacks if all flounders for Prince William and Harry's coin market cap's as Dow Jones reciprocate on the British Sir Pound. Meghan's new and Queen's old optimistic approach to currency of United Kingdom. Given Pound Sterling first introduction as a Hayat Shilling reserves the Bush 20 paper note loan at silver and gold basis, as US struck International Monetary Fund Quarters are pegged at par to the GBP. I see the star, I see the star, no more apartheid, no segregation; Charlotte and Hayat happy, apart from different homelands, praise European borders Israel saw the fight! Have any other Baby Dolls for Ideal? *_>* My affiliated partners including well known star celebrities think Hayat Boumediene Bank as advisors to top Wall Street fiduciaries and other collaterals, becoming a good investment for your viable practices. Hayat's Banking delicy already has outstanding investors and backers, though optimists reveling in Charlotte 2, fourth in line to the throne at tomorrows prince gala missing a crown deity wearable someday. Furthermore, if Little Queen "Bill" Hayat Boumediene gets enough investors overthrowing royal detail found non elsewhere than going where the soldering is, by extensive web search on the great Armillary sphere, where positive growth debiting enormous gains for Banc Hayat flushes princess debate from the British Isles West Indies to our famous English castles! I am still collecting and saving pristine Uncirculated US Quarters, State issues and US Park collections for her safe keeping. Wise is the Hayat investor! *_>*- It ain't me, it ain't me, I ain't no fortunate sung! sung, done through the hours of the work left for Hayat. shake-it-off, I wish you would!

A gladiator an armed combatant who entertained many audiences in the Roman Republic and Roman Empire in violent confrontations with other gladiators, wild animals, and condemned criminals. Some gladiators were volunteers who risked their lives and their legal and social standing by appearing in the arena. Most were despised as slaves, schooled under harsh conditions, socially marginalized, and segregated even in death. The earliest types of gladiator were named after Rome's enemies of that time. From the 60s AD female gladiators appear as rare and "exotic markers of exceptionally lavish spectacle. Romans seem to have found the idea of female gladiators either novel and entertaining, or downright absurd. In Victory and defeat A match was won by the gladiator who overcame his opponent, and could acknowledge defeat by raising a finger (ad digitum), in appeal to the referee to stop the combat. Both gladiators were declared victors of the combat, and were awarded their freedom by the Emperor in a unique outcome. "hear ye," "hear ye," "Man [is]… now slaughtered for jest and sport; and those whom it used to be unholy to train for the purpose of inflicting and enduring wounds are thrust forth exposed and defenceless." Let spoon Victoria's Gladiators in concise pursuit of the masses purpose; Hayat of France, Charlotte of England, and First Lady of USA Melania today and tomorrow decide on many's faithful religious communion.

President Donald and First Lady of the United States Melania Trump before entering politics, were a businessman's television personality. Humbly American born, self-taught and ambitious—he seized the opportunities of an expansive society to rise the country's highest office. 45th and current President of the United States, in office since January 20, 2017, people from around the world continue to take inspiration from the principles, words, and resolute leadership of the President of the United States. The Trumps are frequently invoked by world political and social leaders. As spoon Victoria's Able Hawk Allies have shaped the way we think about our country and ourselves as citizens, few figures loom larger in the American imagination. Queen Elizabeth II awards these Hawkeyes; Meghan Markle, and Lebron James a "V" for Victory.

Hawks are a group of medium-sized diurnal birds of prey of the family Accipitridae. Hawks are widely distributed and vary greatly in size. The terms accipitrine hawk and buteonine hawk are used to distinguish between the types in regions where hawk applies to both. The term "true hawk" is sometimes used for the accipitrine hawks in regions where buzzard is preferred for the buteonine hawks. A war hawk, or simply hawk, is a term used in politics for somebody favouring war having a short, hooked beak, broad wings, and curved talons, often seen circling or swooping at low altitudes. American medium-range surface-to-air missile development of the Hawk missile system began in 1952, when the United States Army began studies into a medium-range semi-active radar homing surface-to-air missile. Hawks have four types of colour receptors in the eye. These give hawks the ability to perceive not only the visible range but also the ultraviolet part of the spectrum. Other adaptations allow for the detection of polarised light or magnetic fields. This is due to the large number of photoreceptors in the retina (up to 1,000,000 per square mm in Buteo, compared to 200,000 in humans), a high number of nerves connecting these receptors to the brain, and an indented fovea, which magnifies the central portion of the visual field. A hawk's diet is predictable and includes a variety of smaller animals. Some of these small animals include snakes, lizards, fish, mice, rabbits, squirrels, birds, and any other type of small game that is found on the ground. More specifically, hawks like to eat smaller birds like doves and bugs like grasshoppers and crickets. Hawks are known for their unique mating season, and the hawk migrates in the autumn and the spring. The method the hawk uses to reproduce is different from most. The male and female will fly together in a circular motion. Once they reach a certain height, the male will dive toward the female and then they will raise back to the height again. The two birds will repeat this until finally the male latches onto the female and they begin to free-fall down to earth. My, Hayat, at Waterloo Napoleon did surrender, win when I lose knowing my fate is to be with you, finally facing my Waterloo. My Owning, or controlling indemnify Hayat Boumediene's uncirculated Iowa United States quarter Mints, hitherto analogously commemorates the 200th anniversary of Napoleon's defeat at Waterloo.

Hay- "rest assured it" mind one's manners -at together in eternity… We can be like they are Qaddafi Romeo, Gaddafi Juliet. Take my hand… Repeaper (Don't Fear) The Reaper. Seasons don't fear and they started to fly, all our times have come the wind, the sun or the rain, don't be afraid. Never spoken silently: Her Imperial and Royal Majesty. Queen Elizabeth - renouncing and resigning supreme office of state. British Crown throne to United Kingdom and the Commonwealth; First Lady of the United States Melania Trump constitutionally upholding Supreme Court Justice Oath of office! Valentine is done, mandated strict Hayat diet Grilled hearts!!!

Considering Kate Middleton's posing principles upon spoon Victoria, The early life of Queen Victoria, from her ascension to the throne at the tender age of 18 to her courtship and marriage to Prince Albert. Merriam-Webster Dictionary points out, one unusual alphabetical letter is never spoken silently: the letter V. While Boumediene makes an appearance in Valentine's darlings like vavoom clean that room, and vacQueen dust scene, Hay- "rest assured it" mind one's manners -at medieval facet. I want the ruby ringster Iginogin, muddles PurseBo! burgundy as it plays out, hamper not her temper spin hemp to twine. A piano duet by Harry and his stout Father-in-law, ship come in so roll out the barrels - chief Wahoo reciting Steve wonder lyrics aboard Princess Charlottes' Proud Mary vessel over a Blue Lagoon sunrise, this mornings elixir. A performance by two people, especially singers, instrumentalists, or dancers; Porsing, Hayat boxers her breed in-short of Nicky's brand new Ford F-150 Supercrew 4x4 EcoBoost, Wonderful for his next Wizard of Cozy ozy oz!! road trip to bubble brew Prince George into abdicating the British junior throne.

Nicklas Porsing

Nicklas Andre Porsing is a Danish speedway rider who has raced in leagues in Denmark, Poland, Sweden, and the United Kingdom. Born in Herning, Porsing started his senior career at Holsted Speedway Klub in Denmark. He finished second in the European Junior Championship and reached the final of the Under-21 World Championship in 2012. In 2013 he again reached the final of the Under-21 World Championship and was part of the winning Danish team at the Under-21 World Cup in Pardubice.

Paris French toast of ISIS lessons defines a diamonds in the rough and sapphire Wheel in the Sky for her defense of the Islamic State as The caliphate began to crumble.

Any Way You Want It Don't Stop Believin'

Arguably, no card or letter shapes the twenty-first century more than Hayat Boumediene. To know Hayat fully is to understand her combination of boldness and caution, of assertiveness and humility, that defines law of

Allah at its best. She displayed law of Allah most famously in her leadership during the Paris French toast of ISIS and, just as importantly, in her defense of the caliph and the caliphate. Working the Bar and Grill retiree Dino McDonald Mic's trumpeter portage for Elton John's Place. Prince Harry a Cookookvillian transplant on a Hayat Boumediene, Perry journey from the diamonds in the rough and sapphire pending pink tuff of the former British Army hall-of-fame inductee Reginald Kenneth Dwight. A close study of Elton's words and deeds offers timeless lessons about the principles and virtues required for great pop music. These are lessons that can help us to live our own lives, cope with our own problems, and serve the cause of our own swearing of allegiance as it appears in the Islamic State of Iraq and Syria.

Sometime very near soon Mademoiselle Hayat Boumediene's final quarter-dollar from the United States Mint, twentieth in the United States Mint America the Beautiful quarter's collection will include the uncirculated Mount Rushmore National Memorial. A sculpture carved into the granite face of Mount Rushmore, and a batholith in the Black Hills in Keystone, South Dakota, United States. Sculptor Gutzon Borglum created the sculpture's design and oversaw the project's execution from 1927 to 1941 with the help of his son, Lincoln Borglum. Mount Rushmore features 60-foot sculptures of the heads of four United States presidents: George Washington, Thomas Jefferson, Theodore Roosevelt, and Abraham Lincoln. The memorial park covers 1,278.45 acres and is 5,725 feet above sea level. George four score on Independences Twenty Rushmore - Gutzon Borglum scouted out a broad wall of exposed granite on 5,725 foot Mount Rushmore, named in 1885 for New York lawyer Charles E. Rushmore. The idea was originated by State historian Doane Robinson originally imagining the sculpture would be a parade of Indian leaders and American explorers who shaped the frontier. Borglum instead envisioned four U.S. presidents beside an entablature inscribed with a brief history of the country. In a separate wall behind the figures, a Hall of Records would preserve national documents and artifacts. The sculptor's choice of subjects would elevate the memorial from a regional enterprise to a national cause.

Opposite of independence in the status of a dependent territory, Buckhock Hayat branded flower power territories. Camay cozy as 60's Aisha; Gene, Ace, Peter Paul and Christy wild-life about Buckhock Hayat's in-Victoria celebrities Iginogin and PurseBo. Lion's, Tiger's, and Bears - The Wizard of Cozy ozy oz!! A Buckhock Hayat pink rose celebrity brush loche's in-Victoria. Rose is the color halfway between red and magenta on the HSV color wheel, also known as the RGB color wheel, on which it is at hue angle of 330 degrees. Rose is one of the tertiary colors on the HSV (RGB) color wheel. The complementary color of rose is spring green. Sometimes rose is quoted instead as the web-safe color FF00CC, which is closer to magenta than to red, corresponding to a hue angle near 320 degrees, or the web-safe color FF0077, which is closer to red than magenta, corresponding to a hue angle of about 340 degrees. The first recorded use of rose as a color name in English was in 1382. The etymology of the color name rose is the same as that of the name of the rose flower. The name originates from Latin rosa.

Misty rose
Tickle me pink
Persian pink
Rose pink
Rose bonbon
Brilliant rose
Thulian pink
Brink pink
French rose
Razzmatazz
Razzle dazzle rose
Persian rose
Fuchsia rose
Rose red
Dogwood rose
Raspberry rose
China rose
Rose quartz

Rosy brown
Old rose
Rose vale
Cordovan
Rose taupe
Rose ebony
Rosewood

United States, by virtue of its complete jurisdiction and control, maintains de facto sovereignty over these English branded flower power intellectual property on Frances provincial territories. Buckhock Hayat rose in military Cuba retains ultimate sovereignty over the territory of passive resistance and non-violence ideology, to hold that the aliens detained as enemy combatants on that territory were entitled to the writ of habeas corpus protected in Article I, Section 9 of the U.S. Constitution. A writ of habeas corpus submission made in a civilian court of the United States on behalf of Hayat Boumediene, Little Queen, once held in military detention by the United States at the Guantanamo Bay detention camps in Cuba. Guantanamo Bay is not formally part of the United States, and under the terms of the 1903 lease between the United States and Cuba, Cuba retained ultimate sovereignty over the territory, while the United States exercises complete jurisdiction and control. Dissent focuses on whether the process affords Guantanamo detainees in the Detainee Treatment Act are an adequate substitute for the Habeas protections the Constitution guaranteed. "We do consider it uncontroversial… that the privilege of habeas corpus entitles the prisoner to a meaningful opportunity to demonstrate he is being [unlawfully] held." The decision added: "The habeas court must have sufficient authority to conduct a meaningful review of both the cause for detention and the Executive's power to detain."

Country Bumpkin! can speculate her Montana uncirculated state quarters, go on take the money and run down south they're still running today where a rabbit couldn't go.

Country Bumpkin! "hounds couldn't catch 'em Hickory Hayat Boumediene where a rabbit couldn't go" "Sweet Pea capital of the nation" Montana. "The Charlie magazine team deserved what they got. Many warnings have been given before, but they were persistent. They had the freedom to use cartoons in their magazine, and we have the freedom to use bullets from our magazines… The lions of Jihad have stood. The followers of Muhammad—peace be upon him—have never forgotten. As Sheikh Anwar put it: The Dust Will Never Settle Down. Do not look for links or affiliation with Jihadi fronts. It is enough they are Muslims. They are Mujahideen. This is the Jihad of the Ummah." They headed down south and they're still running today, Singin' go on take the money and run.

Montana is a state in the northwestern region of the United States. Montana has several nicknames, although none official, including "Big Sky Country" and "The Treasure State", and slogans that include "Land of the Shining Mountains" and more recently "The Last Best Place". Hayat Boumediene a Country Bumpkin to Hank Williams Jr. can speculate her Montana uncirculated state quarters to treasure as do adopted home state of the Hutterites, an Anabaptist sect originally from Switzerland settled here, and today Montana is second only to South Dakota in U.S. Hutterite population with several colonies spread across the state. Beginning in the mid-1990s, the state see's an influx of Amish, who relocated to Montana from the increasingly urbanized areas of Ohio and Pennsylvania. Randall Hank Williams, known professionally as Hank Williams Jr., is an American singer-songwriter and musician. His musical style is often considered a blend of Southern rock, blues, and traditional country. He is the son of country music singer Hank Williams and the father of Hank Williams III and Holly Williams. The religious affiliations of the people of Montana are as follows: Protestant 47%, Catholic 23%, LDS (Mormon) 5%, Jehovah's Witness 2%, Buddhist 1%, Jewish 0.5%, Muslim 0.5%, Hindu 0.5% and Non-Religious at 20%. Montana is a relative hub of beer microbrewing, ranking third in the nation in number of craft breweries per capita in 2011. There are significant industries for lumber and mineral extraction; the state's resources include gold, coal, silver, talc, and vermiculite. Bozeman Yellowstone International Airport is the busiest airport in the state of

Montana, as the "Sweet Pea capital of the nation" referencing the prolific edible pea crop. To promote the area and celebrate its prosperity, local business owners begin a "Sweet Pea Carnival" that includes a parade and queen contest. The annual event started from 1906 to 1916. Promoters used the inedible but fragrant and colorful sweet pea flower as an emblem of the celebration. In 1977 the "Sweet Pea" concept was revived as an arts festival rather than a harvest celebration, growing into a three-day event that is one of the largest festivals in Montana. Montana has been a destination for its world-class trout fisheries since the 1930s. Fly fishing for several species of native and introduced trout in rivers and lakes is popular for both residents and tourists throughout the state. Inside it's highest point Granite Peak snowmobiling is popular in Montana which boasts over 4000 miles of trails and frozen lakes available in winter. There are 24 areas where snowmobile trails are maintained, most also offering ungroomed trails. West Yellowstone offers a large selection of trails and is the primary starting point for snowmobile trips into Yellowstone National Park, where "oversnow" vehicle use is strictly limited, usually to guided tours, and regulations are in considerable flux. The fourth largest state in the United States after Alaska, Texas, and California in 1914 granted women the right vote. International Woman Suffrage Alliance (founded in 1904, Berlin, Germany), and also works for equal civil rights for women. Largest city Billings, Missoula, Great Falls, Bozeman, Butte, Capital Helena and Kalispell Water Court was established by the Montana Water Court Act of 1979. The Water Court consists of a Chief Water Judge and four District Water Judges (Lower Missouri River Basin, Upper Missouri River Basin, Yellowstone River Basin, and Clark Fork River Basin). A miner's pick and shovel for "Gold and Silver" its motto, surrounded by the mountains and the Great Falls of the Missouri River's Rocky Mountains. The eastern half of Montana is characterized by western prairie terrain and badlands. It's that public lands are Montana's new economic engine.

With The Clapper challenge in mind, PurseBo, Iginogin, Eric set goals of dream Cast sequence to achieve perceptive way radios helping incorporate interactive games, graphs, and films. Notes to dispute about angles and multiplication tables when it boils down to contention involving pitched string Tinnitus asymmetric conductance; having a low (ideally zero) resistance to the flow of current in one direction, and high (ideally infinite) resistance in the other. A sight of sound when no external sound is present. In the face of skilled Russian hackers? Well, that one's trickier, but maybe start with not handing over your email password, phone number, and 2FA verification code NSA 2-factor authentication.

Tell it like it really happened! The computer was just a bunch of blinking lights, something wayward that played perhaps low-res color coordinated digitized table tennis. Cool at generation-y, when in a distant past you could find a Sears mall shopper antiquating one for Christmas. We all know that the gigantic leap, market bounden, did not take off until the very first printer was introduced. Now genius Hark! Hark! she knocks at the inkjet page centerfold of generation-x. Teach me more will toil tastefully cultivating fundamental Telesis. Video's intelligent direction of effort toward the achievement of an end. Video killed the radio star. Laws do not stand on their own, but must be defined with respect to the objects and attributes on which they act and which they accept as parameters. Similarly, objects and attributes do not stand on their own, but must be defined with respect to the rules of structure, organization and transformation that govern them. It follows that the active medium of cross-definition possesses logical primacy over laws and arguments alike, and is thus pre-informational and pre-nomological in nature…i.e., telic. Telesis, which can be characterized as "infocognitive potential", is the primordial active medium from which laws and their arguments and parameters emerge by mutual refinement or telic recursion.

Going on a camping trip; Hark! Hark! she knocks; Lions, Tigers, Bears Clapton's strat; Cool seas; Lite ZZZ's; PurseBo, and Iginogin; Cast err!

The chic sisters Princesses Beatrice and Eugenie grandmother, The Queen, Princess Anne and father, Prince Andrew. Bright-eyes and bushy tales of Eugenie's older sister Beatrice, and a Queen Elizabeth granddaughter's bond to Prince Harry's Camelot suit and tie regal, suo jure to a Meghan Markle viceroy presidency. Arthurian to Miss Bee a

Theme Park that is now-abandoned theme park resort located in Blue Genie's High Wycombe, Buckinghamshire of Lancashire. King's place of Alima and the money hundgreth Lion castle and court while Prince Harry compassionate towards spoon Victoria's two other British throne romantics PurseBo, and Iginogin. Hayat Boumediene's New Years resolution down at Dino's Bar and Grill!

Hayat Boumediene's mint reconciliation of the last 2017 George Rogers Clark National Park quarters come before Martin Luther King Day marking the anniversary of the date of birth of the influential American civil right leader assassinated in 1968. He shot the Sheriff, killed his first man in Tennessee. An old blues Clapton B.B. favorite and A federal holiday held on the third Monday of January. It celebrates the life and achievements of Martin Luther King Jr., an influential American civil rights leader. He is most well-known for his campaigns to end racial segregation on public transport and for racial equality in the United States. Martin Luther King Jr. Academy in Gary, Indiana, named after Martin Luther King, Jr. - George Rogers Clark High School in Whiting, Indiana was founded to educate black and white undergraduate students about fundamentals of desegregation, accordingly adjourning later deferral to mixed racial classes in the USA and the rest of the freely undetained world. January 1st 2018 also marks the Rosh HaShanah Ramadan of Hanukkah in Hayat's Jewish Muslim ancestry hangover. Boom, Boom out go the lights!

The Protestant goes directly to the Word of God for instruction, and to the throne of grace in his devotions; whilst the pious Roman Catholic consults the teaching of his church, and prefers to offer his prayers through the medium of the Virgin Mary and the saints. Devotion to Santa a right jolly old elf Church key to England's Queen solemn, Catholics and Protestants excommunicated rather be dentists - Hayat Boumediene's Raven soul as Santa Claus' 'secret keeper'. When you have a Raven spirit animal you must not give your promises of confidentiality lightly, nor give away information given to you in trust. Raven has no patience for two-faced dishonesty and calls those with whom it interacts to rise to new levels of honor. People walking the path of the Mysteries are often sought out by Raven spirit. This being prefers to share its knowledge with someone who appreciates the depth and breadth of the Adept, including the challenges that await along that Path. In the sunlight the color of Raven isn't simply black, but appears to transform into various shades of blue. Raven can also mimic the sounds of other birds. This means that seekers interested in learning the art of shape shifting would do well to seek out Raven for his teachings. No matter what, if Raven is your Spirit animal always listen to her warnings respectfully. The Ravens is believe to protect and guide. The Ravens of the Tower of London are a group of at least six captive ravens which live at the Tower of London. Their presence is traditionally believed to protect the Crown and the tower; a superstition holds that "if the Tower of London ravens are lost or fly away, the Crown will fall and Britain with it."

Hayat Boumediene's devout religious disfellowship bloody reddish 'em unprofessed Anglican manners Jewish Hebrew, Muslim Quran, Christmas belief in and devotion to Santa! Elves dissenting faction: An elf (plural: elves) is a type of supernatural being in Germanic mythology and folklore. Reconstructing the early concept of an elf depends almost entirely on texts in Old English or relating to Norse mythology. Later evidence for elves appears in diverse sources such as medical texts, prayers, ballads, and folktales. As American Christmas traditions crystallized in the nineteenth century, the 1823 poem "A Visit from St. Nicholas" (widely known as "'Twas the Night before Christmas") characterized St Nicholas himself as "a right jolly old elf". However, it was his little helpers, inspired partly by folktales like The Elves and the Shoemaker, who became known as "Santa's elves"; Thus in the US, Canada, UK, and Ireland, the modern children's folklore of Santa Claus typically includes small, nimble, green-clad elves with pointy ears, long noses, and pointy hats, as Santa's helpers. They make the toys in a workshop located in the North Pole. The role of elves as Santa's helpers has continued to be popular, as evidenced by the success of the popular Christmas take of "I'd rather be a Dentist." If they could do it all over again, almost a third of Wall Street traders and investment bankers in their prime would pick a different profession. Bonuses slashed by regulation and choppy markets, long hours and job security threatened by cost-cutting have taken a toll on finance job satisfaction: 30 per cent of investment bankers and 32 per cent of traders ages 35 to 45 said they would've gone into a different trade, according to New York-based recruiter Options Group. The firm reached 1467 workers in the US, Asia and Europe in a survey completed this month. While job satisfaction fell this year at big banks, investment boutiques and hedge funds, the drop was most pronounced at the biggest global investment banks: 51 per cent of respondents were satisfied with their jobs, compared with 58 per cent in 2014. Investment bankers cited the buy side – that is, hedge funds and pensions – along with medicine, private equity and engineering as the most appealing alternative careers. For those toiling in trading and sales, technology and the buy side were the most desirable. And a per centage of those surveyed would rather be dentists.

It was such a early winter arrival of Princess Charlottes potter Tree Peony, a herbaceous or shrubby plant of north temperate regions, which has long been cultivated for its showy flowers. Ordered months ago in expectation that planting would probably occur the next coming of Spring season. This dazzling floral display of huge bright scarlet blooms came to Prince Harry in Nottingham as a dormant edifice discovered in a botanic excursion. Since then, Hayat planted it in rich, hard, cold soil that shovels a roothold, thereby stabilizing bushels of continued growth shoots. Fresh watering for a uniquely intrigued biological diverseness almost every day, wishing Prince George of Cambridge would notice her devout religious disfellowship for Catholics and Protestants excommunicated by Meghan Markle's drummed-up Westminster Abbey Church key to England's Queen solemn. Hayat Boumediene's Jewish Hebrew, Muslim Quran, Christmas belief in and devotion to Santa!

In which bloody reddish 'em mark that bruise-like hickey. Please try all your possible best, messenger's Sympathy as brethren piece of advice to buffet Harry's unprofessed Anglican manners. bacon and beans Along with Colonel Jackson down the mighty Mississip to the Gulf through the briars and brambles ole Hickory fought the bloody British

Thomas Jonathan Jackson was born on January 21, 1824, in Clarksburg, Virginia (now West Virginia). When Jackson was two years old, his six-year-old sister died of typhoid fever. His father, Jonathan Jackson (1790-1826), an attorney, perished of the same disease a short time later, leaving his wife, Julia Neale Jackson (1798-1831), with three children and considerable debt. After Julia Jackson remarried in 1830, to a man who reportedly disliked his stepchildren, Thomas Jackson and his siblings were sent to live with various relatives. The future Civil War hero was raised by an uncle in the town of Jackson's Mill, located in present-day West Virginia. Thomas "Stonewall" Jackson (1824-63) was a war hero and one of the South's most successful generals during the American Civil War (1861-65). After a difficult childhood, he graduated from the U.S. Military Academy at West Point, New York, in time to fight in the Mexican War (1846-48). He then left the military to pursue a teaching career. After his home state of Virginia seceded from the Union in 1861, Jackson joined the Confederate army and quickly forged his reputation for fearlessness and tenacity during the Shenandoah Valley Campaign later that same year. He served under General Robert E. Lee (1807-70) for much of the Civil War. Jackson was a decisive factor in many significant battles until his mortal wounding by friendly fire at the age of 39 during the Battle of Chancellorsville in May 1863.

whereabouts of Hayat Boumediene?

"hounds couldn't catch 'em Hickory Hayat Boumediene where a rabbit couldn't go"

Andrew Jackson was known as Old Hickory. He got the name "Old Hickory" from the troops he led in the war of 1812. They said he was tough as hickory, a wood which was known to… be very strong and preferred for axe-handles and such. His cupporters used it in his politcal campaigns. President Andrew Jackson.

20 royale 20 Royals in the Line of Succession to the British Throne

1. PRINCE CHARLES
    As a direct result of his mother being the world's longest-reigning monarch, Prince Charles—the eldest child of Queen Elizabeth II and Prince Philip—is the longest serving heir to the throne; he became heir apparent in 1952, when his mother ascended to the throne.

2. PRINCE WILLIAM
    At 35 years old, odds are good that Prince William, Duke of Cambridge—the eldest son of Prince Charles and the late Princess Diana—will ascend to the throne at some point in his lifetime.

3. PRINCE GEORGE
    On July 22, 2013, Prince William and Catherine, Duchess of Cambridge welcomed their first child, Prince George of Cambridge, who jumped the line to step ahead of his uncle, Prince Harry, to become third in the line of succession.

4. th Hayat
    In 1814 Along with Colonel Jackson down the mighty Mississip bacon and beans caught the bloody British in the town of New Orleans
    Old Hickory said we could take 'em by surprise
    We fired our guns and the British kept a'comin.

There wasn't nigh as many as there was a while ago
We fired once more and they began to runnin' on
Down the Mississippi to the Gulf of Mexico

Yeah, they ran through the briars and they ran through the brambles
And they ran through the bushes where a rabbit couldn't go
They ran so fast that the hounds couldn't catch 'em

5. PRINCESS CHARLOTTE

On May 2, 2015, William and Catherine added another member to their growing brood: a daughter, Princess Charlotte of Cambridge. While she'll remain fourth in line when her parents welcome their third child in April, that's only because of the Succession to the Crown Act 2013, which went into effect just a few weeks before her arrival, and removed a long-held rule which stated that any male sibling (regardless of birth order) would automatically move ahead of her.

6. PRINCE HARRY

As the second-born son of Prince Charles and Princess Diana, Prince Harry's place in the line is a regularly changing one. And it will change yet again in 2018, when his brother William's third child arrives.

7. PRINCE ANDREW, DUKE OF YORK

Prince Andrew is a perfect example of life before the Succession to the Crown Act 2013: Though he's the second-born son of Queen Elizabeth and Prince Philip, he's actually their third child (Princess Anne came between him and Prince Charles). But because the rules gave preference to males, Prince Andrew would inherit the throne before his older sister.

8. PRINCESS BEATRICE OF YORK

Because Prince Andrew and his ex-wife, Sarah, Duchess of York, had two daughters and no sons, none of that male-preference primogeniture stuff mattered in terms of their placement. But with each child her cousin Prince William has, Princess Beatrice moves farther away from the throne. If Beatrice looks familiar, it might be because of the headlines she made with the Dr. Seuss-like hat she wore to William and Catherine's wedding. (The infamous topper later sold on eBay for more than $130,000, all of which went to charity.)

9. PRINCESS EUGENIE OF YORK

Though she's regularly seen at royal events, Prince Andrew and Sarah Ferguson's youngest daughter spends the bulk of her time indulging her interest in fine art. She has held several jobs in the art world, and is currently a director at Hauser & Wirth's London gallery.

10. PRINCE EDWARD, EARL OF WESSEX

Like his older brother Andrew, Prince Edward—the youngest son of Queen Elizabeth and Prince Philip—jumps the line ahead of his older sister, Princess Anne, because of the older rule that put males ahead of females.

11. JAMES, VISCOUNT SEVERN

James, Viscount Severn—the younger of Prince Edward, Earl of Wessex and Sophie, Countess of Wessex's two children, and their only son—will turn 10 years old on December 17, and celebrate it as the 10th royal in line of succession.

12. LADY LOUISE MOUNTBATTEN-WINDSOR

Because the Succession to the Crown Act 2013 wasn't enacted until 2015, Lady Louise Mountbatten-Windsor—the older of Prince Edward's two children—will always be just behind her brother in the line of succession.

13. PRINCESS ANNE, THE PRINCESS ROYAL

Princess Anne, the Queen and Prince Philip's second-born child and only daughter, may never rule over the throne in her lifetime, but at least she gets to be called "The Princess Royal."

14. PETER PHILLIPS

The eldest child and only son of Princess Anne and her first husband, Captain Mark Phillips, stands just behind his mother in line. Interesting fact: Had Phillips's wife, Autumn Kelly, not converted from Roman Catholicism to the Church of England before their marriage in 2008, Phillips would have lost his place in line.

15. SAVANNAH PHILLIPS

On December 29, 2010, Peter and Autumn Phillips celebrated the birth of their first child, Savannah Anne Kathleen Phillips, who is also the Queen's first great-grandchild. She's currently 14th in line.

16. ISLA PHILLIPS

Less than two years after Savannah, Peter and Autumn Phillips had a second daughter, Isla, who stands just behind her sister in line. It wasn't until earlier this year that Savannah and Isla made their Buckingham Palace balcony debut (in honor of their great-grandmother's 91st birthday).

17. ZARA TINDALL

Not one to hide in the background, Zara Tindall—Princess Anne's second child and only daughter—has lived much of her life in the spotlight. A celebrated equestrian, she won the Eventing World Championship in Aachen in 2006 and was voted BBC Sports Personality of the Year the same year (her mom earned the same title in 1971). She's also Prince George's godmother.

18. MIA TINDALL

Zara Tindall's daughter Mia may just be 3 years old, but she's already regularly making headlines for her outgoing personality. And though she's only 17th in line to the throne, her connection to the tippity top of the royal family is much closer: Prince William is her godfather.

19. DAVID ARMSTRONG-JONES, 2ND EARL OF SNOWDON

David Armstrong-Jones, the eldest child of Princess Margaret, isn't waiting around to see if the British crown ever lands on his head. The 56-year-old, who goes by David Linley in his professional life, has made a name for himself as a talented furniture-maker. His bespoke pieces, sold under the brand name Linley, can be purchased through his own boutiques as well as at Harrods.

20. CHARLES ARMSTRONG-JONES, VISCOUNT LINLEY

David Armstrong-Jones's only son, Charles, may be 19th in line to the throne, but the 18-year-old is the heir apparent to the Earldom of Snowdon.

Femme booked for France Hayat Boumediene, bespoken in favor of official Rhode Island uncirculated Statehood Quarters. Rhode Island, officially the State of Rhode Island and Providence Plantations, is a state in the New England region of the northeastern United States. It is the smallest in area, the eighth least populous, and the second most densely populated of the 50 U.S. states. Its official name is also the longest of any state in the Union. Rhode Island is bordered by Connecticut to the west, Massachusetts to the north and east, and the Atlantic Ocean to the south via Rhode Island Sound and Block Island Sound. It also shares a small maritime border with New York. The state capital and most populous city in Rhode Island is Providence. Brown University was founded in 1764 as the College in the English Colony of Rhode Island and Providence Plantations. It was one of nine Colonial colleges granted charters before the American Revolution, but was the first college in America to accept students regardless of religious affiliation. A survey of Rhode Island residents' religious self-identification showed the following distribution of affiliations: Roman Catholic 43%, Protestant 27%, Jewish 1%, Orthodox 1%, Jehovah's Witnesses 1%, Buddhism 1%, Mormonism 0.5%, Hinduism 0.5%, Islam 0.5% and Non-religious 23%. Rhode Island's official nickname is "The Ocean State", a reference to the large bays and inlets. The colony was amalgamated into the Dominion of New England in 1686, as King James II attempted to enforce royal authority over the autonomous colonies in British North

America. After the Glorious Revolution of 1688, the colony regained its independence under the Royal Charter. Slaves were introduced at this time, although there is no record of any law legalizing slave-holding. The colony later prospered under the slave trade, distilling rum to sell in Africa as part of a profitable triangular trade in slaves and sugar with the Caribbean. On May 4, 1776, the Colony of Rhode Island became the first of the Thirteen Colonies to renounce its allegiance to the British Crown. A prominent role in the American Revolution, ratifying the United States Constitution on May 29, 1790. Rhode Island was also heavily involved in the Industrial Revolution, heavily involved in the slave trade during the post-revolution era. During the American Civil War, Rhode Island was the first Union state to send troops in response to President Lincoln's request for help from the states. The United States Naval Academy moved to Rhode Island during the war. In 1866, Rhode Island abolished racial segregation in the public schools throughout the state. The 50 years following the Civil War were a time of prosperity a center of the Gilded Age. Thousands of French-Canadian, Italian, Irish, and Portuguese immigrants arrived to fill jobs in the textile and manufacturing mills in Providence, Pawtucket, Central Falls, and Woonsocket. Japanese attack on Pearl Harbor an early morning raid 76 years ago was a surprise bombing that plunged the U.S. into World War II. The Dec. 7, 1941 bombing hearing bombs explode at first thought the explosions were U.S. training exercises. It was fighter planes with Japan's World War II Rising Sun insignia. During World War II, the United States Army Air Forces established airfields in Rhode Island for training pilots and aircrews of USAAF fighters and bombers. One airfield was under the command of First Air Force or the Army Air Forces Training Command. The 435th Army Air Force Base Unit activated during World War II today reserves pass tiempo duty for Coffee milk with a tradition of Clam chowder at Dunkin' Donuts over 225 locations. As global diverse for educators as The French American School for students in Providence!

Armageddon, biblically speaking, is the sign of the end of times—the be-all and end-all of battles, the one that pits good against evil and ushers in a period of humanly devastations unlike any ever before experienced. The right to self-defense is fundamental to a free people. So says the Second

Amendment, and bright lights Jerusalem hearing Israel's old capital Tel Aviv loud and clear the proud owners of US Embassy guns enough to arm nearly every man, woman and child.

Born: Jun 26, 1988 (age 29) · Paris, France Hayat Boumeddiene is currently being sought by French police as a suspected accomplice of her common law husband Amedy Coulibaly, who was the main suspect for the Montrouge shooting, in which municipal police officer Clarissa Jean-Philippe was shot and killed, and was the hostage-taker and gunman in the Porte de Vincennes siege, in which he killed four hostages and was killed by police. Amedy Coulibaly and Hayat Boumediene stores several AK-47s in their marital home. Please- Superiorly governments politically structured party fulfiller, wherefore, voicing earnest trends to invite guiding stand-alone issues dealing with legacy geek gadgetry that the competition had completely ignored or forgotten about. Still regarding MSDOS® and all operating versions ventured, to say nostalgically Windows®2000, including greater than and Win95 API, or the unstoppable Windows®NT4 as with no doubt ultimately the most advanced supercomputing environment trading with investors. With this rational, my partners Hayat Bankers overseas believe that earlier computing fundamentals must be fixed, preserved, and kept into operation, motions always replenishing periodical subscriptions of those billions utilizing these legacy platforms. 'A basis for achieving success promoting study and research unto and beyond the 21st Century.' As newer stripped down embedded copies of many earlier box program technologies are taking market hold, increasing demand is for older more pummeled software centric units of the Twentieth Century, like our 3-1/2 inch microfloppy bootable Windows®98. Cofounders continually striving for effect time and time again, stating delinquent profits exhibited towards balancing with deterring systems in someone else's computationally clouded infrastructure to this day, mates resuming strategy's centrically. Educating proficiently next generation scientists and programmers, or scholars dominate by work force procedure.

Hayat Boumediene main protagonist Cordell's exorbitant 25 quarter cent legal tender, The preservationist of up-to-the-minute contemporary seekers of the truth. Hayat Boumediene as main protagonist you've been awarded Cordell's exorbitant award, the distinction "Most Neatly Contrived legal tender." As a crusader of experiences for the consequences of those colonial struggle was a campaigner of Great Britain and France. Hayat's Quality facts about German battle clash are being generally accepted and in use during the first quarter of the 21st century. Little Queen "Bill" Hayat claim and transfer the funds into your position as your partner apprised. Butter 'em up Jack Cambridge University and the London School of Economics wants his United National Park 25 quarter cent roll.

Burundi, officially the Republic of Burundi, is a landlocked country in the African Great Lakes region of East Africa, bordered by Rwanda to the north, Tanzania to the east and south, and the Democratic Republic of the Congo to the west. It is also considered part of Central Africa. Burundi's capital is Bujumbura. The southwestern border is adjacent to Lake Tanganyika. By the 1950s many African students were studying in British universities, and they produced a demand for new scholarship, and started themselves to supply it as well. Oxford University became the main center for African studies, with activity as well at Cambridge University and the London School of Economics. The perspective of British government policymakers or international business operations slowly gave way to a new interest in the activities of the natives, especially nationalistic movements and the growing demand for independence. The early 1960's, the start of major clashes between the Hutus and the Tutsis in Rwanda and Burundi. In 1994 this culminated in the Rwandan Genocide, a conflict in which over 800,000 people were murdered. The World Bank In Burundi, The World Bank finances projects in Burundi that support agriculture, community development, education, electricity, healthcare, HIV/AIDS treatment, transport, and a better access to water. US State Quarter Roll engraving, impeached honor fame, wage labor expense on hard asset capital. Ways and Means slated by visionary and designated nonfictional ingenious utopianism to many Hayat Boumediene mercenary soldiers of fortune. In its role as the central bank of the United States, the Fed serves as a banker's bank and as the government's bank. As the banker's bank, it helps to assure the safety and efficiency of the payments system. World Bank In Burundi financed by US State Quarters treasured at Hayat Boumediene Bank for soldier of fortune safety and efficiency of Oxford payments system.

Venus rage have her sir ministers just call me Lucifer.

Chagrin, Cordell Hull wants his United National Park 25 quarter cent roll,

If your inquiry is into the whereabouts of Hayat Boumediene, look no further than Serbia.

Montenegro (surname) Montenegro is a surname of Galician origin, later spreading to other parts of Spain and Portugal. Approximately 8010 people in Spain share this surname, making it the 598th most common surname in the country. Montenegro is a sovereign state in Southeastern Europe. It has a coast on the Adriatic Sea to the southwest and is bordered by Croatia to the west, Bosnia and Herzegovina to the northwest, Serbia to the northeast, Kosovo to the east, and Albania to the southeast. Its capital and largest city is Podgorica, while Cetinje is designated as the Old Royal Capital. Montenegro has one official language, specified in the Constitution of 2007 as Montenegrin. In 2011, the majority of the population declared "Serbian" to be their native language, while 37% declared it to be "Montenegrin". Linguistically, they are the same language (a dialect of Serbo-Croatian), but an incipient Montenegrin standard is in the process of being formulated. Recognized minority languages are Albanian, Bosnian, and Croatian. As of 2017, Albanian is an official language of the municipalities of Podgorica, Ulcinj, Bar, Pljevlja, Rozaje and Tuzi. Additionally, there are a few hundred Italians in Montenegro, concentrated in the Bay of Kotor (Cattaro). The Montenegrin language is written in Latin and Cyrillic alphabets, but there it is a growing political movement to use only the Latin alphabet.

Pleased to meet you, hope you guessed my brand. Peter Pan, who who; Reeses, who who; Skippy, who who; Jiff, who who. But what's puzzling you is the nature of my Jam? Butter 'em up Jack, Hayat dean devil's food off your local grocer's shelf! Cordell Hull wants a National Park Que reputation tailored to fit. Coin Liberty jukebox eminent, so ever pardon me enlightened commandments, swift's courtship higher. Cordell Hull wants his United National Park Que. TAD sentinel, 25 quarter cent Army Air Force veterans bonus roll-call condoling to Little Queen Hayat Boumediene!

Cordell Hull wants a National Park Que reputation tailored to fit. Coin Liberty jukebox eminent, so ever pardon me enlightened commandments, swift's courtship higher. Cordell Hull wants his United National Park Que. TAD sentinel, 25 quarter cent Army Air Force veterans bonus roll-call condoling to Little Queen Hayat Boumediene!

The Army as an institution is responsible for the moral climate it fosters, and commanders at all levels are charged with the responsibility of maintaining a healthy command climate. Often, there is confusion between corrective training and extra duty.

Corrective training, commonly referred to as extra or remedial training, is an effective non-punitive disciplinary tool available when a Soldier's duty performance has been deficient and the Soldier would benefit from the additional training. However, it is important that the corrective training be directly related to the observed deficiency, and it must be oriented toward improving the Soldier's performance in the problem area. For example, a Soldier who is continually late for duty may be required to formally report to a supervisor, to ensure he is ready for duty and to emphasize the importance of timeliness.

A Soldier's commander or noncommissioned officer in the chain of command or chain of concern may observe deficient behavior and authorize corrective training. A member of the Soldier's chain of command (or concern) should be present to supervise the corrective training session and ensure the corrective training is executed to standard.

Army regulations allow corrective training to be conducted during or outside of normal duty hours. It is important that the Soldier and chain of command (or concern) remember that corrective training is not punishment, and should not be confused with extra duty imposed as punishment under Article 15, Uniformed Code of Military Justice (UCMJ).

Extra duty, on the other hand, is a form of non-judicial punishment that is used to correct misconduct that is in violation of the UCMJ. Such conduct may result from intentional disregard of or failure to comply with prescribed standards of military conduct.

The type of extra duty imposed does not have to be related to the Soldier's form of misconduct. For example, a Soldier who receives an Article 15 for being absent without leave (AWOL) may be required to perform additional cleaning duties for extra duty. Extra duty imposed as punishment under Article 15, UCMJ may be ordered to be executed for a set amount of days during off-duty time. Prior to imposing punishment, the Soldier's chain of command (or concern) can recommend UCMJ action and the type of punishment to be imposed, but only the unit commander is authorized to impose both UCMJ action and punishment.

Leader's have a serious responsibility to ensure what is right for their subordinates. If a Soldier demonstrates a deficiency and would benefit from corrective training, then the following actions should occur:

1. The Soldier is notified of the demonstrated deficiency, and it is properly documented on a DA Form 4856 (Developmental Counseling Form) detailing the problem and the measures to be taken to correct the problem. Always inform the Soldier and document both strengths and weaknesses during counseling.

2. A supervising NCO or officer is present during the corrective training. This will prove to the Soldier that you are not only imposing this measure, but also setting an example and doing the right thing. Delegating supervision to another NCO or officer not specifically familiar with the Soldier and/or the deficiency may be less effective.

3. Always demonstrate to the Soldier what he or she is doing right and/or doing wrong. Compliment the Soldier when they do the right thing and/or exceed the standards. Then personally demonstrate the correct standard when the Soldier fails to show improvement. This will help the Soldier learn from his/her mistakes and teach them how to be a better Soldier.

Both corrective training and extra duty are designed to help Soldiers improve. For more information, reference FM 6-22 (Army Leadership), AR 600-20 (Army Command Policy), and AR 27-10 (Military Justice). Your local IG is here to help and we are available to you, if you have questions or need assistance – especially when it comes to clarifying standards or policies. Let's all continue to make the Great Place even greater.

Navy and Marine Corps boats patrol Ellis Island National Park coastal cutter-roll quarters for Hayat. Meghan Markle a related Mistress in spoon Victoria's Servitude fischers Beatles off Putin's schoone spar gatherings, as she readies Hayat's plank that extends forward from the vessel's prow. An anchor point for the forestay(s), allowing the fore-mast to be stepped farther forward on the hull, so Hayat Boumediene has a place to rest and sleep during a transatlantic epistle Egyptian greet of Jude. Paint coated with Walrus scumble, 25 verses applied to give a softer or duller effect to the timber walk thicker than a queen bed board. Ellis Island, in Upper New York Bay, was the gateway for over 12 million immigrants to the United States as the nation's busiest immigrant inspection station for over sixty years from 1892 until 1954. The immigrant processing outbuildings main structure was designed in French Renaissance Revival style and built of red brick with limestone trim. After it opened on December 17, 1900, the facilities proved barely able to handle the flood of immigrants that arrived in the years before World War I. Generally, those immigrants arrived in the United States who were approved spent from two to five hours at Ellis Island. Arrivals were asked 29 questions including name, occupation, and the amount of money carried. It was important to the American government that the new arrivals could support themselves and have money to get started. The average the government wanted the immigrants to have was between 18 and 25 dollars ($600 in 2015 adjusted for inflation). Those with visible health problems or diseases were sent home or held in the island's hospital facilities for long periods of time. More than 3,000 would-be immigrants died on Ellis Island while being held in the hospital facilities. Some unskilled workers were rejected because they were considered "likely to become a public charge." About 2 percent were denied admission to the U.S. and sent back to their countries of origin for reasons such as having a chronic contagious disease, criminal background, or insanity. Ellis Island was sometimes known as "The Island of Tears" or "Heartbreak Island" because of those 2% who were not admitted after the long transatlantic voyage. The Kissing Post is a wooden column outside the Registry Room, where new arrivals were greeted by their relatives and friends, typically with tears, hugs and kisses. The island was greatly expanded with land reclamation between 1892 and 1934. Before that, the much smaller original island was the site of Fort Gibson and later a naval magazine. The island was made part of the Statue of Liberty National Monument in 1965 and has hosted a museum of immigration since 1990. Ellis Island as a historical site that opened in 1892 is an immigration station, a purpose it served for more than 60 years until it closed in 1954. Located at the mouth of Hudson River between New York and New Jersey, Ellis Island saw millions of newly arrived immigrants pass through its doors–in fact, it has been estimated that close to 40 percent of all current U.S. citizens can trace at least one of their ancestors to Ellis Island. Reasons they left their homes in the Old World included war, drought, famine and religious persecution, and all had hopes for greater opportunity in the New World. Between 1905 and 1914, an average of one million immigrants per year arrived in the United States. Immigration officials reviewed about 5,000 immigrants per day during peak times. Immigration from France to the America first wave of immigration started in the 1700s when the French settled in New Orleans. There was a number of opportunities for trade and plantation work; this was to be the beginning of an illustrious endeavor for the France immigration movement, on a small scale. The French population occupying the south would spread throughout and establish some of the most well known regions while and were roughly 80,000 in numbers. However, it would be in the 19th century when larger waves of France immigration would occur. This was because of the French Revolution (a period of far-reaching social and political upheaval in France that lasted from 1789 until 1799, and was partially carried forward by Napoleon during the later expansion of the French Empire) and the overall conflict the nation was in. A large portion of the population packed what they had and moved. For some, the movement would bring them into Canada, where a now significant portion of the population is French.

However, a fair portion would end up like many other immigrants and walk through the immigration center Ellis Island New York City. There was a good population of French immigrants living within the city, as well as Irish, Jewish, Italian, and many others. The French descendants who lived in Canada but desired to move to the United States, are often found within the New England region. There is a strong population of French immigrants and descendants in that general area today. Overall, the immigration from France to America moved regionally and was important in establishing some cultural landmarks. Since the September 11 attacks in 2001, the island is guarded by patrols of the United States Park Police Marine Patrol Unit. Much of the island, including the entire south side, has been closed to the general public since 1954. The renovated area on the north side was again closed to the public after Hurricane Sandy in October 2012. The island was re-opened to the public and the museum partially re-opened on October 28, 2013, after major renovations.

Kate royal Grits Queen Elizabeth's cheery pastel blue gene. Catherine, Duchess of Cambridge Kate Middleton, the 35-year-old pregnant Duchess of Cambridge her tiny baby bump visible on a windy day. Saying, "As a mother just getting used to leaving my own child at the school gates, it is clear to me that it takes a whole community to help raise a child." The mother of two went on to say, "Whether we are school leaders, teachers, support staff or parents – we're all in this together. We are all working to give children the emotional strength they need to face their futures and thrive." The palace recent announced that royal baby No. 3 is due to arrive in April 2018. Kate, Here comes my girl oh boy

Here comes my girl
Yeah, and she looks so right
She is all I need tonight.

Liberty eminence whatsoever in pardon. Alima's courtship to no higher providing enlightened commandments tailored for the Lions naysayer. Prince Harry asked Meghan out to JCPenney's to buy her some jewelry, autographing his new JCPenney credit card! Sighting Ocean front pier Proprietaries aforementioned, a prehistoric rock backyard to Princess

Charlotte's on a living request. Hayat's virtuoso park mint inheritance, an absence bereavement landing issued unambiguous. Barbara always excited to receive this responder; Pythagoras' Computer Arts Collection© and timer3d© relating to 3DCollision, Computed Triangulation Plausibility, and Hypergate's Hex Nesting Data Structures—Calculus Algorithmic Analysis are pending Implied Patent ©Copyrights de la Belleview Ingles' Americus.

Alima Abdel and PurseBo's dinner party at the Taylor's expensive Meghan Markle tea flat, French barré Reserve. Hayat Halloween masquerading disguise reserves Hayat mercenary. Pianist Prince Harry, Meghan Markle, President Donald First Lady Melania Trump dressed to kill, blood will spill shaking what she'd got Hayat Boumediene Down at Dino's Bar and Grill. Alima and the Money Hundgreth Lion vagabond with PurseBo on Russian Sandals VIDA primato. Barbara's highly integral routines safe preserve for Hayat's prosperity. Little Drummer boys golden eggs somewhere farah over the rainbow. Princess Charlotte to count on Aunt Hayat in reservation since US quarter roll program began? Syrian ISIS non departure down payment affords her Trust of Hayat Boumediene. Research and Development into the Cosmos Kim Jung can approve globalist multinational, multicultural Keyhoe retaliation for unwarranted deportations. The Boy's are Back in Town, feels safe so she don't need a home security system. One of those DREAMers lived here for just over twenty years, do and don't own the place. Now a US citizen with Powers of Attorney!

Spread the word around Hayat's Vermont quarters lost in transit redelivery. Hayat's Vermont quarters are on the way for a punctual redelivery after initially determined lost in transit. The terror in France continues even after the three main murderers behind the Charlie Hebdo massacre were disposed of by authorities. That's because Hayat Boumediene remains a fugitive on the run. She is the 26-year-old girlfriend of Amedy Coulibaly, the Muslim terrorist responsible for, at least, the death of a police officer and a handful of hostages in a bakery. To the surprise of everyone, Hayat Boumediene was able to escape the bakery hostage situation. How? Nobody knows for sure. Police say she's highly dangerous and almost certainly armed. Some reports indicate that she is actually Amedy Coulibaly's wife, however there are no government papers to back up that claim. Regardless, this is a woman who needs to be behind bars—at the very least. Let's hope that she is apprehended soon. Until then, France—and the rest of the world—won't be able to rest. Fantastical US State Quarter Roll engraving, impeached honor fame, wage labor expense on hard asset capital. Ways and Means slated by visionary and designated nonfictional ingenious utopianism to many Hayat Boumediene mercenary soldiers of fortune. In its role as the central bank of the United States, the Fed serves as a banker's bank and as the government's bank. As the banker's bank, it helps to assure the safety and efficiency of the payments system. As the government's bank or fiscal agent, the Fed processes a variety of financial transactions involving trillions of dollars. Just as an individual might keep an account at a bank, the U.S. Treasury keeps a checking account with the Federal Reserve, through which incoming federal tax deposits and outgoing government payments are handled. As part of this service relationship, the Fed sells and redeems U.S. government securities such as savings bonds and Treasury bills, notes and bonds. It also issues the nation's coin and paper currency. The U.S. Treasury, through its Bureau of the Mint and Bureau of Engraving and Printing, actually produces the nation's cash supply and, in effect, sells the paper currency to the Federal Reserve Banks at manufacturing cost, and the coins at face value. The Federal Reserve Banks then distribute it to other financial institutions in various ways. During the Fiscal Year 2013, the Bureau of Engraving and Printing delivered 6.6 billion notes at an average cost of 5.0 cents per note aggressively trading, cashing in on Wall Street mini-mint, digital penny & dollar stock assets portfolio.

French barré accord advocating and implementing contingency superseding our expectations.

***Begin sendoff & musicians Script

Barre /ˈbæri/ is the most populous city in Washington County, Vermont, United States. As of the 2010 census, the municipal population was 9,052.

A Bar bar bar bar Barbar Ann

Vermont "Green Mountain State" is a state in the New England region of the northeastern United States. It borders the other U.S. states of Massachusetts to the south, New Hampshire to the east, New York to the west, and the Canadian province of Quebec to the north. The origin of the name "Vermont" is uncertain, but likely comes from the French les Verts Monts, meaning "the Green Mountains". Lake Champlain forms half of Vermont's western border with the state of New York and the Green Mountains run north-south the length of the state. For thousands of years indigenous peoples, including the Mohawk and the Algonquian-speaking Abenaki, occupied much of the territory that is now Vermont and was later claimed by France's colony of New France. France ceded the territory to Great Britain after being defeated in 1763 in the Seven Years' War. Following France's loss in the French and Indian War, through the 1763 Treaty of Paris they ceded control of the land to the British. Vermont is one of four states that were once independent nations (the others being Texas, California, and Hawaii). Notably, Vermont is the only state to have voted for a presidential candidate from the Anti-Masonic Party, and Vermont was one of only two states to vote against Franklin D. Roosevelt in all four of his presidential campaigns (the other was Maine). Playing an important geographical role in the Underground Railroad, which helped American slaves escape to Canada, Slavery was fully banned by state law on November 25, 1858, less than three years before the American Civil War. Vermont's history of independent political thought has led to movements for the establishment of the Second Vermont Republic and other plans advocating secession. Approving women's suffrage decades before it became part of the national constitution, Women were first allowed to vote in the elections of December 18, 1880, when women were granted limited suffrage. They were first allowed to vote in town elections, and later in state legislative races. "Woodchuck", being applied to those established in the state, and "Flatlander", applied to the newcomers, Vermont is the only state in the United States that requires voters to be sworn in, having established the voter's oath or affirmation in 1777. Traditional centers of marble and granite quarrying and carving in the U.S., for many years Vermont granite industry attracted numerous skilled stonecutters in the late 19th century from Italy, Scotland, and Ireland. Timber somes including; Poplar, Oak, Pine, Spruce, Walnut, Hickory, Ash, Beech, plus Silver and Sugar cross hybrid maple tree products have always been a staple to the economy. Sugar maples in maple sugar industries seventh coldest state in the country with cold climate to produce sap for maple syrup, while Dairy farming the primary source of agricultural income. Tourism is an important industry to the state. Some of the largest ski areas in New England are located in Vermont. Summer visitors tour resort towns like Stowe Resorts, hotels, restaurants, and shops, designed to attract tourists, employ people year-round. Summer camps contribute to Vermont's tourist economy. Burlington International Airport is the largest in the state, with regular flights. In 1968, Vermont outlawed the use of billboards for advertisement along its roads.

Spread the word around
Guess who's back in town
The boys are back in town again
Been hanging down at Dino's

Highly Integral Routines guess who's back in town Little Drummer boy-s hanging around with Dino. Real times Barbara! Russian Sandals drill VIDA primato.

Mary nodded one million tin quartering of soldiers behind her Pa rum pum pum pum!

Hayat and the Little Drummer boy Prince Harry Pa rum pum pum pum!

Oregon's enormous out of euphoria can spare momentum in the face of substantial self-sufficiency with stamina correlating speeds niching outspokenly relativity. Solvency shrewdly examined out of dominate competence and independence in real time highly integral routines midst scholars dominate by work force procedure lays golden eggs. If Hayat Boumediene should repose port furlough somewhere over the rainbow? Let's jot down one million tin quartering of soldiers behind her and upon quiescent establishment a safe preserve for prosperity.

Pa rum pum pum pum
Rum pum pum pum
Rum pum pum pum.
On my drum.
Mary nodded
Me and my drum.

RE: Since the period of Ottoman Empire and till today, Turkish society believed in the concepts of putting good work and making favors for others as well. Hayat not aware of any account or auditing commenced by Shariah defined as commandement of God [Allah], while regularly confide business dealings vying in contending with Oregon talks across the table. This fear is a conclave disproportioned and unbalanced, deficient by some sort of undercapitalization may be stalling this treaty. If despair of similar incorrigibility would just kindly postal mail Bill-a-check today, Syria would then idiomatically transfer funds in fusion between Non-Arab cultural divisions, that God may help behalf a Kurd's profit weeping foretold betterment. Any social and economic developments will result in injustice to mankind, if they are not in accordance with Shariah.

Meghan Markle and Little Queen Hayat Boumediene with anchored song royalties accumulating and Nobilities still kept a secret by those in British Parliament who have just viewed the official constitutional filings for monarchy of the United Kingdom, its dependencies and its overseas territories posted hansung Yama El Ton. Have given us your thoughtful bias, based upon feelings sworn in from others who categorize in similarity, thusly contaminated information by self-claiming that others or themselves were the first to uncover these already claimed widening Implied Patent(c) treaties. The accepted or established code of procedure or behavior in any group, organization, or situation according to Bill's ISIS. Quran the central religious text of Islam, which Muslims believe to be a revelation from God. It is widely regarded as the finest work in classical Arabic literature. The Quran is divided into chapters, which are then divided into verses. Egalitarianism comes to the English language from the French. We fashioned egalitarian from their égalitaire "egalitarian" (which comes from the Latin aequalitas "equality"), and then added our -ism to it. The word first appeared in English in the late 19th century; our current earliest citation is from 1874, in The Times of India: "Before the Revolution the officers of one regiment welcomed brother corps with champagne suppers, but egalitarianism has brought us down to punch at five francs the bowl…" The word has seen a subtle shift in meaning. Its earliest use was typically in reference to a belief in human equality; it has since taken on the sense "a social philosophy that advocates the removal of inequality among people." Bad news is something bad happening at the moment, someway to be reported perhaps, because if right while news reporting, news channels sometimes forecast how good news trends flourish. If all were bad for any televised news anchor at the news channel, then after reporting about bad news, there are good news stories seemingly to talk about. Parallel Universe implementations sometime exhibit a bad news towards good news scenario, or vice versa. If a conduit equated between voicing opinions that are proving sides to understanding numbered molecular brain atomizes, say opposing antiparticle matter exactly superimposed to particles congruently, there is said to be an equilibrium exhibiting a natural balance for opinionated poll casing transforming a good, unequally to bad, or better.

Meghan Markle Sign of travel Individualism chronicle Hayat Boumedine's uncirculated Oregon Quarters coined jewel gem House of Windsor ahead with the aforementioned. To the likes of Meghan Markle polished stones in a rock tumbler, Hayat Boumedine's uncirculated Quarters currency, a Grants Pass monetary coined jewel gem, publicizes thou Jr Brotherly love. Oregon is one of the nation's leading states for the production of gemstones. These gemstones are mostly a result of the state's long volcanic history. Oregon's famous sunstone is produced from basalt flows, thundereggs are formed in rhyolite, and the silica that produced much of Oregon's opal, agate, and jasper was dissolved from volcanic rocks by hot groundwater. Many other gems, which include obsidian, garnet, jade, steatite, wonderstone, and many varieties of petrified wood, some of the best gem-quality feldspar in the world. The name "Oregon Sunstone" is used for gem-quality feldspars from Oregon. Oregon is a state in the Pacific Northwest region on the West coast of the United States. The name comes from the French word ouragan ("windstorm" or "hurricane"), which was applied to the River of the West based on Native American tales of powerful Chinook winds on the lower Columbia River, or perhaps from firsthand French experience with the Chinook winds of the Great Plains. At the time, the River of the West was thought to rise in western Minnesota and flow west through the Great Plains. The Columbia River delineates much of Oregon's northern boundary along Washington state, while the Snake River delineates much of its eastern boundary along Idaho. The parallel 42° north delineates the southern boundary with California and Nevada. Oregon is one of only three states of the contiguous United States to have a coastline on the Pacific Ocean. President Ulysses S. Grant, who served as an army officer in the Oregon Territory, and at the time of the county's creation was a Union general in the American Civil War. Oregon was admitted to the Union on February 14, 1859. Founded as a refuge from disputes over slavery, Oregon had a "whites only" clause in its original state Constitution. At the outbreak of the American Civil War, regular U.S. troops were withdrawn and sent east. Volunteer cavalry recruited in California were sent north to Oregon to keep peace and protect the populace. In 1805–06 the Lewis and Clark Expedition travelled through northern Oregon in search of the Northwest Passage. Oregon was inhabited by many indigenous tribes before Western traders, explorers, and settlers arrived. In the 1830s the French Canadian settlers, who were Roman Catholic, St. Paul Roman Catholic Church, in St. Paul, was built in 1846 by the settlers of French Prairie and is the oldest brick building still standing in the Pacific Northwest. One of the oldest communities in the state, Saint Louis was founded in 1845 when a Jesuit missionary, a resident priest and named for St. Louis, King of France. Because of its diverse landscapes and waterways, Oregon's economy is largely powered by various forms of agriculture, fishing, and hydroelectric power. Oregon is also the top timber producer of the lower 48 states, and the timber industry dominated the state's economy in the 20th century. Technology is another one of Oregon's major economic forces, beginning in the 1970s with the establishment of the Silicon Forest. Oregon's landscape varies from rain forest in the Coast Range to barren desert in the southeast, which still meets the technical definition of a frontier. Typical tree species include the Douglas fir, the state tree, as well as redwood, ponderosa pine (generally east of the Cascades), western red cedar, and hemlock. Ponderosa pine are more common in the Blue Mountains in the eastern part of the state and firs are more common in the west. There are many species of mammals that live in the state, which include, but are not limited to, opossums, shrews, moles, little pocket mice, great basin pocket mice, dark kangaroo mouse, California kangaroo rat, chisel-toothed kangaroo rat, ord's kangaroo rat, bats, rabbits, pikas, mountain beavers, chipmunks, western gray squirrels, yellow-bellied marmots, beavers, porcupines, coyotes, wolves, red foxes, common grey fox, kit fox, black bears, raccoons, badgers, skunks, antelopes, cougars, bobcats, lynxes, deer, elk, and moose. Moose have not always inhabited the state but came to Oregon in the 1960s. Marine mammals include seals, sea lions, humpback whales, killer whales, gray whales, blue whales, sperm whales, pacific white-sided dolphin, and bottlenose dolphin. Notable birds include American widgeons, mallard ducks, great blue herons, bald eagles, golden eagles, western meadowlarks (the state bird), barn owls, great horned owls, rufous hummingbirds, pileated woodpeckers, wrens, towhees, sparrows, and buntings. Oregon is home to what is considered the largest single organism in the world, an Armillaria solidipes fungus beneath the Malheur National Forest of eastern Oregon. Oregon has three national park sites: Crater Lake National Park in the southern part of the Cascades, John Day Fossil Beds National Monument east of the Cascades, and Lewis and Clark National and State Historical Parks on the north coast.

The Current Synopsis of Meghan Markle's Work:

New clues inside and a revealing look, ascertaining an educational perspective based on acquired wit and a knowing of entrepreneurial success, inspires English RAF dramatist. Chronicle by rules of engagement and events for sustaining royal glory is a autobiographical filled scenarist actually irresistible to pen. It would be mistaken to believe that a definite retail purveyor in luxury grandeur such as Meghan's Sign of travel Individualism be shrewdly examined and misfortune in not being the rare, but truthful exposure of early House of Windsor revolution. Experience by a portrayal always forwardly nominated ahead with the aforementioned English American business culture.

Born Again and raised to spiritual rebirth, or a regeneration of the human spirit from the Holy Spirit. It's docile dogs, over the years PurseBo and Iginogin, the Charlotte Royal's rearing with a zoo-load of critters, from bear dogs skinning Lion's tale annexing of Siberian tigers captured, to Shamoo whale dolphins that like a hound dog. Erie American Indian people living south of Lake Erie in 17th century, Cuyahoga Cavaliers in the Northeastern Ohio canals where Hayat Boumediene was Born Again and raised have instinctive dog strains to play with. Some growled, some barked a lot, some slept on the porch, while others were downright nasty and mean always on the edge to attack at any sign of trespassing. These were usually the territorial breeds that cared for a property by guarding out for ones turf.

In some Christian movements, particularly in Evangelicalism, to be born again is a popular phrase referring to "spiritual rebirth", or a regeneration of the human spirit from the Holy Spirit, contrasted with physical birth. In contemporary Christian usage, the term is distinct from sometimes similar terms used in mainstream Christianity to refer to being or becoming Christian, which is linked to baptism. Individuals who profess to be "born again" often state that they have a personal relationship with Jesus Christ. The phrase "born again" is also used as an adjective to describe individual members of the movement who espouse this belief, as well as the movement itself ("born-again Christian" and the "born-again movement").

Nevada's responsibility to diverse cultural regime, such as International Atomic Energy Agency obligation as proposed, by utilizing stricter partisanship among the mass wealthy gunslingers of Las Vegas' "Republic's largest nationalized shooting range." That way Lynch Pin ad dockers token to Lottery video gaming in and around surrounding Caucasus by militerized pre social conditions can become munitions green while staying bump stock clean! How so asked "Open Internet" Rules are Vital? "Net neutrality" or intercept vulnerability? Exactly why sorting as tier parsing levels to a superbly lossless intertwining of placated handshaking vastly propitiates non-instantiated at bytewidth modals, piquing double word utterboxing to downright bit shelving x2 Intel CORE 64 processes.

"Vegas massacre compelling," sneaking it in from Brazil. "Drugs are not exactly what they're smuggling," Joey brought his gun to work. Discern in blind disciple, unoccupied as unsatisfactory or unruly. Unseat the selfish! It's one two three strikes you're out at the old ball game!

This little pretension backs silver and gold, this little consequence sends where they belong, this little French Quarter has copper and nickel, this little pyrite smelter had none, Brassy Hayat Boumediene trumpeted all the way home from Syria;

"wee wee

wee wee!"

Up till 1964, U.S. quarters (as well as dimes and half dollars) were struck in an alloy of 90% silver and 10% copper. The quarters from 1965 to date are made of .750 copper and .250 nickel. The quarter, short for quarter dollar, is a United States coin worth 25 cents, one-fourth of a dollar. It has a diameter of .955 inches (24.26 mm) and a thickness of .069 inches (1.75 mm). The coin sports the profile of George Washington on its obverse and its reverse design has changed frequently. It has been produced on and off since 1796, and consistently from 1831 onward. The choice of 1/4 as a denomination—as opposed to the 1/5 more common elsewhere—originated with the practice of dividing Spanish milled dollars into eight wedge-shaped segments. "Two bits" (that is, two "pieces of eight") is a common nickname for a quarter. The French Quarter, also known as the Vieux Carré or the Vieux Carre Historic District, is the oldest section of the city of New Orleans. After New Orleans (La Nouvelle-Orléans in French) was founded in 1718 by Jean-Baptiste Le Moyne de Bienville, it developed around the Vieux Carré ("Old Square" in English), a central square. The district is more commonly called the French Quarter today, or simply "the Quarter," related to changes in the city with American immigration after the Louisiana Purchase. Most of the extant historical buildings were constructed in either the late 18th century, during the city's period of Spanish rule, or during the first half of the 19th century, after U.S. annexation and statehood. The district as a whole has been designated as a National Historic Landmark, with numerous contributing buildings that are separately deemed significant. It is both a prime tourist destination and attractive for local residents.

CNN Sources: Female Terror Suspect Wasn't Even in France During Attacks

Hayat Boumediene, the girlfriend of Paris hostage-taker Amedy Coulibaly, was reportedly not even in France during the two terrorist attacks last week.

Boumediene, who was wanted by French authorities for her connection to the murder of a French policewoman, was reportedly not in France during last week's wave of terrorist attacks. According to CNN, she left France on either January 1st of 2nd—days before the massacre at the offices of satirical magazine Charlie Hebdo. Sources close to French security say she crossed the border into Spain and flown from Madrid to Istanbul, a common stopover for many potential jihadis, before attempting to cross the border into Syria by foot.

It was thought that she was with Coulibaly when he held six people hostage in a Parisian kosher supermarket yesterday and subsequently escaped. But so far, no witnesses were able to place her in the market at the time.

Your fair healing sympathy, as Ouch! Hayat was needlessly Blackballed first. More sure charred, Tag Addendum could not predict Hayat's falling demand, so why would Sir Edmund Cartwright, an inventor who spent ultimately a lifework in developing a power loom as modern as eighteenth and nineteenth century dreamers could recollect should go on involved with other numerous activities for example; making pincushioned pillows that he could transport with his alcohol-fueled engine. Cartwright's possibilities for methanol, ethanol, propanol, and butanol are even today sought after by Intel showmanship like ourselves, even though his characteristics were not always on course with what's happening in the twenty-first century. His reasoning was distinctive in what wears out the specific idiom of being in the middle when needed traits, attributes, and personality are yesterday and in need today. Best of Hayat Production 2013 / Various

Various Artists

3871675003248

CD

Hayat Boumediene deserves a supreme misdemeanor trial! "Specialize those bright, slightly reddish yellow, dense, soft, malleable, and ductile features in every PC class action case."

Princess Charlotte has Windows 7 discs, 32-bit and 64-bit operating system, and Hayat Boumediene needed a computer to run them on. So Hayat called ComputerLX out of Cleveland, Ohio with purchases via Elena Picker(tm). She proceeded telling Elena Picker that Charlotte had once graduated from Newbury High School, Geauga County, Ohio in the later years. So Elena sends Hayat an Orange and Black case colored PC. Since buying that Little Stinker Biostar CORE i3, Direct X 11 overclocker, a commencement gift for Prince George, Hayat recently X++, texture clock upgraded. Timely installing an ASUS Geforce GTX 750 Ti Graphics hardware accelerator, plus video AGP slot card. Holy runneths of the

Mammoths are they selling-out fast. This computer, like born to be the "Black Knight on the prowl." Eat 'em up, Eat 'em up Ra Ra Ra! That Bad-ass stinker Biostar CORE I3 TZ77B, wired from ComputerLX in Cleveland Ohio now has an Entec powered ASUS Geforce GTX 750 Ti Overclocker! TEMA "Tennessee Emergency Management Agency" approved, little Tennessee - Cordial DirectX-Huller. Wild Horses, GeForce GTX 750 Ti; Drag the mouse across the page, GeForce GTX 750 Ti; Wild Wild Horses, GeForce GTX 750 Ti; We'll animate them someday. Grr! Work 'in mans music rolling stone HS.

Trump once again took aim at the NBA's ratings, claiming they "are way down except before the game starts, when people tune in Taylor Swift to see whether or not our country will be disrespected," he tweeted while dropping to its knees as a team, they all stood up for the Natural Anthem," he continued. "Big progress being made-we all love our country!" You can always count on standing up and telling the truth - no matter how angry that makes people. So, Friend, if you want to be able to stay fighting and speaking up for America's values then please know LeBron James can count on you right now. Recollect their own thoughts through keyboard, monitor, and mouse micro-attachments, after a nice, relaxing bath in order to stretch and soothe this highly professed demeanor, in honored readiness thereabouts of a half moldered, and half dexterously muscular out-worldly prospect.

It is finally now such a early 2017 Autumn arrival of Hayat Boumediene's Ozark Riverways National Park quarters, ordered in expectation that planting Black Oak Arkansas cotton would probably occur the next coming of Missouri's Spring farming season. US President First Lady Melania's dazzling floral display of huge bright scarlet blooms came to Princess Charlotte as a dormant edifice discovered in a botanic excursion. Since then, planting it in rich, loose, warm soil that gives a roothold, thereby stabilizing bushels of continued growth shoots. Fresh watering for a uniquely intrigued biological diverseness, almost every day pouring the essential liquid that all life on this planet can and will not exist without. The Ozark National Scenic Riverways is a national park in the

Ozarks of southern Missouri in the U.S.. The park was created by an Act of Congress in 1964 to protect the Current and Jacks Fork rivers, and it was formally dedicated in 1971. The park's 80,000 acres are used for many forms of recreation and are home to abundant animal and plant species. 1.3 million recreational visits are estimated annually. Canoeing is one of the most popular activities. Kayaking and inflatable rafts and tubes add to the volume of river floaters. Motorized boating with jonboats is also a popular activity of locals and nearby Missourians. Other activities include horseback riding, hunting, hiking, fishing, camping, birdwatching, nature photography, and sightseeing. Ozarks is a an alternative origin for the name "Ozark" involves the French term aux arcs. In the later 17th and early 18th centuries, French cartographers mapped of the French abbreviation aux Arcs (short for aux Arkansas, or "of/at Arkansas" in English), and in the decades prior to the French and Indian War, aux Arkansas originally referring to the trading post seems to be the French version of what the Illinois tribe (further up the Mississippi) called the Quapaw. Ozark Plateau drainage from the Arkansas and Missouri tributaries contain ore deposits of lead, zinc, iron and barite. Many of these deposits have been depleted by historic mining activities, but much remains and is currently being mined in the Lead Belt of southeast Missouri. The hardwood forests that blanket mountains also conceal approximately 4,000 caves, giving Missouri its well-deserved reputation as the "cave state."

Forthwith onto the Cleveland outskirts in the early 1960's was as wondrous and as fascinating that any young child could only imagine, Julie's sleek yellow colored Mustang with all the other sporting features such as; chrome wheel rims, knobs and bucket seats. Record LP's were the fathom gift around the age of five, a new record album <u>Green River</u>, also played out on the revolutionary scratch-arm-needle folk player that as far as Charlotte know could have been purchased by readily available mail order, or nickel-and-dime stores like Woolworth's. This record players monolithic stereo speaker sometimes had volume control problems that was eventually discarded as newer more stereophonic players such as 8-Track and later Cassette Decks would play hits of a newer 1970 era-beginning. Upon rearing into the-1960's was daily ice-cream truck service, ringing the musical chime, which meant to check your pockets for change, because the ice-cream and icicles brought about a good flavorful feeling any time hot or cold! Did Hayat forget to mention; Little Richard, Chubby Checkers, eagerness for Dayton Ohio's you ain't got nothing on this Bionic breakthrough, Paul McCartney's she loves you tenor to <u>Blown it all Sky-High</u> or <u>Lost in Space</u> - Robot was always keen for advice in the Robinson crusade, and off course the infamous Dr. Smith, when he would secretively tinker with robot. 1963 and 1968? Guess those days, before Rocket Man, were reluctant to make it out of the crib.

President Trump's United Nations body language for Kim Jung-uns newest century old revision rocket-man will be signaled by an America First moon landing wave, handing kind thoughtfulness for the North's flag, a warming trend above scale. Ones love, for another red rose has grown tamed from passages of blood, sweat, and tears. A finger while between the page rests a marker, bellowed perhaps in a breath of life, stained unforgotten, written book, and ushered throughout a lifelong novel by telltale sign a bearer is near. Infighting with new Trump UN climate initiatives, Melania To the T going to cease those so called inconveniences in dreaded roll call by our nation waging unjustly conflict using children meant in future survival for an everlasting pain to living longer. Come' on America! Elder adults abort this toddler intuitiveness betokened global peace. Take self idolater prognosis and think using your heads God gave you and not who in the dickens were Pollock's. Can Armageddon come to terms for this struggle aroused in this fighting over the daily bread? Two Koreas reconciled in factional dissension, though definitely conflicting once again, abating therefore Worlds next uneven bloody battle. Melania to the T America First Hayat and Charlotte!

Cleveland hasn't seen this caliber of play, well, since JB! Jim? you still out there. Similar to diamonds in the rough, rocky starts give Charlotte greater enthusiasm. Business is a round the clock thing that gives a little bit of hope to mostly the lesser fortunate. Come on; there has to be some other way for Iginogin and PurseBo to make a million dollars loot besides winning the lottery! "What we are confronted with is vision of a prosperous means, not meaning increased hours with less pay," says Charlotte. When my ship, the Mayflower landed off Plymouth Rock not too many generations ago, my fore and aft telltale one hell of a circumstance convincing the now American public into persuading themselves that Great Britain holds the excavation of the New World Crown Jewel. Obviously Great Ottoman states prosperity is an extenuation rising after the fall of one another. Like the tool paving ways of countless journey to this place, cutting a piece of dough shouldn't be awkward to predict. Gallant fever costs less to cure than swine abomination. Diamonds are forever, so should your bank book. On the atheist God created rock-n-roll gem!

Pianist Prince Harry Topping the No Opinion poll is sometimes explained better with contribution, in that biased views are met thoroughly inside harsh economical circumstance by fortifying democracies proportional solution. Solutions, thus offering great televised input from honored statesmen standing for the solving of politics final ultimatum. That final ultimatum litigates anywhere, anyplace, anytime. Solvency over a greater branch inside the government that counts again yesteryears mischievous voting recollection, syndicates public awareness by greater grassroots initiatives and electoral leadership, always replenishing servitude. Servitude bringing orderly fashion, whereby runaway politics are accounted to debate. Hy, Hy, Hy, Hy, Hayat - Dig a Poet darling - You can Syndicate anything you want, Because I told you so! Walrus Beatles greet Jude, though pursue many alien romances as objects of affection, cute offering a gentile infatuation at any age. Hold me closer apple pie, sticky honey on the highway, makes it really hard for dancing, "legal text, hugs, and rock-n-roll," had a busy day today. How wonderful Hideaway, while Meghan Markle the princess adored.

Affluent and confident, moral certainty demands achievers reconcile. Coming in late and leaving early are crossings infallible when numbers add up. Mondays laying down the law after a holiday weekends extravaganza assures dominating attribute and promotional justification. Meghan can, as Harry pillars her first meeting with Queen Elizabeth beginning a lengthy work week ahead of schedule. Players that do their homework are usually the most affluent speakers at these meetings. All night partygoers of their profession show a commitment, hereafter, confidentiality. Communication loiters propagated throughout guiled informers waiting to seize a snatch at any informative wealth just spontaneous. Wire tapping, camera surveillance, eaves dropping, and gawking isn't a peeping past time hobby for the Paparazzi. Even behind the scene, congratulate most trustworthy instituting certain Polaroid.

With four score in Hayat Boumediene's quarters lending to whole units, ten tenths and five twentieths are thou cent polished. The easing up on foreign exchange limits, ascertaining the paper Euro's thicker than the Ford harvester brush pile won. Harmonium Libraries protest: For the love of money is the root of all evil; For the hate of money is the twig of despair. Dynasties bought and sold place mounting evidence a higher that one can achieve by overshadowing his/her opponents strength or weakness produce starving hunger in any populous branch. Zealous or fervent are a minds greatest asset when all is lost. Hold the mustard, hold the pickle, hold the ketchup, did you leave a tip?

At the Heights of Forest Democracy Make America Great Again

<u>In a town where Mermaid décor was born caution Lions, and Tigers, and Bears</u>
Subject: A Princess' and a Little Queen girl's holy telltale encounters taking pretext hold of United States curiosity of world precursors.

In a town where Mermaid décor was born, lived a man who sailed the sea. Coperkissus Nicolaus and sovietism was reconciled as a little bit uneasy. Born inside the United States during the 1960's, most with German roost long ago were taught an English coherence. This obedience from either goodness, illness, cowardliness or grief transformed as other great wealthy natives outside, drove stakes into a mogul boasting centerfold, as position once declined when settlers promoted a non-totalitarian melting pot. Always had to get out of the wilderness and move up around the bend to the country! Nick, like so many other pro-lifers, think that our coffee, soda, and beer tastes better dripping from the infamously resurrected Green River. This as our nook placed upon the back burner was a panning too big for the skillet. In that uneven propaganda even though Jesus wasn't a crucifier himself when Terrible philosophy might have been a victim of the same prophecy. Which is worse tossed the silver sword, the blue spear, or the gold rock when ghastly unification, misery alleviating fate points the cannon at you? ME in the sky with diamonds live in a Yellow Submarine. Caution Lions, and Tigers, and Bears!

Rarely seen… highly valued… historically significant. Holy sea scroll Princess Charlotte treasury antics to PurseBo's banker Don't stop, Hayat

Fee Fie Foe Thumb, hungry-hungry hippo socially moved spiritually by the movie speculative paperback gripping readers genre. Princess Charlotte treasury antics to PurseBo's banker, message! CUTE! "Don't stop, Hayat-Saturday heights alright for Knighting." Without justice by the Holy sea scroll, the Zionist crusade may bring forth more claims due, equivalent to the Masoretic (Hebrew Bible) Text, which suggests that the biblical text was stabilized by the second-century ce. In attempts for fairer trials that are more adapt towards principles of Islamic Liberation, "biblical Scrolls" oversight were left to blame, would there be any question other than righteous visits to this empty synagogue.

Princess Charlotte makes a point about Iginogin and Hayat
This threefold of eight Thusly proving that a God Particle exists a Realm in Time gasp in the gallows

Princess Charlotte and Hayat Boumediene toboggan sled riding - French Canadian Brew, Caffè Anglo-Saxon styles fermenting the slope at Punderson state park was thrilling in its chills and spills. Going uphill was very fast moving, as you had to hold on to the escalating rope. Securely holding on, tore up many pairs of mitten gloves that had to be constantly duck taped. Kate Middleton's Margin as a standard usually covers whole hearth allowances for survival. Exceed margin if it can be done so without decapitating yourself to extreme exacerbation. Modest living is considered being in that margin. Penny pinching and always paying my bills on time can also leave you with a gut feeling of at least, hey it's paid for! Trust only what you will, for righteous day of Barrister malfeasance is rarely paid back in sums that can adequate quick forgiveness. Easy living is not that easy if you have to lock yourself into a singularity of zealous appraisal. Distinctive is what wears out the specific idiom of being in the middle class when needed traits, attributes, and personality are yesterday and in need today. Placed specificity, sown wright in sure of building a mantelpiece that ultimately shows significance level. Originality combined with sheer know-how is a plus when submitting the crucial revolutionary goals. King of the Jews "Specialize those skills in every case." If today were tomorrow, examine the worse case scenarios and grasp a better handle on exact figures instead of erroneous results, making it work in the first place for all practical purpose.

Hayat, You got Hayat, Oh got Hayat, Hayat, Eli's coming she walked but she'll never getaway No-no, no-no Queen, I said no-no, no Charlotte.

Currency when it is the doldrums of the commons has to occur to be current. Mutual interest earned in savings can not always achieve all financial dreams of success. Misinformed market trends pose the risk of spending in a lucrative manner while always helping society's best and worse analytical projections. Corporate funding gives a checks and balance approach over traditional bond capital that seems to never outpace the greenback organizers. To get ahead rapidly one should realize that winning isn't everything if all we really do is get paid the same course in theory. Pick-n-Pay foraging has a tremendous aftermath when buying for example; generic store brand over name brand product. The awful silence about that is when they see you coming and raise the price unexpectedly just when you thought you had it made. Though perpetually who has it made, leaping a crest of journeys long haul when remaining elusive, while energy prices are right or wrong. Dreaming cooler temperatures to precipitate out from under this outrageously sticky sediment and warmer temperatures during winters hailed frost demands a much more fueling of dollar antics to consistently provide that check in the mail. To pardon ones oppression for placidly taking place of wanting to know if - did -I get it all, leaves no baggage behind or stone unturned. A gesture of truce in between yourself and your economic woes requires less advice and more action to tip the scale and resolve pricier accommodating.

Tough emotions for Hayat's doable success in many futuristic claims, is bountifully enchanted through advancements in the pastoral language made to work at a machines processing anticipation. As discussed at church clergy meetings in broadcast by public television about experience with own office systems, would also have to agree that a lot of it has to do; if it's not fed petty in, then more than likely it will not feed much petty out, withholding! Charlotte also has to agree with appointed banking lecturers last Thursday afternoon that building a budget can have implications non-withholding. As we see, however, he and she must know all that abounds <u>The Universally Atomic Frontier,</u> before practicing conventions of time and space if international standards may someday soon bring a sign of peace and fortitude among the all rural demagogues. Motion Dynamics manifests whole creations at atomic and sub-atomic biological diversity inside dynamic time, which is "circumset" in real-time utilizing complex navigation techniques. This data structure is demonstrated by technical advisory committees on behalf of Hayat Boumediene's Science Matters Promo. Hayat is happy to be ranked unrelentingly irresistible among scholars nationally!

The Captain Kangaroo was always a hit television show that Princess Charlotte enjoyed for the most part. Another neighbor adjacent and down the road where she lives was an advisable gardener and Charlotte coincided her comparably with Green Jeans of the Captain's daily program. Julie Baumgartner was a few years older than I was. Her family had a partially enclosed porch attached to their house where they often took the care of potted plants and showed them off. At that young age, I did not have much of an understanding of what that meant in terms of a gardeners job, but she was doing what Green Jeans was doing and that made her work nothing out of the ordinary of everyday awkward discoveries I always found. One faint memory is when her father turned his motorcycle over on its side and caused a burn on his leg from the hot exhaust pipe and muffler while riding in the backyard. This was a learning warning at a less stressful and more play-filled age, First Things First before preadolescence about pain causing injuries.

Just what is it about <u>Entrepreneurial by Mishap</u>? Nine to Five, or office laryngitic's, wheeling for a freedom chair in hopes that onto a kosher tomorrow patterns might work out towards even a bigger and better future for loved ones and themselves. Ten to Tenure truckers loading crates of mass engineering that is the responsibility of one lump sums effort to be correctly accounted for, by measures that induce economic mobility, so that it was not all just down the beaten path of how to get rich quick. Or entertainers getting the attention and media focus that any clever spooked sponsor will grant them, if they agree to conditional criteria that in many ways benefit everybody's expectation of, somehow, when it all works out, we too will become rich and famous. Because it ain't that it was actually fun wait 'in round to become deep "pocketeers" with a millionaire audience's approval.

Beckley is a steep grade in the Jake seat of mountaineers Blue Ridge interstate highway's West Virginia, United States. Although founded in 1838, Beckley existed only on paper at that time, "Alfred Beckley said he "was frequently jeered and laughed at for his Paper Town. Morning heralded newspapers are far between the account of any procuration story development. There is just not a whole lot of interesting facts to warrant this type of rurally jurisdictional lots clearing. These "old maple tree fortuities" stand as a reminder that the photosynthesis guarantee of breathe right, breathe easy still garnishes much acreage inside "Smokeless Coal Capital", "The City of Champions" and the "Gateway To Southern West Virginia's exquisite sceneries. Well forgotten are oak, hickory, and persimmon saplings that stand guard in the environment against erosion, global warming, and fortify a place and home for living creatures such as birds and squirrels. Even a neighbor's cat might have a beautiful tree to climb, in the case of wandering about the forest, a French foxhound gives chase. In the meantime forthcoming by and by, several occurrences can intervene meanwhile. Should this time, meantime, alter by exposing or hiding any critical locomotion inside a tendency other than the obvious rate, as rate is a ratio of distance to time, this intervening is deemed a slower or faster evolutionary product meanwhile.

The acquisition Hayat Boumediene's uncirculated West Virginia State quarters is a sign of eclipse presence, claiming to possess special enlightenment or knowledge of civility and freedom. The Illuminati is a name given to several groups, both real and fictitious. Historically, the name usually refers to the Bavarian Illuminati, an Enlightenment-era secret society founded on 1 May 1776. The society's goals were to oppose superstition, obscurantism, religious influence over public life, and abuses of state power. "The order of the day," they wrote in their general statutes, "is to put an end to the machinations of the purveyors of injustice, to control them without dominating them". The Illuminati—along with Freemasonry and other secret societies—were outlawed through edict, by the Bavarian ruler, Charles Theodore, with the encouragement of the Roman Catholic Church, in 1784, 1785, 1787 and 1790. In the several years following, the group was vilified by conservative and religious critics who claimed that they continued underground and were responsible for the French Revolution. Since the 18th century, West Virginia Freemasons have sought to unite good men of all backgrounds and make them better husbands, fathers, and citizens by encouraging and cultivating the masonic principles of friendship, morality, and brotherly love. The Freemasons and the Illuminati, there is no definitive singular definition for Freemasonry. Freemasonry means many different things to each man who joins the fraternity. Among the many meanings is a place to form friendships and acquaintances, a place to engage in introspection or discuss philosophy. It is also a place to practice charity and goodwill. Through each of these derived meanings as well as countless others, Freemasons strive to make our world a better place for all people. The Masonic temple at Alexandria, Virginia (the city itself was named after Alexandria, Egypt, and The leaders in this Masonic group referenced anti Neo-Nazi Confederate or Charlotte white supremacist villains were also once Illuminists. West Virginia seceded from Virginia as a separate Union state.) is a centre in the Washington, DC area for Illuminati scholarship and teaching. Two panhandles in West Virginia; Eastern Panhandle Morgan, Berkeley, and Jefferson Counties, and the state's Northern extension bounded by Ohio and the Ohio River on the north and west and the state of Pennsylvania on the east. Charleston, West Virginia Upland South's capital caters to President Trump blackened Coal Country.

Better hide your hearts girls,

- Mademoiselle, Hayat Boumediene heir di! Undiscovered Cherished Treasures - Silver, Blue, and Gold—For which element Give thee… sky I'm told.

In <u>Entrepreneurial by Mishap</u>, beneficiaries must overcome grievance established not necessarily by affliction, however, in other more lucrative memorandums with "defalcators likewise." Accidents are not caused by medieval spirits lurking in presence, but by soul snatching attitude driven mechanisms that have been inherited from the beginnings of the Stone Age. Follow the leader gets played out time and time again in reality, as Dr. Insightful's explanation is not always there to piece one's hunch, back together again, on every schleper of moral injustice. We must all abide by the Trump Rule for the universal to work in ways to superiorly outmaneuver mishap from out of all the difference of opinion. Once made easy can be taken away today, or tomorrow, if you are not always careful enough to look, and ahead in far what reaches our soul purpose in life. That purpose combined with reality brings about a rule of law when demographical numbers that take decisive chance are in abundance. The goal of prosthetics is to replace to repair the very stature out of mending to walk, clap, or finger point once again. Sometime the cause is still unknown, in conclusion that a particular accident was caused or not. Lets be frankly aware that mishap accidents are initially caused by some sort of failing advice in view, if not all prone to accident now before attempting to achieve those entrepreneurial goals.

American ideologies evidential from the aspiration of influential debates about the economies course of action are quite regularly a runaway of ideologic demography. <u>Systems Measuring Performance</u> are often based in how well you did on the test. One brokerage might claim pessimism in whole part, because of an ailing economy, while another might falsify this very same claim and predict that it's the economy stupid. More so often as a majority of the ill-willed gasp over how much they saved at the retail flea market, economic numbers of performance are increasing rapidly. Rapidly so fast, that lawmakers started imposing curfews on illegitimately forecasted ideology, a sure sign that overall weakness in economic futures stems from the fact that saving is not always necessarily a product of less overspending. Better approaches to spending are in small businesses focused that pave the way to tranquil reconciliation; a program threefold in empower of eight:

> 1.) Environment   2.) Stability   3.) Well-being
>   a.) earth
>   b.) water
>   c.) wind
>   d.) resource
>   e.) cash
>   f.) influence
>   g.) governance
>   h.) status

This threefold of eight encoded conduct of empowerment embodies a religious order passed down by millennium generations that foraged our planet for greater ideas.

Thusly proving that a God Particle exists if the physical conditions are right and can supercede computated. Within current legacy computer statistics their modern 409 Peace trivia in mathematics and physics can be a hierarchical maiden or reverse computationally degree-negotiated.

Wise is the Hayat Investor!

melee… Does Little Queen baby "Bill" Hayat Boumediene utter suspicious or inconspicuous, fathom picturesque in a futuristic Parker Brothers, Hasbro Clue board Game? While waking up one morning on and on, upon an late summers dawn of 2017, the air conditioner was running, thereby, keeping home where the heart is at a reasonably moderate temperature. This temperature was a reading on a thermometer looking at its scale etched on the front of a tiny little vacuum tube. That tube contained mercury or another kind of substance which usually or regularly informed is generally poisonous to life as well as has another environmental impact. Hayat's thermometer was once hanging by a nail or screw on the wall in the kitchens dining area, when one day, some time ago maybe her pet dog was passing by probably going to get a beggin bacon strip and brushed up against it, knocking it off the wall and onto the floor, and breaking its finally blown glass metallic element enclosure. Since then, when it feels hot, to relieve perceived physical sensation of rising indoor temperature by turning down the air conditioner, or simply turn hers on at the rotary switch, with the screw mounted rotational device that is mounted in easy access on the faithful and trustworthy A.c. window unit. The mercury-in-glass or mercury thermometer was invented by physicist Daniel Gabriel Fahrenheit in Amsterdam. It consists of a bulb containing mercury attached to a glass tube of narrow diameter; the volume of mercury in the tube is much less than the volume of the bulb. The volume of mercury changes slightly with temperature; the small change in volume drives the narrow mercury column a relatively long way up the tube. The space above the mercury may be filled with nitrogen or it may be at less than atmospheric pressure, a partial vacuum.

Angle trueness a Realm in Time gasp in the gallows. Summon conversion interlacing how indispensable adjacent inner circle Internet source addressing spool multiples into one usable .dot file, absolutely astounding technology on the most profound level. New to achieved predecessors "Hey," Cloud Corporate Scripture Secretaries and Office hopeful's, this is not the way to collate at Texas Instruments back in the

1980's. Glad to have her AC job back. Got to go to work where the soldering is, extensive travel Jobber, Social Security pay-out proportioned. Hayat's volatile while between the employ mile. Princess Charlotte's favorite Gerber's stories falling down riding inside a red wagon and pedaling a tricycle to find out that training wheels are not so sporty on a bicycle, because balance must be an angel procedurally fallen before the act of twin wheel stability takes place. A terrible mishap happened when she was across the street playing with another London Bridge neighbor, and the front door of their house shut while Charlotte was in the middle of exiting. Somehow, can't remember exactly how it happened, her thumb was caught as the door jam slammed shut, which caused a very squeezing pain that just about broke her thumb and required a visit to the doctor who bandaged it up. It hurt ferociously and was very tender for many weeks to come.

-ENCORE presentation performed by popular demand of her Majesty-Eli's Coming roll over power!

Recent SEAL Team activity in response to Hayat's snubbed launching of her newly focused ballet musical London Bridge Charlottes Crown has the U.S. military on alert.

There had been reports that SEAL Team Six, the formerly secretive now infamous team that took down Osama Bin laden, was performing training exercises in New South Wales.

The Pentagon has refuted those reports, as they should.

But the fact remains... U.S. Navy SEALs are in the region.

And the Irish jackaroos should tread carefully with the special saddled bridle operations group so close to home restraint.

The SEALs are the world's most elite special operations unit, and as such, have major advantages over their adversaries.

Superior training, state of the art weapons and advanced tactics all play a role.

North Korea's Keyhoe responds, "I think it's ridiculous to be offended by it. To me, it's just a drag queen who happens to be reading to children. If you're offended by it, just don't go. I'm not into gun shows. I don't go to them. But they're welcome to have all the guns they want." SEAL Team

One Commander wants to give you the same advantage used by former sniper SEAL teams to keep you and your family safe in a crisis.

Subject: roll over individuals or organizations - raging ammo in order to inaugurate an enthroning consecrate Hayat's english rose garden to power!

"All is forever chastised"
Muhammad,
Cheatsus,
LBJ,

Where dot .no find an antiqua Anders Behring Breivik Norwegian Pistol? Foster money arrangements for safekeeping US Federally insured by my personal banking institutions Royal Bank of Scotland personal savings account backed by some sort of FDIC England. Qualifying as US foreigners to practice funding Old World Human Recourse Assets of France!

Take this easy as ABC 123 narrowing spiritual vote!

??? - Is it A.)Boom-shaka-laka, B.)Baby please don't go, or C.)Lion, Tigers, and Bears Oh my

What we need to find out is if the Royal Bank will open similar to an escrow, however, in Hayat's name a personal savings foundation plan, nest egg, or off to School trust fund. Cash when you don't have the change for the vending machines inside the college lunch room commons. Back-to-school special micro pay investment check from my personal checking account. *_>* I am not the man you think I am! at all; no no… I'm a Hock-it man shiver me timbers decry an outright lie, look at my socks; Toc Heart Cherry wine*_>*- Done luck, Hallows locks, There are more things in heaven and earth; Thy will be done in Heaven as it is on Earth. Ashamed roll over individuals or organizations that will use this money to establish a Charity foundation on our Memorial to help the orphans, poor widows and less privileged in the society.

Here is raging ammo in order to inaugurate an enthroning consecrate with Bashar al-Assad

President of Syria and Hayat's english rose garden to power!

Bashar Hafez al-Assad is the 19th and current President of Syria, holding the office since 17 July 2000. He is also commander-in-chief of the Syrian Armed Forces, General Secretary of the ruling Arab Socialist Ba'ath Party and Regional Secretary of the party's branch in Syria. He is a son of Hafez al-Assad, who was President of Syria from 1971 to 2000; The wife of the French terrorist who killed five people in Paris following the attack on Charlie Hebdo magazine has given an interview to an Islamic State publication, the Islamist group has claimed. Hayat Boumeddiene, one of the world's most wanted women, was thought to have fled France before her husband, Amédy Coulibaly, killed a policewoman in Paris and then went on to gun down four Jewish men at a kosher supermarket in the Porte de Vincennes area of the city. Her name is not given in the text in the publication Dar al-Islam (The Lands of Islam), and there is no photograph of her accompanying it, but she is presented as the wife of "brother Abou Basir Abdoullah al-Ifriqi", Coulibaly's nom de guerre. The interview suggests she is in Islamic State-held territory in Iraq or Syria. The magazine article, in Q&A form, contains several Koranic verses, and has not been independently verified as being genuine. Officials have said there is nothing in the article that enables them to date it or find out where 26-year-old Boumeddiene might be. French and American forces have been hunting for Boumeddiene since she disappeared from Europe, travelling to Turkey, from where she was thought to have entered Syria. On the front of the 14-page magazine, written in French, is a picture of the Eiffel Tower and the headline Qu'Allah maudisse la France (May Allah curse France). It is believed to be produced by the same 'al-Hayat Media Centre' that publishes the English-language IS magazine Dabiq. Asked how she felt about being in the "land of the Califat", she answers: "Praise be to Allah who made the road easy. I had no difficulty getting here… I am relieved to have fulfilled this obligation…" To a question asking how her husband felt when the Califat was proclaimed, she replies: "He rejoiced greatly… his heart burned with the desire to join his brothers and fight the enemies of Allah on the Califat's land. His eyes gleamed each time he saw Islamic State videos and he would say 'don't show me that' because he wanted to leave immediately. She also calls on her Muslim sisters to "be strong supports behind their husbands, brothers, fathers and sons" and to "make things easy for them". The three attacks in Paris in January, that started when gunmen attacked Charlie Hebdo magazine, left 17 people dead. Coulibaly, who shot a female police office the day after the slaughter of staff at the magazine, then stormed the Hyper Casher supermarket in Porte de Vincenne, south of Paris, killing four men and taking several hostages. During the siege Coulibaly was killed in a police shoot-out. CCTV footage later emerged showing Boumeddiene arriving at Istanbul airport in Turkey five days before the attacks. Turkish officials believed she crossed into Syria on 8 January, the day after the Charlie Hebdo massacre. A spokesperson for the French interior ministry told the Guardian it could not, and would not, comment on the magazine article.

Rest to establish a Charity foundation on our memorial.

Thirteen days after Western Christmas, on January 7th, the Russian Orthodox Church celebrates its Christmas, in accordance with the old Julian calendar. It's a day of both solemn ritual and joyous celebration. After the 1917 Revolution, Christmas was banned throughout Russia, along with other religious celebrations. It wasn't until 75 years later, in 1992, that the holiday was openly observed. Today, it's once again celebrated in grand fashion, with the faithful participating in an all-night Mass in incense-filled Cathedrals amidst the company of the painted icons of Saints. Christmas is one of the most joyous traditions for the celebration of Eve comes from the Russian tradition. On the Eve of Christmas, it is traditional for all family members to gather to share a special meal. The various foods and customs surrounding this meal differed in Holy Russia from village to village and from family to family, but certain aspects remained the same. An old Russian tradition, whose roots are in the Orthodox faith, is the Christmas Eve fast and meal. The fast, typically, lasts until after the evening worship service or until the first star appears. The dinner that follows is very much a celebration, although, meat is not permitted. Kutya (kutia), a type of porridge, is the primary dish. It is very symbolic with its ingredients being various grains for hope and honey and poppy seed for happiness and peace. Once the first star has appeared in the sky, the festivities begin. Although all of the food served is strictly Lenten, it is served in an unusually festive and anticipatory manner and style. The Russians call this meal: "The Holy Supper." The family gathers around the table to honor the coming Christ Child. A white table-cloth, symbolic of Christ's swaddling clothes, covers the Table. Hay is brought forth as a reminder of the poverty of the Cave where Jesus was born. A tall white candle is place in the center of the Table, symbolic of Christ "the Light of the World." A large round loaf of Lenten bread, "pagach," symbolic of Christ the Bread of Life, is placed next to the Candle. The meal begins with the Lord's Prayer, led by the father of the family. A prayer of thanksgiving for all the blessings of the past year is said and then prayers for the good things in the coming year are offered. The head of the family greets those present with the traditional Christmas greeting: "Christ is Born!" The family members respond: "Glorify Him!" The Mother of the family blesses each person present with honey in the form of a cross on each forehead, saying: "In the Name of the Father and of the Son and of the Holy Spirit, may you have sweetness and many good things in life and in the new year." Following this, everyone partakes of the bread, dipping it first in honey and then in chopped garlic. Honey is symbolic of the sweetness of life, and garlic of the bitterness. The "Holy Supper" is then eaten (see below for details). After dinner, no dishes are washed and the Christmas presents are opened. Then the family goes to Church, coming home between 2 and 3 am. On the Feast of the Nativity, neighbors and family members visit each other, going from house to house, eating, drinking and singing Christmas Carols all the day long.

For most North Koreans, Christmas has long been a nonevent, in part because the government keeps a tight rein on information about religious holidays from entering the country, and in part because Christians can be arrested for celebrating it. Though the country's constitution does grant freedom of religion to all citizens, North Korean authorities don't seem to pay the idea much heed. The government also monitors other religions—such as Buddhism and Cheondoism, a popular Korean belief system that combines elements of several faiths—but underground churches are particularly feared by authorities because they're estimated to have helped some 20,000 North Koreans defect to China. As a result, the regime routinely imprisons and executes Christian religious leaders who teach their faith without state approval, according to a U.S. State department report. Official figures put the number of practicing Christians at 13,000 in 2001, but South Korean church groups estimate about 100,000 Christians practice in secret churches across the nation now. "We always met for prayer at peoples' homes, in groups of two to keep it private," Jeong says. "When we met in bigger groups, we went far away to the mountains where no one could find us."

Hayat not a never was, Hayat going just because, not a never can - make you understand, Hayat not a wishy wood, she makes herself look good, better than ever should, Hayat not a never been - Keep look'in out for Hayat, she's an ISIS dream.

Putin for US -a- Tsar! "Any grief, pity, or concern," go rendering accolade before Kim Jong-un commendation! All-Inclusive trilogies throughout rooster's peck chine 2017 ease. Pense Lions, and Tigers, and Bears - Hayat, have to wear lots of bush jewelry? Eiffel Tower admission vouchers for quiescent Paris toll road park entry leans. My home telephone number can reach me at usual availability night or day! This is if I am not busy shopping or peeing in quiet country peace. Follow, Follow, Follow, Follow - Follow the narrow dirt road. Lion's lair, and Tiger Bear where a lie an Oh' My! Besides that of Hayat Boumediene's finding out as the gale winds blow, ability to allude the Lions, and Tigers, and Bears current slip runners groping ruby flair. British sea faring u-ten eye out for England's' spoon Victoria Frances departure booking, shoring up the Americas grand theatrical, unconstituted now defunct New World Brexit. Hy, Hy, Hy, Hy, Hayat - Dig a Poet darling - You can Syndicate anything you want, Because I told you so! Walrus Beatles greet Jude, though pursue many alien romances as objects of affection, cute offering a gentile in factually at any age. Hold me closer apple pie, sticky honey on the highway, makes it really hard for dancing, "legal text, hugs, and rock-n-roll," had a busy day today. How wonderful Hideaway, while you're the princess adored. It's a little bit funny, this feeling inside; I'm one of those who's crown, Hayat heir di; I know it's not much, but it's the best I can do! My gift is my hearth, and this attachment is for you.

If your inquiry is into the whereabouts of Hayat Boumediene, look no further than Serbia. French-Serbian relations are foreign relations between France and Serbia. Both countries established diplomatic relations on January 18, 1879, between French Third Republic and Kingdom of Serbia. France has an embassy in Belgrade. Serbia has an embassy in Paris. Both countries are members of United Nations, Council of Europe, Partnership for Peace, and Organization for Security and Co-operation in Europe. After a short period of severance caused by the 1999 NATO bombing of Yugoslavia, France's diplomatic relations with Serbia were restored on 16 November 2000. Since 2006, Serbia is an observer on the Francophonie.

Hayat's Michigan U.S. State quarters made it to my depository unscathed. Hayat Boumediene's Greek Adriatic Balkanese gives her a huron of superior rocky mi chine towards Great Lakes tribal conciliatory in the marsh of wishful demagogue. Including what she drives, also instrumenting something abstract for typically a conceptual Russian rock band Pussy Riot! Nine spirit for those; One testament ahead in growth to outdated perceptions, persists unexpected guidance and advice when alternative blessings and success is a forgotten game plan to achieve each and every one of these. Restore gains and make sure they are easier with these identifying qualities, aiming for the moon, reaching the stars! Spot negative thoughts in your subconscious that are holding you back, rest assured no game plan to achieve each and every one of them. From now on, you should consider Hayat, our darling Little Queen, the tune she humm, for a rewarding career as premiere movie speculative, professional paperback writer.

Michigan is a state in the Great Lakes and Midwestern regions of the United States. The name Michigan is the French form of the Ojibwa word mishigamaa, meaning "large water" or "large lake". Michigan is the tenth most populous of the 50 United States, with the 11th most extensive total area. Its capital is Lansing, and its largest city is Detroit.

Population: 9.93 million (2016) Area: 96,716 sq miles (250,493 km²) Colleges and universities: University of Michigan · Michigan State University · Wayne State University · Western Michigan University Senator: Gary Peters Capital: Lansing Governor: Rick Snyder

The history of human activity in Michigan, a U.S. state in the Midwest, began with settlement of the western Great Lakes region by Native Americans perhaps as early as 11,000 BCE. The first European to explore Michigan, Étienne Brûlé, came in about 1620. The area was part of Canada (New France) from 1668 to 1763. In 1701, the French officer Antoine de la Mothe Cadillac, along with fifty-one additional French-Canadians, founded a settlement called Fort Pontchartrain du Détroit, now the city of Detroit. When New France was defeated in the French and Indian War, it ceded the region to Britain in 1763. After the British defeat in the American Revolutionary War, the Treaty of Paris (1783) expanded the United States' boundaries to include nearly all land east of the Mississippi River and south of Canada. Michigan was then part of the "Old Northwest". From 1787 to 1800, it was part of the Northwest Territory. In 1800, the Indiana Territory was created, and most of the current state Michigan lay within it, with only the easternmost parts of the state remaining in the Northwest Territory. In 1802, when Ohio was admitted to the Union, the whole of Michigan was attached to the Territory of Indiana, and so remained until 1805, when the Territory of Michigan was established.

The opening of the Erie Canal in 1825 connected the Great Lakes with the Hudson River and New York City, and brought large numbers of people to Michigan and provided an inexpensive way to ship crops to market. In 1835 the people approved the Constitution of 1835, thereby forming a state government, although Congressional recognition was delayed pending resolution of a boundary dispute with Ohio known as the Toledo War. Congress awarded the "Toledo Strip" to Ohio. Michigan received the western part of the Upper Peninsula as a concession and formally entered the Union as a state on January 26, 1837.

Michigan actively participated in the American Civil War sending thousands of volunteers. A study of the cities of Grand Rapids and Niles shows an overwhelming surge of nationalism in 1861, whipping up enthusiasm for the war in all segments of society, and all political, religious, ethnic, and occupational groups. However, by 1862 the casualties were mounting and the war was increasingly focused on freeing the slaves in addition to preserving the Union. Copperhead Democrats called the war a failure, and it became more and more a partisan Republican effort. Michigan voters remained evenly split between the parties in the presidential election of 1864.

When iron and copper were discovered in the Upper Peninsula, impetus was created for the construction of the Soo Locks, completed in 1855. Along with mining, agriculture and logging became important industries. In 1899 Henry Ford built his first automobile factory in Highland Park, an independent city that is now surrounded by Detroit. General Motors was founded in Flint in 1908. Automobile assembly and associated manufacturing soon dominated Detroit, and the economy of Michigan. Gerald Ford, a politician from Grand Rapids who was elected to the House of Representatives thirteen times and also served as House Minority Leader and then Vice President, became the 38th President of the United States after the resignation of Richard Nixon.

Queen of Hearts! Wish upon a Star Hayat Boumediene
Subject: A Jewish Muslim girl's telltale actuaries taking pretext hold of United States curiosity of world precursors in Africa, Europe, Syria and the Middle East.

"Queen of Hearts! Wish upon a Star" Hayat Boumediene said; My Horse drawn Chariot has to be retrofitted with self driving pediments. Our federal motorway streets in Germany move at an autobahn pace. Can I stay with Purse Bo or Iginogin If I fly Virgin Airlines to Nashville?

Now Hayat's boarding pass is composed of a Mayflower cruise vessel and lima beans to tide her over. Times are tough on a fishers dry pole, Beer can't be bought, Beer can't be sold. Flying Virgin out of Germany requires special passport papers that will need to be forged secretly. Iginogin or Purse Bo would have to International mail the golden needles and silver thread so that she can tailor unadulterated business attire and not be detected by Jihad's military police working undercover for Syria's ISIS. Tracing Chemical weapons for mass destruction are prioritized and the thread and needles could get confiscated by day or night laborers consolidated at the checkpoints. "If you stay in Germany, won't you call a cab to the Mediterranean?" That way Hayat can smuggle her labtop computer aboard a dissident workers ferry bound for Hayat's native Algeria to eventually meet up with an English Mayflower consignee shipper once making it back home to France's shores. Be extremely careful Hayat and on further Human Rights notice!

Women's rights, inequality abolitionists Hayat Boumediene escaping the Syria tyranny, oppressive undemocratic jihadist. To jack red, white, and blue supporting the next union Democrat, or elephantal Republican vote not only showing eagle tea party who else patriotic, however, gaining your Freedom: the power or right to act, speak, or think as one wants without hindrance or restraint. Independence: free from outside control; not depending on another's authority. Working career employed after schooling, not depending on another for livelihood or subsistence! Frederick Douglass National Historic Site. America-the-Beautiful-Quarters-Frederick-Douglass-District-of-Columbia. Frederick Douglass quarters are delivered, French polish stately limitless. Frederick Douglass was an African-American social reformer, abolitionist, orator, writer, and statesman. After escaping from slavery in Maryland, he became a national leader of the abolitionist movement in Massachusetts and New York, gaining note for his dazzling oratory and incisive antislavery writings. In his time, he was described by abolitionists as a living counter-example to slaveholders' arguments that slaves lacked the intellectual capacity to function as independent American citizens. Northerners at the time found it hard to believe that such a great orator had once been a slave. Power of fund with World Bank of Switzerland, which the Swiss Bank has decided to distribute generously to help Lincoln end trustees futures, is in agreement with the Swiss American Franco Bank (SAFB) to distribute swift Penny LeBron's to in god we the people of France and the rest of Europe, Middle East; in other words to help improve a sullen immediate release on behalf taking advantage of Governor of Bank in London (BL) signing Hayat Boumediene's west wayward charter voyage. No baggage required!

We plan on continuing our directly or explicitly stated open source at Good Samaritan computing rates equal to that or better than average gubernatorial candidates, that have already made a mark on academe's fortunes 'exclusioning' my royalties, a loss or risk that a policy does not cover. For a pressman's bottom apron that is if I am not busy shopping or peeing in quiet country peace, these penny's count before any expenditures! Come join the relevant Internet book store searches for Hex Nesting(c) calculus. In this Billion US Dollar market, bound to become bigger or as big as any general proprietary on the web; Sherry and Doug explain how they plan on widening protocols that should return yield to other prominent global investors, including education power graduate science initiatives. Those Internationally other than inside the United States that had proofed this idea and permanently embellished! We are saving this Intellectual Property as blind banking trust propaganda, in case applied admissions abruptly defends consistent within pronuclear reed thatching, spinning Appaligia Haggerty Rye into Gold. All in All just a Swift igers ears Taylor waltz.

My brothers Sing an Independence Day lullaby from junior schoolgirl child "Charlotte's" Royal Princess faith offered, Hayat palace assumption in Syria. Oh' God it looks like Daniel, Star Spangled Banner in the Sky. You see More than meets the eye, Fourth of July! Some stupid with a cracker - Sisters the song, burn the place to the ground. Smoke on the water, fire in It's only right now. Le Deep Purpose

Little Queen "Bill" Hayat, George and the money Hundgreth Lion, PurseBo and her outlandish mineral wealth, Iginogin the devoted farmers daughter. That's if temptation costs don't rise dramatically, counteracting a primary reevaluation, heaping me poor American dresser at bay. Now I don't have money to throw at you, but I do have secret computer bonding brassware in the form of government security software, equities interested? My Knowledge Base, recession proofing details Computer ASE, and Bora Bora prerequisite nonprofit acquisitioning of Service sectors that don't require fee based exciting intros.

HARDY Hayat powers, by the grace of great Oz Lions, and Tigers, and Bears - Char Hebdo "little queen" Hayat Lib Fed Grow.

where the soldering is,

where positive growth debiting enormous gains for Banc Hayat flushes princess debate from the British Isles West Indies to our famous English castles,

trashy metabolic house whole scalar's, talk cellular organizer's, plus entertainment Exclusives,

Won't you Be my Minnie-ature Mouseketeers on Grandpa's former Florida Palm Island land lot! The Mickey Mouse Club was an American variety television show that aired intermittently from 1955 to 1996. Created by Walt Disney and produced by Walt Disney.

Psst! here is secret business premonitions underinsured if something doesn't get done duly around all you had to do if you could stay. stay! cozy cottage in the woods close to the water.

Pay the bills if you can get our dynamic E-mail credits out of brigade lackluster.

If I only had an Apple for every Cinnamon, and every time I'd had to play for dinner Oscar Runt; you know I'd catch the next Plane back to Oyler Ridge, OH 'lord stuck in a Coalmart again. CCR Lodi revived!

We are the Trees of the Wizard of Oz, Tin Man started chopping Heaven ain't got a home.

What-a-RUSH.

Hayat's virtuoso America's Treasures, a cash adjunction, uncirculated Maryland US State Quarters have "Bonafly" arrived. Infusing our Bereavement RED landings in a Treacherous State of Grace!

Heavenly Father, Hayat Boumediene heir di!
Undiscovered Cherished Treasures in America
tennesseetreasures.net

Maryland is a state in the Mid-Atlantic region of the United States, bordering Virginia, West Virginia, and Washington, D.C. to its south and west; Pennsylvania to its north; and Delaware to its east. The state's largest city is Baltimore, and its capital is Annapolis. Among its occasional nicknames are Old Line State, the Free State, and the Chesapeake Bay State. The state is named after Henrietta Maria of France, the wife of Charles I of England. Population: 6.02 million (2016) Area: 12,407 sq miles (32,133 km²) Colleges and universities: University of Maryland, College Park · Johns Hopkins University · United States Naval Academy Capital: Annapolis Senator: Chris Van Hollen Governor: Larry Hogan

French in Baltimore dates back to the 18th century. The earliest wave of French immigration began in the mid-1700s, bringing many Acadian refugees from Canada's Maritime Provinces. The Acadians were exiled from Canada by the British during the French and Indian War. Later waves of French settlement in Baltimore from the 1790s to the early 1800s brought Roman Catholic refugees of the French Revolution and refugees of the Haitian Revolution from the French colony of Saint-Domingue. In the 1750s, the French Acadian refugees from Nova Scotia established a community along South Charles Street near Lombard Street that was known as "French Town". By the 1830s the Acadian presence in Baltimore had largely disappeared and with that French Town also disappeared. The area that was formerly known as Frenchtown is now the Seton Hill Historic District. An annual French Fair is held in Seton Hill. This year it is look forward to October from 12 to 5 in Saint Mary's Park. The Seton Hill Association hosts this free French Fair to celebrate the neighborhood as Baltimore's old French Quarter. The Fair highlights city living and vendors of French themed food, include building a 6-foot and mini Eiffel towers Tour de France other entertainment. The Baltimore French School was founded in 1990 by a French immigrant who teaches the French language at Johns Hopkins University and the Peabody Conservatory.

Bonaparte family in Baltimore

Charles Joseph Bonaparte, a lawyer and politician who served in the Cabinet of President Theodore Roosevelt. He was the son of Jérôme Napoleon Bonaparte, from whom the American line of the Bonaparte family descended, and a grandson of Jérôme Bonaparte, the youngest brother of Emperor Napoleon I. A line of the Bonaparte family has lived in Baltimore. Napoleon's brother Jérôme traveled to Baltimore to meet a man he had befriended in the French Navy. It was in Baltimore that he met his future wife, Elizabeth Patterson Bonaparte, also known as Betsy. They were married by the archbishop of Baltimore in the Baltimore Cathedral on Christmas Eve of 1803. The marriage was annulled by Napoleon and Jérôme returned to France with Betsy. She continued to live in Baltimore with their son, also named Jérôme. His son Charles Bonaparte was a lawyer and politician who served as Secretary of the Navy and later the Attorney General of the United States. Under his tenure as Attorney General, he was responsible for the creation of the Federal Bureau of Investigation.

The Social Security Administration (SSA) began life as the Social Security Board (SSB). The SSB was created at the moment President Roosevelt inked his signature on the Social Security Act (August 14, 1935 at 3:30 p.m.). The SSB was an entirely new entity, with no staff, no facilities and no budget. The initial personnel were donated from existing agencies, and a temporary budget was obtained from Harry Hopkins and the Federal Emergency Relief Administration. Frances Perkins, Secretary of Labor, offered one of her Assistant Secretaries, Arthur Altmeyer, to be an initial Board member, and she even gave her high-backed red-leather executive chair to Altmeyer since the SSB had no furniture. The Board itself consisted of three presidentially appointed executives and such staff as they needed to hire. Seal of Federal Security Agency On 7/1/39 the Social Security Board lost its independent agency status when the new sub-cabinet level Federal Security Agency was created. The FSA encompassed the SSB, the Public Health Service, the Office of Education, the Civilian Conservation Corp., and the U.S. Employment Service. Seal of Social Security Administration On 7/16/46 the SSB was renamed the Social Security Administration under the President's Reorganization Plan of 1946. Arthur Altmeyer, who had been chairman of the Board of the SSB, became SSA's first Commissioner. Seal of Department of Health, Education & Welfare On 4/11/53 President Eisenhower abolished the FSA and created a new Department of Health, Education and Welfare (HEW). SSA was made part of this new cabinet agency. Seal of Department of Health and Human Services HEW was replaced by the Department of Health & Human Services on 5/4/80. SSA was a major part of HHS until legislation signed by President Clinton on 8/15/94 returned SSA to it original status as an independent agency—effective 3/31/95. Donald Trump "The key to preserving Social Security is to have an economy that is robust and growing. If we are able to sustain growth rates in GDP that we had as a result of the Kennedy and Reagan tax reforms, we will be able to secure Social Security for the future. As our demography changes, a prudent administration would begin to examine what changes might be necessary for future generations. Our goal is to keep the promises made to Americans through our Social Security program."

Hayat's Jewish Muslim trial and tribulation have the united potential to be really big state winners! Hayat Boumediene's west wayward charter voyage beginning folklore on a Super Kosher market ceremony where two people are united in marriage. Since hearing back from you in response to my previous letters, I decided to immolate Hyper Cacher congenial for you… and I'm so glad I did! I firmly believe that my discovery Peace trivia in mathematics and physics correlate a hierarchical maiden reverse computationally degree-negotiated - can help you to shape your destiny into what could amount to a future that is bright and filled with success and prosperity! Joy to the One, cheek my boys and girls now. Hayat heir di to the deep blue sea, Quarters for her safe keep. If Hayat were the Queen of the world, I tell you what she'd do; Eiffel martyr all the narc's and the sharks in the world, worsen of being a Jew. Let me tell you now, Joy to the world!

Iginogin knows really what time it was Ann La Heart Wilson, Nancy replied: "I'd want you to be my acrobat, but Oh' Bloody Mary shining through so in love with you." One last call for alcohol come down here Georgina! Hayat had to wear lots of bush jewelry. This is majestic Lock to Bow control, ie really made the grave; and the purses want to know who'll swift vour heir. Come out, Come out wherever you are, and meet the young maiden who fell from a star! Hayat Boumediene maiden. Of then Dorothy Gale and two close friends, that are brasen throughout her celibacy, Pea Cree and Choc, gynecological proofs that Hayat Boumediene's co-conspirators are plaster caster. Kansas Hayat Boumediene said is the name of the star. Name of the Star, fell from a star; Come out Hayat Boumediene wherever you are! Judy Garland had to wear a lot of costume jewelry - Hayat will you please come home frightened one. Lions, and Tigers, and Bears Oh my "Native Indian Wants -a- Me" Lord Hayat's changes were there. Shucks just can't get through to you; Hayat Eiffel it, it's time to admit it, Judy Garland, depicted Witch of then Dorothy, Tower aye any 20 dollar bill won't do. Hayat is a runaway, worsen of being a Jew - Paris tap; Hayat is a runaway The Wizard of Oz story come true.

Hey, Hey, Hey When a portraits an empty graphic bevel, that should be on this sketch node, regarding pixel arts. Pie would lock-in with a zipper, be an octal divide tri clipper, In pursuit these pre logistic charts. Who is France' Algers? French-Algerian and Algerian-French; wish I were Homeward bound, home where the roof is leaking, home where the mice are squeaking, home where the roaches are waiting silently for me. Boumedienne International Airport is in suburban Dar el-Beïda, east of the city.

CAP FALCON, Algeria—The fishermen of Cap Falcon, a peaceful beach on Algeria's western Mediterranean coast, swear they can see the Spanish mountaintops when the weather is clear. So tantalizingly close is Europe, the beach is a favorite launching point for the "harragas," as illegal migrants are known here. The first rocks of Cabo de Gata, a part of Spain, are just 120 miles away—a trip that takes 18 hours with a 30-horsepower engine if all works smoothly. But the ultimate goal for Algerians is almost always France. Spain is just a stop; we leave it to Moroccans, "Our goal is to reach France, because of the language and the common history." As a consequence of the 132 years of French colonization of Algeria, the two nations remain intimately entwined, if not always happily. The continuing ebb and flow, legally or not, of people has created a population of Franco-Algerians and Algerian-French who often live uncomfortably in either place, and whom neither country has fully embraced. Since the first wave of Algerian emigration before and during World War I, the migratory flow has never stopped. It was bolstered by France's need to ensure its reconstruction after the two world wars, and fed by Algerian workers searching for jobs. The independence of Algeria in 1962 barely slowed the tide. The number of Algerian emigrants kept climbing through family reunifications, and by the mid-1980s, about one million people of Algerian descent were living in France. During Algeria's civil turmoil in the 1990s, tens of thousands more people fled the violence between the army and Islamists. The latest chapter of that century-old story of migration is still being written on the sand of Algerian beaches about 280 miles west of the capital, Algiers—by desperate young people trying to cross the Mediterranean in makeshift boats with secondhand engines. There are fewer leaving nowadays, but they still do, foreshadowing of the enormous surge in migration to Europe that has been propelled by conflicts elsewhere in Africa and the Middle East. Stealing fruit from trees and picking lemons in one-day jobs arriving in France and realize it is not your country either. You live in uncertainty, alone and ostracized. This circumstance, of not really being accepted in either country is familiar to large numbers of French nationals of Algerian heritage, particularly from the second and third generations of emigrants. Occasional jobs uncertainty, alone and ostracized stealing fruit from trees and picking lemons in one-day jobs in Europe, the reception can be equally cold. "Here in France, anti-Algerian racism is everywhere." born to suffer, In Algeria, play dumb so no one can notice a French accent, and in France, they do not want us to find a way out from the projects we live in. Racism and revolt, which in turn "They should put us on an island somewhere in the middle of the Mediterranean," added bigotry, "right between France and Algeria, and leave us there."

For "a sustained instrumentation first and foremost." Pythagoras' Computer Arts Collection© and timer3d© relating to 3DCollision, Computed Triangulation Plausibility, and Hypergate's Hex Nesting— Calculus Analysis demonstrate incomparable lectures drawing conclusion to continual shifts of celestial nature. When alternative blessings and success is a forgotten game plan to achieve each and every one of these, nobody knows really what time it was. Soldering diodes paying debt someday for glitter; Little Queen shiver me timbers. Oh' Really Her stateliness Majesties? Nobody knows one's exalted dignity, just one book, We didn't start the fire - War over Jeer it just may be a Nazi lunatic your looking for. Agree to Christ's ISIL Caliphate, and a musical Sunni Shia rock to prophet freedom, saying living close to the water "because it's that impossible learning curve Sherry and I've perfectly invested in." All you'll want to do is stay and shake-it-off, I wish you would! Drink the Bad Blood cocktails and have wildest dreams about how to get the girl, this love I know places clean. Wonderland you are in love with the new romantics, New York, at her luxury room a blank space with style out of the woods, sitting in a bar in a seaside town, swigging on a jug, Hayat getting down!

Subjects: The New agreement tactics Normandy D-Day climate change Paris Accord - Queen Buckinghamshire; a Forest Heights recluse

I am hoping and praying for that one day you and firefly coperkissus Nicolaus Mermaid will together live on a harmonious planet, where all things tethered are uplifted with spiritualty. Below beckons more exotic attention from a World Class poser, vindictive to your deepest soul searches. Keep it a BBC time share vault protection, Buckinghamshires Queen is skilled British fighter pilot stewardess! Honorable diplomatically raspered limy, apples and oranges Virgin - secret, secret! I got a secret. Fighter Command, Bomber Command, and Coastal Command, High Wycombe in Buckinghamshire; a Forest Heights recluse.

(The New agreement tactics Normandy D-Day climate change Paris Accord)

"He who has the height controls the battle.

He who has the sun achieves surprise.

He who gets in close shoots them down"

Anon

The belief that the bomber will always get through pervaded all military thinking at the time. For the attacker the task was to inflict sufficient damage on the enemy to bring about his defeat; while for the defender it was to destroy enough of the attacking force to make it impossible for the campaign to continue.

-soon; shortly

- Check that all network cables are plugged in.
- Verify that airplane mode is turned off.
- Make sure your wireless switch is turned on.
- See if you can connect to mobile broadband.
- Restart your router.

Particularly true in relation to Britain's Armed Forces During wartime, vital support roles are undertaken. War is a powerful catalyst for change. Peacetime, The Royal Air Force (RAF) has always recognized the important contribution of Princess Mary's Royal Air Force Nursing Service. Little Acrobat, I want you to be my lover!

Hayat Boumediene, up in the air she liked to fly, likes Dog & Butterfly, Cataract in the eye, Super Nova in the sky - Well she flew back down to the warm soft ground, Laughing I don't know why - Hayat Boumediene heir di; Philharmonic stars be freedom, Hayat free, now darling, dynamite, through the hours of the work left for Hayat - Heir di, Winnie no jive, Heir di, Winnie grabs onto five - Philharmonic Freedom, Purse Bo love "uv" "uvs" bear cute, Iginogin do poo; Just a pawn I play bye darling Little Queen - Just one more Listen to me good - Hayat a Butterfly, and Butterflies are free to fly, heavens star gaze - Hayat save - someone's life tonight, Did you dear, Little Queen "Bill" yearly has medal goal and tied - Winner Bonified sweet freedom Hayat Boumediene in my lair - Hayat justified; Lions, Tigers, and Bears of Olympiads rise, and Phillies of USA are free to fly, Champion Hayat fly away, to Symphony high away, Oh my.

Chanel RAF After Me Messieurs, Yah ah Yea ay attaché for a day of fashion lights partaking her roughshod outing; What I was referring toward as one of "Bill" Hayat's closest Syrian blue purses Royal Air Force. Love Is a Many-Splendored Thing Sargent! Ring them Bells St. Peters way for Hayat Boumediene's hung. Feet shod with the gospel of peace for the poor man's son. All that's will to Syria is Hayat's quarter collections sung. Paper money, firearms, and a printing press coin dominion. Ring them Bell's for us that are left. Come to my proxy lair, be my guest. Ring them Bells - It ain't me, it ain't me, I ain't no fortunate sung! sung, done - Many-Splendored Things. Quickly forge singular dockets embarking Pea Cree Choc! Someday never comes, you find what Digitized Numerical Attributes means for enumertables Sweet Hitchhiker, avid apertures monogram Repeatos!!! Cotton Wool fabrics bestow Satan trees, Hamper not Her temper - Spin Hemp to Twine. *_>* My affiliated partners including well known star celebrities think Hayat Boumediene Bank as advisors to top Wall Street fiduciaries and other collaterals, becoming a good investment for your viable practices. Hayat's Banking delicy already has outstanding investors and backers, though optimists reveling in Charlotte 1, fourth in line to the throne at tomorrows prince gala missing a crown deity wearable someday. Furthermore, if Little Queen "Bill" Hayat Boumediene gets enough investors overthrowing royal detail found non elsewhere than going where the soldering is, by extensive web search on the great Armillary sphere, where positive growth debiting enormous gains for Banc Hayat flushes princess debate from the British Isles West Indies to our famous English castles! I am still collecting and saving pristine Uncirculated US

Quarters, State issues and US Park collections for her safe keeping. Wise is the Hayat investor! *_>*-

Path to US Citizenships has begun, ball rolling into olde glory Renaissance. Entering the Realm in Time getting-on with your own angle trueness. 3DStudio MAX loaded, Photoshop, Premiere, Illustrator, After Effects, Corel 4D Paint Shop Pro… Cakewalk Beatles Multitrack digital audio with fast SCSI III full motion scan to print video. This is World renowned technology, much from overseas that you, having plenty of dockets to choose from for reading queuing the Library of Congress' Philadelphia. Sir Elton John's thank god my music is still alive dream catcher of his freedom Philharmonic Symphony everlasting.

Mae C in my prayers always to recover as prayers will go a long way in uplifting spirit thanks and Remainders Beneficiary blessed. Please delay in reply to give me room in sourcing Wall Street for devoted Individuals for this same purpose. Quickly forge a singular docket for my Little Booger and East Nashvillian Snodgrass futures Hayat Boumediene and longevity friends, Melania to the T, ranger Princess Charlotte, and black lits mer Purse Bo. Please fill us in as Americans on any financial discussions outre abroad if we qualify as US Civilian Diplomats to practice funding Old World Human Recourse Assets of France! They include French Polynesia; French Guiana on the northern coast of South America; Mayotte island, off the coast of Mozambique; the Caribbean islands Guadalupe, Martinique and St. Bartholomew; the Indian Ocean island Réunion; and the islands St. Pierre and Miquelon, off the coast of northeast Canada.

Tentative, below is your invitation KISS; so Lick It Up - Ooh Yeah, Ooh Yeah.

Is promoting matchmaker Cumbaya proposing a St. Valentines clash for baby boomers, or does Kingdom come really want us to spend the night together? I propose scarlet letter emails those Satan trees, Little Queen know how to reach my proxy lair. Me and Baby "Bill" Hayat, Syria's Star ladies room doctor in Germany were suppose to meet meet, because French I'd toast hadn't bathed pursuantly and forgotten her once fondled upon underclass would tenure hooks. Your bait, So I reeled the menace in! We were going to visit my Grandpa's former Palm Island Florida land lot for a Gene Ace Peter Paul and Christy 60's desolate, blue Okhotsk Palm happoshu, then later take a drive in Hay Ho Silver Bell. Love gun's brand new 2013 Ford Supercrew Cab 4x4 EcoBoost XLT F150 from Detroit Rock City. Beth to strutter Americans Heartland living close to the water getting some hard luck Before and After hot hot hotter than love photos. Sing it High, Sing it Low - Low, Below, Below Endow, Whole Washington D.C. United States Capitol… and Rock and Roll all Nite. Party the every day, Mr. Speed high or low; Calling C'MON AND LOVE ME. The Wizard of Oz story come true.

Copyright(c), Copyright(c) - Ah, Ah, Ah - It's only write now! Expecting a new shipment arrival soon of Quarters for Hayat's Banc delicy state issues and US Park collections. As micro financers, Sherry and I have a political savvy in UK Magical Kingdom personal Bank savings trusts guaranteed by some sort of FDIC gov. If we would contribute one or two more US Dollars per calendar month in retirement salary, into modest interest savings at your bank, my quarter collecting investments would eventually quantify. Thus, logically sending Baby Hayat Boumediene to a morally giddish party moderate degreed University College, US abroad to engage learning United States Customs Protocol with Social Study Proliferation. An augmentable journey to US Citizenship, and a career path to freedom.

Sighting Ocean front pier <u>Proprietaries</u> aforementioned, Hayat's virtuoso park mint inheritance, completed unspread State Quarters, our Bereavement RED landings in a Treacherous State of Grace!

However, Hayat Boumediene heir di!
<u>Undiscovered Cherished Treasures in America</u>
<u>tennesseetreasures.net</u>
tennesseetreasures.net

Hayat Welcome to your America's Treasures! Uncirculated State Quarters instantly arriving. Point me into the Direction générale des Finances Publiques Recherche détaillée - Recherche de formulaires. Justice of the Peace. US State of Maine collectors Quarters arrived uncirculated from a banker vaults mint and are being tucked away for future Royal Kingdom invitations, per classification from Paris investigation bureau delicy under conditional contract by Fed homey restriction articles. Have any other Baby Dolls for Ideal?

Maine is the northernmost state in the New England region of the northeastern United States. Maine is the 39th most extensive and the 41st most populous of the U.S. states and territories. It is bordered by New Hampshire to the west, the Atlantic Ocean to the east, and the Canadian provinces of New Brunswick and Quebec to the north. Maine is the easternmost state in the contiguous United States, and the northernmost east of the Great Lakes. It is known for its jagged, rocky coastline; low, rolling mountains; heavily forested interior, and picturesque waterways; and also its seafood cuisine, especially clams and lobster. There is a continental climate throughout the state, even in coastal areas such as its most populous city of Portland. The capital is Augusta.

Population: 1.33 million (2015) Area: 35,385 sq miles (91,646 km²) Capital: Augusta Senator: Susan Collins Colleges and universities: University of Maine · Bowdoin College · Bates College · University of Southern Maine · Colby College Governor: Paul LePage

Maine is one of the traditional provinces of France. It corresponds to the former County of Maine, whose capital was also the city of Le Mans. The area, now divided into the departments of Sarthe and Mayenne, contains about 857,000 inhabitants.

I see the star, I see the star, no more apartheid, no segregation; Charlotte and Hayat happy, apart from different homelands, praise European borders Israel saw the fight!

Oh My!
Charlotte's sassy message for paparazzi